Charles grew up in a small seaside town in Suffolk, England. He is a divorced, devoted father of two. He started writing short stories at the age of ten and has since expanded his genre to World War II. He has family connections in both the Allies and Axis during the war. This is the reason for his extended interest in that era. He has grown to have great respect for resistance groups who, without any military experience, took up arms for their country.

My two beautiful sons;
Paul Fournel and Marcus Lankester.

Charles.G.Fournel

RISE OF THE MAQUIS

A French Resistance Story

AUSTIN MACAULEY PUBLISHERS™

LONDON • CAMBRIDGE • NEW YORK • SHARJAH

A CIP catalogue record for this title is available from the British Library.

ISBN 9781528986960 (Paperback)
ISBN 9781528986977 (ePub e-book)

www.austinmacauley.com

First Published (2020)
Austin Macauley Publishers Ltd
25 Canada Square
Canary Wharf
London
E14 5LQ

Synopsis

With Europe in turmoil due to the tyrannical reign of Germany, a small group of brave resistance soldiers fight from the inside to save France from being taken over completely. Together, this ragtag group of individuals including an English Special Operations Executive (SOE), band together to form an alliance; this band of brothers is a family thrown together through necessity. Hiding in plain sight, they form a bond that no one, not even Hitler, can break. They even have the support of Pablo Picasso, but will it be enough to get through the war unscathed? With their black-market supplies and procured weapons at the ready, these men and women will fight for their country, for their freedom and for their lives.

Prologue

Paris 1942

As the slim elegant girl in her early twenties with the long plaited blonde hair, wearing a dark navy overcoat, buttoned to the top, walked down the dim, damp cobbled streets, there was an essence of disaster, despair and decay in the air. The young female walked down the street as Nazi troops stood on every street corner of this once glorious capital city. Her hand was holding a steel flick knife in the pocket of her long dark overcoat and she gripped it ever tighter every time an invading soldier looked in her direction. She had had friends who had been brutally taken advantage of by these 'disgusting parasites' and she would be put in front of a firing squad before that happened to her. A German SS officer gave her a smile and salute as he passed her and she just gave a forced, small smile back without stopping.

As she nervously walked down a dark, secluded alleyway, she consistently looked behind her; she was alone down here and sighed as she came out the other-side. The young women checked the street before her, it was silent, not a person or soldier in sight. She crossed the road still looking for any sign of life and after a final check she slipped into the garage opposite; the door closed behind her with a quiet thud. The inside of the garage had next to no light but the confident girl knew where she was going, she opened the red metal door with peeling paint and descended the concrete stairs before her, before opening another metallic door, which opened up into a room, alight with lit candles and humming with activity. She walked through the rooms with the many people giving her nods of welcome. She walked past a group of young men, all smoking and holding various machine guns. One of the young men, holding a Mark II Sten gun, most likely from one of the American or British secret weapon drops, wearing a tartan jacket and flat cap, smacked the girls' rear as she passed the group. She stopped in her tracks and faced the offending man, who had a wide grin on his face. She gave a seductive smile and walked elegantly over to the group, reached into her black purse which she was carrying and before anyone knew what was happening, the young man had a German Luger pistol pointing at his testicles at nought point-blank range. The young man now had a shocked look on his face, his rolled cigarette falling from his mouth. The girl smiled with her red-stained lips and returning the gun to her purse, she turned and wandered un-fazed into the open room. She may look like a young professional business woman but this was war and she was in the resistance.

Chapter 1

Corporal James Garner was a rough Englishman, this was not his real name, but the name he had been assigned and was now the only name he had; it had been so long that he had almost forgotten his original name. He had been the owner of a high-end street chemist, before being assigned as a Special Operations Executive (SOE) in a small, quaint village named Farndale in Yorkshire. He had moved to inner London when he proposed to his long-time lady friend, Kate Mayfield. Not long after that, his new apartment home in Islington, London, was destroyed during the blitz, which also killed his new fiancée.

He had short brown cropped hair and a thick stubble covered chin; he looked like a man who had lost his way as he sat slumped over the beer-stained glossed wooden bar. He took a large swig of his German 'Private Stock' whiskey and lit a filter-less Woodbine cigarette, with a fine vine-engraved silver lighter. It was the same lighter that his father had used during his escapades in Germany in the first world war and gifted to his son when he himself had also joined the Royal British Armed Forces as an SOE. Garner inhaled the tobacco fumes; it was a little bit of home in this foreign country.

Two years ago, he had been part of a three-man SOE team, who were dropped by parachute behind enemy lines in the eastern, mountainous area of France, known as Morvan. British intelligence had told them previously that the south of France was too dangerous for a drop, as it was controlled by the French collaborating Vichy regime. The SOEs primary objective was to assassinate a Nazi General, named Dietrich Hugo Hermann Von Choltitz, Hitler's second-hand man in Paris; he would, surprisingly, later be known as the 'Saviour of Paris'. Unfortunately, James' superior Sergeant Carl Hurten, who was the only one of the three who could speak German and French fluently, lost their much-needed MAS 36 sniper rifle during his drop and broke his back as he was slammed against a cliff face by a sudden gust of wind, killing him instantly. The dedicated corporal and his good friend and brother in arms, Private Henry Farrows, had mutually decided to continue with the mission to the best of their ability. They made their way the twelve miles West, towards the capital of France, Paris, dressed as everyday Parisians, with a satchel full of plastic explosives. They used their disguises to press on with their secondary objective, to obstruct the Nazi occupation in Paris by detonating explosives at Nazi fuel depots and to sabotage armoured vehicles and military outposts. This happened steadily until an explosive device detonated prematurely and killed his good friend, Henry, along with the Nazi fuel depot target. Since then James had given up all hope. On entering the French capital city, they had been given a secret room at the back of a common Nazi hangout, La Belle de Nuit nightclub. The establishment was secretly owned by a pair of Jewish businessmen who clearly supported the Allied forces, feeding them any information gathered on the occupying forces by a secret radio, B2, that they kept disguised in a black briefcase hidden in the office, as well as helping the French resistance to the best of their ability. The Paris nightclub was run for the exiled Jewish owners by a French Madam. James had used this to contact the SOE headquarters in London, via Morse code, to report the failure of his mission and the passing of his two comrades; this is also where he was informed that his extraction would not be possible. All this was done unknown to the large German clientele.

The Secret Operations Executives (SOE) were known as Churchill's secret army; they would be dropped behind the enemy, fighting the occupying forces from within in a less conventional manner. The chosen men would have had previous jobs in all fields and be employed in the British army for an intensive four weeks of weapons, explosives and obstacle training, before being dropped behind enemy lines. They would train up and recruit resistance groups, obstruct enemy communications and supply lines, as well as anything else to help the allied cause.

The nightclub kept Nazis happy with singers such as Marie Magdalene Dietrich and Maurice Auguste Chevalier, and allowed them to cohort with the French waitresses who were serving them as much as they could drink, which was often too much, of the widely available, un-rationed French champagne.

"It is not healthy to drink alone, friend," said a man in a strong French accent, appearing next to James. Without looking up from his drink, James replied dutifully:

"Not too healthy to speak English in a place full of Krauts either." He downed the remainder of his beverage.

"The Germans mind their own business," replied the stranger.

"Jean-Claude, two more whiskeys, s'il vous plait," he requested from the French barman; he spoke in English but translated with hand signals. The barman refilled James' glass and got out another glass to fill for the French newcomer.

"Cheers," said the English soldier, raising his glass before downing the contents in one go.

"*Santé,*" retorted the man, sipping on his own beverage.

"So, who are you?"

"My name is Pierre and we are big fans of yours," said the man sipping on his alcoholic beverage.

"We? Who the hell are we?" James asked, getting a bit fed up with this Frenchman's cryptic speech. James turned to look at the guest; it was the first time he had looked at this man. He was a clean-shaven middle-aged man, who had long black hair going down to the bottom of his neck in a ponytail and deep brown eyes. He was wearing a sky-blue polo neck jumper, a brown wool-lined leather jacket, much like James' own coat, which he had used to complete his disguise as a Parisian. The man flipped open the collar of his coat to reveal a dark steel lapel pin showing a cross with two crossbars. He had seen this before, graffiti on the Paris walls, often with the slogan '*Vive la Resistance*'; this was the symbol of the 'Maquis', or more commonly known as the French Resistance.

"Maybe we should go and talk somewhere a bit more private," suggested Pierre looking at the crowd behind them. James followed the man's gaze. In the lower circular auditorium were between twelve and fifteen tables each with at least three smartly dressed Nazis and SS officers, wearing grey, black or green uniforms, depending on their rank and position in Hitler's Third Reich. They were flirting with the waitresses, laughing and joking; the occupying forces were totally oblivious to the two men at the bar, but still too close for comfort.

"Jean-Paul, or whatever your bloody name is, give us the rest of that bottle and put it on my tab." James just received a quizzical look from the French barman, until his new associate, Pierre, translated. The young barman put a cork stopper into the top of the bottle and passed it over the bar to the undercover Englishman.

With the bottle of whiskey cradled in his arms like a new-born baby, James led the resistance member down a narrow passageway adjacent to the stage. He flung open a wooden door with the word '*privé*' on the outside. This room was the dressing room and inside were nine skimpily clad French burlesque dancers. Pierre stood in the doorway and said, "Ooh la la." James just smiled; the first time he had come back here, he was not too sure where to look, but by his third visit and fifteen slaps later, he soon learnt his place. James slid open a hidden door, disguised as an old large vintage poster of the famous singer La Madelon. He looked back to see Pierre successfully flirting in French with a young blonde burlesque dancer; James had received more than a couple of slaps from this particular girl; she was a beauty, and she seemed taken by this confident Frenchman. *Must be the French charm,* thought James as he cleared his throat to get the Frenchman's attention. Pierre turned and then bowed to the young performer with an "*Excusez-moi*" and strode directly past James into the dirty dust-filled room, which looked like a spacious storage room cluttered with rotting wooden step ladders and dust sheets. There were three stained and worn mattresses' in one corner and directly opposite sat a worn settee with obviously broken springs and a matching sofa; in front of them was a wooden plank resting on a pair of cinder blocks, making an uneven, makeshift coffee table. On the flaking walls were some pin-ups of scantily clad women showing their wares, which were left by the last residence, who, judging by the pictures, was an American.

Once James had closed the hidden doorway and locked it shut with a heavy wooden latch, he sank himself into the settee and put his legs up on the makeshift table, where there sat a Nazi Luger P08 handgun, a former SS officer peaked cap and a Hitler youth knife. Pierre picked up the revolver and examined it admiringly.

"Yours?" asked the Frenchman, cocking the gun, it was in full working order.

"My partner's," replied James, seeing in his mind's eye how his good friend had acquired the Nazi tool of war and saved his life at the same time.

The duo had been taking their time completing their secondary objective, blowing up Nazi fuel depots and military vehicles in turn. James was fitting an explosive charge to a Nazi twenty-millimetre heavy artillery weapon, it was a powerful weapon with four barrels that could cause major damage to troops and vehicles and could take out a whole military battalion with great ease and anything else that got caught in the menacing war machines sight, including any aircraft that would fly overhead. James and Henry had previously taken out the two guards, both using their McLaglen Peskett close combat weapons, a great piece of kit which could be used as a multiple of weapons such as a garrotte, cudgel or knife and could easily be concealed. Henry garrotted the first Nazi soldier, as James beat the second over the head with the steel weighted ball end, beating the soldiers face into a messy pulp. James had just set and fixed the device onto the weapon, in prime position to permanently disable it, he was just about to set the timer, when a voice in a strong German accent said, "Do not be moving and your arms being up!" James slowly raised his hands and turned to see an SS officer in a smart coal grey uniform and the common 'Toten Kopf' on his officer's hat, he also wore an edelweiss patch on his left arm indicating that he was a mountain troop officer, most likely on regulated leave and spending his pay in Paris. The officer had a chin of stubble, he had most likely spent the whole night exploring the famous Paris brothels in the popular Paris Red Light district, as many soldiers did, and had not been back to his lodgings to shave. With a crooked nose, piercing blue eyes and long blonde hair sticking out from under his hat, James remembered thinking 'true master race' as he looked at him. He was pointing the same Luger pistol that was now in Pierre's hand, directly into James' face, his finger poised on the trigger. The mean looking officer froze on the spot all of a sudden, James thought he was unsure of what to do, normal German protocol was to shoot the perpetrator on the spot, but then the man made a gurgling sound and dropped to his knees with blood flowing from the corner of his mouth, his menacing eyes looked up to James before he fell forward to reveal a British bayonet stuck into the base of his neck, an aggressive looking Henry Farrows stood behind where the Nazi special forces officer had once stood, he took the officers weapons, as his 'trophies of war', which was his provocative. The following day his friend had passed and James started to hit the bottle hard.

"A terrible tragedy," said Pierre, as if reading the man's mind. "We all know of your loss." The Frenchman paused for a moment. "How would you like to take your revenge, for the loss of your comrade in arms, my friend?" he asked, replacing the firearm onto the table, this offer was very enticing and made James sit up straight and lean forward to hear what this Frenchman had to say clearly.

"Take a seat and tell me more," said James, directing the man to the sofa, Pierre neither accepted nor declined the request and just perched himself on the armrest of the seat.

"We are the Paris resistance—" started Pierre.

"Paris resistance? Paris does not have a resistance," interrupted James, sitting back again in disappointment, once again sinking into the settee. He had been fully briefed about the resistance cells in France and according to the general who had briefed them back over the channel in London, the resistance in Paris was non-existent and the residents of Paris preferred to roll over and become 'Hitler's bitch' when the French government had retreated south and would bend over backwards to appease the Nazi Führer. The intelligence couldn't be wrong to that extent, if Paris had a resistance force, British intelligence would have known about it and would have informed his team.

"We are following the brave Marie-Madeleine Fourcade, fighting the treacherous collaborating Vichy regime, down the south in the 'free-zone' of France. We can no longer live under the Nazi Jackboot!" They had been briefed on Marie-Madeleine Fourcade, before they had left England, she had become a French resistance leader in 1941 and with that she had over three thousand agents under her control who fought the French governments Vichy regime who had decided to collaborate with the Nazis and were allowed to control the southern part of France. They may have named it the 'free-zone', yet they still followed the Nazi law, it was a gallant strategy.

James stayed silent, trying to size up the Frenchman in front of him, was he bold or just a fantasist? Could he be trusted or was this a Nazi ploy to flush out foreign agents? He had heard of German agents pretending to be SOE agents to flush out resistance sympathisers. "I understand, you must think about it, my friend. You are a strong man we can use in the resistance. If you agree to join our noble campaign, meet me tomorrow in the alleyway behind this building, at seize o'clock." Pierre paused before cautiously clarifying himself, "Eh, six hours tomorrow."

"In the morning?" asked James, he had not woken that early for a long time.

"Non, afternoon."

"Eighteen hundred hours then."

"*Oui. Dix-huit.*" With that Pierre took his leave and left James to his thoughts and the remainder of the bottle of whiskey.

Chapter 2

James had not slept well during the night, he woke multiple times to find he had only slept a couple of hours, this continued until midday when he eventually rose from his stained mattress. Pierre's words had been going through James' head all night, yet as the day's light shot into the desolate room through the beams of the wooden planks which boarded up the window. The words became clearer in his mind and he knew for the first time, since the tragic demise of his friend, what he had to do.

He shaved over a bowl of stagnant water with a straight razor, he had not shaved for a fortnight, it was rough and sore, he didn't have any shaving soap to make it any easier. He then got himself dressed in a maroon red Polo neck jumper, wanting to blend in, he had taken his lead from the Frenchman Pierre and pulled on a pair of green combat trousers, with pockets halfway down each leg, in which he carried a set of brass knuckles. The Frenchman had a somewhat fanatical enthusiasm which was not sitting well with James. James tugged at a dirty dust cover, to reveal a regal pine hat stand and hanging on it like decorative ornaments from a festive tree, hung a pair of rimmed Tommy military helmets, a single Nazi helmet, a couple of boxed gas masks, brown wool lined leather jacket and grey flat cap. James put on the cap and leather jacket which fitted as if they were made for him because they were by the talented hand of the Royal army tailors of Great Britain. He hesitated before picking up the Hitler youth dagger and slipped it into his black military boots. Finally, he grabbed his aggressive, yet effective McLaglen Peskett close combat weapon, which he slipped into his belt strap and concealed by the leather jacket. Instead of making a beeline for the bar, as he would usually do, he strode to the check-in counter and said in broken French the password "*Courrier śil vous plait,*" the girl, no older than nineteen years of age, smiled politely at this Englishman's attempt at French, but understood him well enough to recognise the password and passed the man an envelope bulging with French Francs and German Reichsmarks, the only two currencies accepted in Nazi-occupied France. This password was for the operations funds that were kept under the counter of this establishment, in case they were searched in an all too common spot check by the occupying forces and they could then pass it off as wages. If the Nazis discovered it on the SEO, they could have it confiscated, with no explanation, even if their cover had not been blown. James took out a small wad of French Francs and German Reichsmark notes (both were now being accepted in the invaded city) and handed the remaining notes in the envelope over the bar, to pay off his tab for the previous night, even though the bill was still months overdue. He strode out of the La Belle de Nuit nightclub into the foggy streets of Paris. The sun which had earlier been streaming into his hidden room had gone into hiding behind a blanket of the grey clouds which now adorned the sky. The mist was so thick, James was unsure whether it was, in fact, fog or rain, it clung to James' clothes like a transparent cobweb and the dampness penetrated his skin to the bone. James casually made his way down the cobbled street to a quaint, family run, traditional French café and in his best French, which was not even good at a child's level, he ordered a coffee and croissant, he had always been curious if a croissant tasted different in France. As he drank the steaming hot liquid and ate the homemade, warm pastry, it gave a slight understanding of how the French were coping with this occupation of their land. He sat back and lit a Woodbine, inhaling the smoke, right now for him, life was okay.

He had taken his time in this comfortable café, he lost track of time and as he left he was surprised to find that it was four o'clock. The weather had turned once again, the sun had battled through triumphant and burnt away the fog, the air had warmed up, with only the slightest breeze which crept through covertly. James spent the following couple of hours, walking down the small cobbled back streets of Paris admiring the hidden architecture of his picturesque city, he took in as much sun as he could before steadily making his way for his appointment with Pierre, he had no idea what he could expect. James became cautious as he slowly walked through the narrow back alleyway of the La Belle de Nuit and turned a corner to see Pierre arguing in French, which James did not understand a single word of, with a beautiful French brunette, seeing him the arguing ceased and he was sure he had interrupted some sort of lovers tiff.

"Ah, James, you made it, my friend," said Pierre shaking the man's hand warmly. "Are you ready to help us take back this great land?"

"Well I guess so," said James nervously. "I think some introductions may be necessary," he suggests, keeping his eyes on the girl, who he naturally assumed was Pierre's partner.

"*Mon Dieu!* Of course, how rude!" the Frenchman over-exaggerated. "James, this is one of our brave resistance females, Constance Bonnaire." She was a very fetching female in her early thirties with shoulder length dark brown hair and deep-sea-green coloured eyes. She was wearing a white blouse under a yellow overcoat with a belt around her slender waist and a tight black skirt which stopped just below her knees, showing her shapely black stocking covered legs and yellow heeled shoes which matched her overcoat.

"*Bonjour, mademoiselle,*" said James bowing his head to her, she just ignored this stranger's attempt to become an acquaintance. James just shrugged it off, at least it wasn't a slap in the face, which seemed to be the custom of any French maidens he attempted to know. He turned to Pierre, who was staring angrily at the female, at her rudeness to their guest.

"You said I would have a chance to get my own back on these Aryan bastards, so just tell me what you want me to do?"

"Well, my friend, your first job will be to drive Constance here to the town hall, where the German Ambassador, appointed by Adolf Hitler, himself, Otto

Abetz has decided to reside. He has a fondness for three of our French treasures, our cheese, our wine and our women." James could understand this Germans taste for the delicacies, James also had a fondness for cheese, the occasional glass of wine didn't hurt, yet he preferred whiskey and the French maidens were certainly true beauties but seemed immune to his British charm. Pierre revealed a wicker basket which contained a bottle of Petrv Merlot red wine, and a wooden box containing Camembert cheese. This display outraged James.

"So we are going to feed this bugger, this Generaloberst?" he said loudly, he could hardly believe this, they were going to send this Colonel General a gift. Pierre smiled and revealed a hidden compartment at the base of the bottle of wine, revealing two blocks of plastic explosives.

"Before Constance gets out of the car, she will crush this acid trigger detonator," he said showing a detonator, it was a time pencil which James had seen many times before, it just looked like a copper tube the size of a standard pencil, these were often used on covert missions. "From then on you will have seven minutes for Constance to deliver the package and then it will be your job to get her out of there. Safely," instructed Pierre. James couldn't believe his ears, he had heard that the resistance took risks, but this hairbrained scheme seemed to have one obvious flaw.

"And they won't be suspicious by some local, dropping off some of your so-called treasures?" James questioned suspiciously.

"Non!" replied Pierre. "Many officers try to impress the Generaloberst by sending young French girls with cheese and wine, we have put in a letter and addressed it from a young lieutenant, he has gone missing at the bottom of the Seine, three days ago." It was evident that Pierre was impressed with himself. "He won't have heard about his missing lieutenant yet."

"Come England," said the young French maiden, taking the wicker basket. She had a sweet, strangely warming voice and she led James back into the street and to a beautiful dark navy blue Corrino sports car. James admired it, he knew his cars and, even though he had never driven one, had always considered this one to have the heart of a race car in the body of a streetcar, which meant it wouldn't draw much attention to itself, but it would be the perfect car for a quick getaway.

They drove in relative silence, except for the '*gauche*' or '*droit*' for left or right. They finally came to a street, on the left-hand side there was a line of numerous luxury three stories terrace buildings, each with a swastika flag flying from the flagpole erected above the doorway and on the opposite side of the road, each of the romantic light poles had a Nazi flag hanging from it.

"These used to be the homes of the French government before the cowards fled," explained James' French associate. The Third Reich decorations and the abundance of Nazi soldiers roaming this area told James that this was now the residential area of the 'master race' elite which made James feel very uneasy. They eventually reached the end of the street, facing them was a single colossal building, it was at least five times larger than any of the terrace building and at least two stories higher, with six pillars decorating the outer entrance which held up a balcony with a carved swastika cradled in a wreath and an eagle above, two large banners hung from the walls, one of the black Nazi swastika in a white circle on the blood-red background and the second had two black SS symbols next to each other, in the same sized circle on the same red background. James parked the car opposite the large building where five muscle-bound Nazi soldiers stood guard at a pair of black doors. James watched in complete silence as Constance took a pair of pliers from the glove compartment and crushed the end of the detonator, she hastily screwed the end of the bottle back on, concealing the detonator and explosives inside. Constance then pulled her blouse down a little to reveal her small cleavage and without a word exited the vehicle and strode over the road. James looked at his beige Omega watch, it took the female resistance member under a minute before the guards let her enter the premises.

James watched as the seconds tick by. His adrenaline was raised by the second. Every minute that passed felt like an hour. James had been the driver on operations countless of times before, but that was mostly with his old friend and SEO comrade or other fellow soldiers he could trust, but never against such an overwhelming occupying force. He looked around the area as casually as he could, realising that this area was, in fact, a square with a park in the centre encased by the high-class buildings. There was just one single road in and out of this cul-de-sac, this worried James, if they were unable to get away before the alarm was sounded, they could have some trouble getting away, there was no other exit from this area. He checked his watch again, there were two and a half minutes left on the fuse, James felt himself gripping the cars steering wheel tightly, he could not tear his eyes from the second hand of his watch as another minute slipped by, only ninety seconds were left. Something caught his attention from the corner of his eye. Constance had exited the lavish building. James breathed a small sigh of relief. It was another thirty seconds before the elegant French female entered the car.

"I say, girl, you are cutting it close," said James with his stress level clearly heard in his tone.

"Go! *Vite!*" said the women closing her car door. James obliged happily, as he turned the bend to head to the exit road, there was a sonorous explosion as the large building was engulfed in a ferocious fireball. James took a glimpse of his watch, it had gone off thirty seconds earlier than anticipated, but right now that was not his primary concern. The Nazis existing had wasted no time in blocking off the only exit, with a pair of BMW R75 motorbikes with sidecars, each fitted with an MG34 machine gun, now aiming into the square, along with a dozen or more heavily armed soldiers armed with Beretta 34 submachine guns and about three or four vicious German guards with Doberman dogs, growling, barking and pulling at their chain leads. James knew that if he hesitated, even for a second, then neither of them would survive this ordeal. He put his foot flat down on the accelerator hard, revving the engine to peeks and drove directly towards the centre of the makeshift roadblock as fast as possible, the German forces opened fire at the approaching vehicle, riddling the chassis of the car with bullet holes, but this did not stop the car or the British soldier driving it. They burst through the roadblocks, scattering the bikes as autumn leaves in a strong breeze as soldiers dived for cover. James was struggling to keep his composure and felt himself breathing rapidly.

"Pull off the road here, and hide behind those trees," said Constance in the best English he had heard her, or anyone in France, speak. James was too shaken to truly notice. He pulled the car off the road, up a grassy knoll and parked up behind a thicket of trees, hiding the vehicle from sight. He turned off the engine and sat back trying to regulate his breathing. His counterpart, Constance, on the other hand, seemed unnaturally relaxed. She reached into the glove compartment and pulled out a pair of crystal shot glasses and after a second quick rustle around, she pulled out a thin pewter hip flask and poured a clear liquid into the two glasses. Constance passed one to James who accepted it without question and after a quick toast by the French female to the 'liberation of France' they downed the strong Russian vodka. The strength of the liqueur took James by surprise and made him cough as Constance, with a schoolgirl smile, refilled the glasses. The second glass, James was prepared for the strong kick the beverage offered. He took out his packet of Woodbine cigarettes, he had three left, he offered one to his female companion who accepted one gratefully and he took one for himself before James could even reach for his silver lighter, Constance lit his cigarette for him. James looked at her and her sea green eyes reflected the light of the flame as they looked into each other's eyes, she gave the most beautiful of smiles and looked away bashfully. James was confused, was she flirting with him? He was sure she was Pierre's girl, what was she playing at? After the pair had finished their tobacco products and given themselves enough time to settle their nerves, Constance broke the uncomfortable silence.

"There is a shed over there," she said in her perfect English, pointing to the other side of the small ridge they were on. "We keep a car there for emergencies, we must change cars, the whole Nazi army will be looking for this one. We can walk there; we will get some of our resistance fighters to repaint this one and cover the bullet holes."

"Your English is amazing!" exclaimed James; this was the first time he was composed enough to hear her perfect pronunciation. "Where did you learn that?"

"I spent two years travelling around England and Scotland." She smiled fetchingly, then her voice became soft, alluring and almost in a teasing way, she said, "Come on, England." *She was definitely flirting*, he thought to himself, as she opened the car door.

It was an easy two-minute walk to the rickety wooden shed, which was little more of a rundown shack with panels missing from the walls and the remaining ones covered in mould, there was also a large number of missing slates from the roof. After they had crept down the crevice and found their way to the old shed, James went to see the vehicle. To his immense disappointment, sat in the centre of the old shed was a rusting ford truck, it was quite a downgrade. All the paint had either faded or flaked off to leave the rusting body on show. The windows were packed with dirt, it was in a real state, James couldn't be sure that it would even start. The pair entered the cab, the keys were already in the ignition, James wouldn't be surprised if they were rusted in place. With not much hope James turned the key and the engine rumbled to life, he could not believe it, this 'wreck' actually worked as a new well-oiled machine. He shook his head in disbelief as he revved the engine to warm it up so it would not fail them the moment they were on the move. He followed Constance's directions, making his way steadily back into the centre of the occupied zone in Paris and he hoped to a resistance stronghold or at least a safe house where they would be safe and hidden from the invaded enemy troops.

Chapter 3

It had taken the duo another hour and a half of driving at an average speed, so as not to draw attention to themselves, these types of vehicles were common enough not to be noticed by the roaming Nazis plus James did not want to overexert the old knackered engine of this 'rusting piece of junk'. Constance directed him to a derelict cast-iron building, just north of the La Belle de Nuit nightclub. There was no evident sign of life but James could tell they were being watched, he scanned the buildings but he could see no one until they entered the large building where he saw five or six men all holding shotguns in the rafters, yet this did not make James feel any less at ease as he parked up. Constance got out of the van, ignoring the armed men aloft and led James down a small narrow stairway, to a reinforced metallic door.

She knocked, two slow knocks followed with three in quick succession. The sound of a heavy-duty metallic latch could be heard unlocking from the other side, it opened a couple of inches as a grim looking man observed the two guests. Recognising Constance, the man opened the door fully, it creaked loudly, he stood aside, allowing the couple to enter. They walked past many men and women of countless ages all armed with various weaponry which they nursed tentatively and casually, but he did note a sense of awareness, that these people were ready to move out at a moment's notice. This damp cellar was lit by various candles, strategically placed on crates and small uneven shelves to allow the maximum of light to be released. The atmosphere down here was totally different to the one of oppression on the outside. Many men and women greeted Constance in a friendly manner, suspiciously looking James up and down, he ignored their stares and just nodded to them politely.

"James, my friend." Pierre smiled shaking James' hand, he gave Constance a peck on the cheek before she left the two of them to talk alone. "Your success is all over the radio, the Nazi powers are flooding the airwaves, they are in a state and before the day is over the führer will have heard. Our resistance is growing with every victory," he continued excitedly, James was sure this guy was a bit too into himself.

"Well, if I am going to continue helping you with your… movement." James chose his words carefully, remembering the narrow escape they had just previously. "I'll need some kind of weapon, more than my close combat weapon." He pulled out his wooden McLaglen Peskett close combat weapon from his belt. "And I could do with some more cigarettes."

"Of course, I will have to introduce you to Édouard, he can get you whatever you need, do you have any money, my friend?" James thought for a moment, he didn't have much of the operations funds left, then he remembered his SEO trouser belt, he undid his belt and took it off, Pierre watched him puzzled. James tore off a thin strip from the inside to reveal ten gold full sovereign coins fitted on the inside, this was common kits for SEO, to be used for bribes and as emergency funds.

"Will these do?" the Englishman asked his French comrade with a sly smile, Pierre looked shell-shocked by the immense wealth that had just been disclosed to him.

"Yes, my friend, but these black-market people do not just ask for money, but also favours." James took out one of the sovereigns and replaced his belt before following Pierre behind a tattered old curtain in an annexe of the underground headquarters, he had noticed a few of these around. On the red brick walls, wooden shelves had been fitted and they were stocked to their full capacity with everything from silk shirts, bottles of alcoholic beverages, weapons, ammunition and explosives, most James recognised as Nazi guns. This was almost surreal, it was a storage room of hard to get, illegal merchandise, unavailable under Nazi occupation, James was in awe.

"Édouard, let me introduce you to our new hero, James." Pierre introduced him proudly, putting a hand on James' shoulder. A bald-headed man who wore an eye patch on his left eye and a malicious looking scar which ran over his smooth hairless crown. He was in the middle of a process which looked like stocktaking, bent over a table with a large oxblood leather-bound ledger. The gruesome man eyed up the Englishman being presented before him; he was making James feel even more uneasy.

"So this is the English soldier who rid us of Abetz?" the man finally said, his voice was deep, gruff and tired, just how James had expected. "You have done the resistance a great service."

"Édouard, he needs some things. A gun and cigarettes," said Pierre.

"Can he speak for himself?" the man almost growled. Pierre stepped back with a little nod; James would have never expected his French associate to be nervous of anyone. "Leave us, Pierre, I am sure we can arrange something for him." Pierre skulked away and left the men to conduct their business. "Guns and cigarettes are not cheap. We accept Francs, Reichsmarks and items of a similar value, German, French, English, we don't care." James flicked one of the twenty-four-carat coins onto the table.

"What about gold?" he smiled seeing the man's single eye widen and light up, as he picked up the gold sovereign and fingered it, before replacing it on the table. "Very nice," he said as if it meant nothing to him, yet seemed unable to tear his gaze from it. "But I am not as trusting as Pierre and his little sister Constance." James stumbled a step back in shock, Constance was Pierre's sister, *not* his lover! This explained James' suspicion; she had been flirting with him. "I have a small problem, which you could help me with," the man continued, not taking his eye off the golden disk on his desk. "And if you do this for me, you will have earnt my trust, a pistol and these." He pulled a carton of ten packets of Lucky Strike cigarettes off the shelf and put it on the table next to the gold coin.

"What kind of problem?" queried James, eyeing up the cigarettes, whilst swiping up his gold coin and slipping it in his pocket, Édouard's eye lingered on James' pocket for a moment, as if he could remove the coin with the power of his mind before he replied.

"There is a Gestapo major, who has taken it upon himself to arrest my men, making business very hard and dangerous. He carries a black notebook with him wherever he goes, it has names and photos of all my men. I want you to kill him and get the book." James laughed to himself, the man made it sound so easy.

"A bit of a big order to kill a Gestapo officer," said James. The Frenchman rose to his full height, he must have only been a couple inches short of seven foot tall.

"Well, then I cannot help you," he said.

"Okay, calm down," said James. "How do you expect me to kill this guy, without a gun?" asked James casually, Édouard smiled showing a set of yellow broken teeth, it was evident he always got his own way. He turned to a shelf and handed James a walking cane with a silver coloured knob handle.

"A gift from your RAF," he smiled as James examined the cane quizzically.

"A gift? I am sure this helps the war effort," James said sarcastically.

"Turn the top to the right." James did as he was instructed and the nob popped up subtly, James pulled at it to reveal a hidden eight-inch blade, concealed in the cane. James smiled, he had heard of blade canes before, the blade was normally longer, more like swords, but he never thought he would be holding one and the size was perfect for a stealth mission.

"Anything else?" asked James, replacing the blade.

"The Germans call me '*Der Französische Kaufmann*', the French merchant, this Major is the one who took my eye. Let him know I sent you before you kill him," commanded Édouard grimly.

"You've got it," James said with determination. "Where will I find him?"

"He is a common visitor to the red-light district, he enjoys to sample the wares, every Thursday at nine o'clock, he is always on time and that is in two hours from now," said the man.

"Hold on a second," said James, suddenly nervous that it was after curfew. "I'll need a map." The large man smiled broadly, once again showing his stained uneven teeth. He got out a folded piece of silk from the back of his ledger, drawn on it was a map, James listened to Édouard give him directions on how to get from the headquarters to Paris' famous red-light district, before he handed the Englishman a grey tartan suit, explaining that it made the cane less suspicious. He then passed James a gold lapel pin with an enamelled swastika in the centre. James questioned this abruptly.

"What the hell is this, you have got to be kidding me!"

"The only businessmen able to afford our French working ladies are Nazi collaborators, so you must have some Nazi association. It will help you get close to the major and stop any nosey German soldier asking for your identification paper. Members of the Nazi party are the only ones allowed out after curfew and the only ones who would have the nerve to break curfew are friends with some high-ranking officer, so most soldiers will be too scared." Édouard had obviously given this a lot of thought and if it stopped James being hassled, then that was fine with him.

Once he had had a shave and changed into his itchy grey suit, with a black fedora hat and his cane, he viewed himself in a cracked full-length mirror, he looked like a new man.

"I have heard that you are doing a favour for Édouard," said a French female voice. James turned with a start to see Constance leaning against a wall, wearing a green Polo neck and tanned brown tight cropped trousers, looking at the changed man. James reached into his pocket and got out his last Woodbine. Constance shook her head and laughed out loud "A true Nazi businessman would never carry a packet of cigarettes and would never smoke anything but true Arian cigarettes." She said handing James a silver cigarette case, which he opened to reveal twenty typically German 'Atikah' cigarettes. "And I get this for you, a present for your first mission, I even got Édouard to engrave it for you," she said, James closed the silver case to see the elaborate letters J and G, James gave a small smile, it was a moving gesture. Constance then reached into her pocket and produced a small thin block wrapped with a blue sleeve. "*Chocolat,*" she explained in French.

"You had better keep it for when I get back." James smiled. "We don't want the bloody krauts to take it if they search me for some reason." James thanked the French maiden and was about to go and give her a peck on the cheek when her brother, Pierre, appeared from around the corner and James swiftly reconsidered.

"We have all heard the news from Édouard, my friend," he said proudly. "I have arranged for a car to pick you up outside the red-light district at half past nine, you shouldn't have any trouble, but you can never trust these, how do you say? Lady of the night?" James lit the last of his English cigarettes and gave a quick nod. The mention of the red-light district made Constance give her English comrade a look with a raised eyebrow, which made James blush lightly and avoid her gaze.

"Any chance of a drink before I go?" inquired James, his adrenaline was beginning to pump through his veins for the second time that day. It was imperative that he seemed calm and casual throughout this mission. Constance passed him her pewter hip flask of Russian vodka which James gratefully accepted and took a couple of large swigs from before returning it. It had the desired effect for James, he felt a weight lift from his shoulders, then he and Pierre walked to the reinforced door, with the occasional '*Bon chance*' from various resistance members. Pierre and James shook hands and James exited the headquarters, up the narrow stairway, through the cast iron building and after checking the streets for any occupying patrols before disposing his English cigarette and stepping out into the cool open air of the once picturesque capital city of France.

Bloody brilliant! thought James, *I started as a chemist, became a SOE for the British military, joined the French underground and now I am a French Nazi party businessman*, the more he thought about it the quicker his adrenaline rose. He began walking with haste but casually enough not to stand out, he was gripping his cane in his left hand ever tighter and through the corner of his eyes watched every German soldier as he passed. He was either exceptionally brave or overly stupid for accepting this mission, even James himself wasn't too sure of which one he was.

As he passed a dark alleyway, he saw movement, James stopped in his tracks and looked down the alleyway, he couldn't see anything through the darkness but he was positive he had seen some movement, his eyes must be playing tricks on him. He took another couple of steps and he saw it again, unmistakable this time, this was beginning to scare him, someone or something was watching him through the darkness and did not want to be seen. He swiftly stepped into the shadows and watched and waited. Then like mice which had been hiding unmistakable from a predator a group of five or six children between the ages of six to twelve years old, continued to graffiti the wall with anti-Nazi slogans and '*Vive De Gaulle*'. *These would be the next recruits for the Maquis*, thought James as he began to relax and smiled as he stealthy observed the spectacle unravelling before him. Even these young children were fighting the occupying forces in their own special way, they would be the ones who would chuck stones at German vehicles as they passed by, young enough to be ignored as a real threat by the invading soldiers. Making sure not to be seen by these potential resistance youths, James continued his mission.

It took him only another fifteen minutes to reach the red-light district from the headquarters, James checked his watch, the time was five minutes to nine, there was nobody apart for a few over made up women, standing in one corner waiting for their next punter. James got out a German cigarette from the silver cigarette case and lit it, as he inhaled the smoke, he had to confess the Germans made good cigarettes. He roamed the courtyard looking in all the red lit-up windows, stopping at one of the brothels with a skinny, black haired beauty in the window, flaunting her wares. James admitted to himself that she was very alluring, but his quest was in the forefront of his mind.

As Édouard had said, on the dot of nine o'clock walked in the thin, black-suited Gestapo officer wearing a jet black uniform, a silk white shirt, with a black tie, large-brimmed hat and a circular pair of thin-framed spectacles, on his little finger of his left hand he had a silver band ring with a skull adorned with a couple of swastikas, he was a good-looking, yet maybe overly thin, a clean-shaven man with true Arian features and a red Nazi armband on his upper left arm, displaying the much hated black swastika in a white circle. He strode confidently into Paris' red-light district. James subtly watched the Nazi regime agent, looking into the red-lit brothel windows as if he was window shopping for a new settee, checking each prostitute before deciding on his choice of the brothel that would suit him that particular night. James strode over to intercept the German Major before he could enter. The Nazi officer looked offended when this 'businessman' stepped in his way and asked using hand signals, for a lighter. The Gestapo Major grudgingly dug into his pocket to assist the stranger, as James stealthily unlocked the hidden blade from the walking cane. The officer lit James' cigarette with a match from a match-book, which James recognised from the La Belle de Nuit nightclub, they were displayed all over the bar where James had spent most of his days before the resistance. James nodded his thanks and then in his best pronunciation said,

"Der Französische Kaufmann sends his regards," the officer looked taken back and shocked, unsure of what was happening. James drew the eight-inch blade from its wooden cane sheath and impaled the officer with an upward thrust, piercing the majors' organs as it easily passed through the man's ribs. James caught his victim, so the noise of the body falling would not make a sound that would attract any unwanted attention. James carefully dragged the Nazi victim to a dark corner of the plaza, as blood trickled from the corner of his mouth. He then rifled through the soldier's inner pocket and found two small pocketbooks, he could not be sure which one his associate, Édouard, wanted, so decided to take all three and fitted them into his own inner jacket pocket. James checked his watch again, his timing had been almost perfect, the car Pierre had arranged will be picking him up in the next few minutes. James replaced the blade into the cane and locked it back in place. He walked from the red-light district adjusting his suit as if he had been a client of one of the working girls who frequented this area. He stood on the pavement and looked for his lift, there was not a vehicle in sight, he checked his watch again, the pickup should have been here two minutes ago, but they were going to be in an occupied zone after curfew, so some slight delay was to be expected.

James saw the rectangular lights of a car's headlights approach, he prepared himself. As it slowly came closer, he could make out the insignia on the side of the dark car, as it approached him, he recognised it as a Nazi 1938, Skoda 903. They couldn't know about the Gestapo officer's demise yet, could they? Had some nosey prostitute seen what had happened and squealed? Had his body been discovered by some whore's punter? All these worst-case scenarios ran through James' head as he watched the car, it slowed to a crawl as it advanced towards him. He did not speak a word of French or German; any attempt of communication would undoubtedly blow his cover. He began to walk away from his rendezvous point and he could hear the low growl of the six-cylinder, eighty bhp engine as the Nazi staff car followed him along the road. James was getting nervous, he looked behind him and saw a Nazi soldier walking along the pavement closing down behind him, he cautiously unlocked the top of the cane, he would not be taken alive and Pierre's guys would be here at any moment to back him up, he was sure of it, he could not believe how much faith he had in his French comrade. The car revved as it sped up briefly and swerved across the pavement, only three feet in front of James, stopping him instantly in his tracks. The back-passenger side door opened and a German officer in dark green, full dress uniform stepped out and approached James, the sentry walked behind him and passed James, he saluted the officer who, raising his hand, returned the salute, before turning back to James as the sentry began to walk past the car.

"*Guten arbent*," said the man, the undercover SEO agent understood enough German to know that this was a greeting, so he put his hand to his hat out of politeness. *Hopefully his officer just wanted a cigarette,* thought James. The officer took a few steps closer to the grey-suited man, James slowly began to draw the blade from his cane as the officer looked around before James could act the German officer said in a low whisper, "James, it is Pierre." James froze, he squinted his eyes and through the dim street lighting he could identify his comrades' features, he relocked the blade into the cane. James could not be entirely sure what was going on, why was his associate dressed as one of the occupying forces? How was he a passenger of a Nazi staff car? Had this all been a setup? Had he just been clearing house for Hitler?

"Come, get in the car, my friend," motioned Pierre. James thought better than to argue and Pierre entered after him. In the front seats sat two more men, both dressed in Nazi uniforms, he recognised the driver as one of the resistance soldiers, from the headquarters, if it had all been a setup, James would be hung as a spy. The second of the men was no older than nineteen years of age and gave James a 'Cheshire cat-like' smile, which he was sure was meant to be friendly but was more unsettling. "Luc! Eyes forward!" commanded Pierre; the boy did not move, until Pierre repeated it in French, smacking the lad around the back of his head; it was evident the boy did not speak English. The car continued on its journey.

"What the bloody hell is going on?" asked James.

"Be calm, my friend, the only way we could pick you up is to be disguised like Nazis," said Pierre. "The curfew starts at nine, it be the only way to pick you up," urged the Frenchman. James accepted this explanation, to be honest, he had to admit, he couldn't think of another way to escape undetected after curfew. James looked out of the window as they passed the shops, even though he had not been in this city for too long, or even this country, it was evident that they were not heading back towards the resistance headquarters.

"Where are we going? This isn't the way back!" he said trying to determine where they were.

"We cannot return to the headquarters in a Nazi car and uniforms, we would be shot!" Pierre laughed.

"We have a small house in the woods, where we can hide the car and change the clothes," said the driver of the car in a strong German accent, James looked at Pierre who could read the concern on James face.

"This is Yosef Böhmer," smiled Pierre. "He is the best mechanic and driver in the resistance. You can trust him; he is a German Jew." Yosef then continued.

"We then just walk back into the city, tomorrow disguised as mushroom pickers." Then the man in the front passenger seat sat up straight and then leaning forward in his seat said

"*Merde! Point de contrôle!*"

Pierre and James peered through the windscreen and through the fast-approaching darkness they could see a Nazi military checkpoint up ahead of them.

"It is okay, Yosef will get us through," reassured Pierre, sitting back, he was not at all worried in the slightest. As the intimidating checkpoint came closer into view, they could identify eight guards wearing their long green overcoats and their coal scuttle shaped helmets. As the car slowed James sat back, he did not want to show the German guards the tension he was feeling spreading throughout his body. The conversation between the Jew and the guards could have only lasted a couple of minutes, but to James, it felt like a lifetime or more. Pierre eventually wound down his window and the soldiers instantly stood to attention and raised their right arm in a fascist salute, Pierre just raised his right hand and wound the window back up. James only felt free to breathe again, when the barrier was finally lifted and the occupying soldiers waved the car to continue on its way.

The resistance inhabiting the matt green Nazi vehicle continued along the nearly deserted streets, it was like driving through a desolate ghost town as the dim street lights played with the shadows on the paved streets. They continued to drive along the cobbled roads until they turned onto a mud path towards a wooden, log cabin with a connected wooden log shed. They drove the car into the shed and after disembarking the vehicle, they covered it in a large dirt cover and then dispersed wooden crates and straw on and around it, enough to conceal and disguise the vehicle so any passing soldier would not identify it as a Nazi staff car. The four personnel then entered the log cabin and lit a couple of petroleum lanterns.

The men changed into some casual, normal everyday clothing, concealing the Nazi uniforms under some loose floorboards which they disguised beneath a tattered red rug. Luc turned on the wireless radio and banged it as if it would force it to work quicker.

"You need to let it warm up," groaned James, tiredly, as the fatigue hit him, it had been a stressful day and he was ready to hit the sack.

"Quelle?" asked the young man

"He only speaks French, my friend," explained Pierre, before translating for James. The radio eventually came to life on the 'BBC radio Londres' channel which introduced itself by playing the beginning of Beethoven's fifth symphony, which when translated into Morse code spells out the letter 'V' for victory. This was a British radio broadcast which played internationally. James had listened to this program before, the London SEO headquarters often slipped in coded messages for missions behind enemy lines which meant nothing to anyone except the particular agents involved in that operation. They all sat back in the rickety chairs with a cigarette and the calm slowly swept over them as they listened to the soothing music, whilst Pierre cooked a pot of roasted chicory and grain coffee substitute over a cast iron hob.

James revealed the two booklets he had retrieved from the corpse of the recently executed Gestapo officer. Pierre opened the black leather book and each page had a black and white picture of a different man, with a name, what they sell and the area in which they occupy their black-market business, this had to be the book Édouard wanted to retrieve. The second book was slightly smaller but no less thick with the word '*Taschenbuch Bririsches heer*' in the decorative and elaborated German text. Pierre took one look at it and passed it over to Yosef, who looked at the three men with an expression of pure shock, his face as white as a sheet.

"It says '*Taschenbuch Bririsches heer*', which means 'Handbook of British Army'; I have heard that all officers who have been on the front line have one of these. They are instructions about British forces, look, it has regiments, their weapons, armour and uniforms of the British forces," Yosef said. James grabbed the book and flicked through it, the amount of information, from the parts he could read, was scary.

"Some traitorous spy, like that bastard William Joyce, are to thank for these no doubt," sneered James.

"We have ours just like they have theirs," said Pierre in thought as he took his turn to examine the book.

That night each man took a turn on watch as the others slept. The following day they would be walking back into Paris with the rouse that they had been mushroom picking in the French countryside.

Chapter 4

The following morning the troop of four left just after nine o'clock, the curfew initiated by the Nazi high command ended at seven AM, but to fortify their alibi of leaving that morning to go mushroom picking, they had to leave their hideout a bit later. There were two old wicker baskets already waiting for them both half full of various edible mushrooms to complete their cover story, they buried the books they had retrieved beneath the assortment of fungi.

Halfway along the dirt track, on the way back to the big city, they stopped in their path, all horrified. There was a single large oak tree, in this forest of pine trees, and swinging on one of the lower branches were three dead men, hung by the neck with piano wire nooses. The first was a ragged man in his late fifties to early sixties with silver hair on his balding head, the other two were young men in their early twenties, with messy dark hair, all had a steel look of terror etched onto their faces. Pierre shook his head in despair.

"I knew these men," he said. "They were good men, their only crime was to sell the occasional rotten potato." He got a puzzled look from James. "He and his sons owned a potato farm down in the valley. They did nothing to deserve this! They picked these mushrooms for our cover." James saw his associate begin to well up.

"*Traîtres,*" spat the young Luc, he had an emotionless glare in his eyes and seemed unnaturally undisturbed by the scene.

"They were not traitors!" Pierre shouted at Luc in English before remembering his associate didn't understand him and then saying, what James assumed was the same in French.

"Why would the Nazis hang them?" murmured James, in confusion, this was a too hostile a punishment for non-active resistance members and not public enough to make a statement.

James got out the Hitler youth knife, from his boot, to cut down these poor victims, but Pierre grabbed his arm "We cannot do it, my friend, if we get caught we will be hung next to them and we must get Édouard his prize," he urged; it felt a bit harsh but this was war, and Winston Churchill had always said the SOE was "the ministry of ungentlemanly warfare", and this proved it. After a few moments of silence and a brief Jewish prayer by Yosef, they continued on their long walk back, all feeling partially saddened by the atrocity they had just passed. The group trekked back and passed through the checkpoint without any hindrance, which was a relief to all. There were many shops with the large windows boarded up with planks of wood and the word '*Juden*' painted in thick white paint along with the 'Star of David' to indicate that these were Jewish

29

owned businesses. James could tell by Yosef's face that this scene of countless closed down shops, whose owners he had most likely known from temple and had now been shot or shipped off to a concentration camp, was greatly distressing him, but they dared not stop, not even for a moment, to too many of the Nazis it would be construed as a sign of compassion towards the Jews and they didn't want any trouble, not now that they had got back into the city. It had been decided that Yosef, who was visually the oldest should take Édouard's cane and support a limp as an excuse, so apart from the knife in his boot, James was unarmed and this did not fill him with confidence.

They began to walk past a park adorned with plants and trees, if it was anywhere else you may forget that there was even a war on, but not here. There was a small crowd of people growing at the front of a wooden platform. Decorated with the offensive swastika flags, a wooden banner at the back had the SS logo painted on it. In the centre of the stage stood a Nazi colonel, in front of a free-standing microphone, at the foot of the platform, stood six armed Nazi soldiers separating the growing crowd from the wooden scaffolding. There were a dozen young boys and girls, wearing brown uniforms and a swastika armband, indicating that they were members of the Hitler youth, handing out propaganda flyers to the public, James was handed one which he made out to be reading, but it was all in French and he couldn't make out a single word of it. The four men blended into the assembly and listened to the ranting German officer who was speaking loudly in French.

"He is saying that the Jewish terrorists in Paris are to blame for the death of Otto Abetz," translated Pierre, "and that they have struck again." He paused as he listened to the Nazi officer. "The parasite Jews last night murdered a Gestapo officer and, he says, the only way to assure the safety of Paris is to stamp out the Jewish infestation and to execute all who aid them." He translated the officer's speech, word for word. This made the group of four feel very uncomfortable, even though Yosef had not registered himself as a Jew, as was the law and so was not made to wear the 'Star of David' armband, it would be wrong to say he had no Jewish facial features and unfortunately many of the occupying forces had a keen eye for such an appearance.

"We must go," urged James in a hoarse whisper, feeling more and more uncomfortable with the situation. His comrades couldn't have agreed more. And they slowly began to separate from the throng, making sure not to draw attention to themselves and continued their hike back to the headquarters of the Paris resistance. James began to breathe a little lighter as Pierre knocked the code on the reinforced door.

James dug into his basket of mushrooms and retrieved the small black book from the bottom and delivered it, along with the borrowed walking cane, to the rough looking Édouard, flipping it casually onto his paper covered table.

"I think this is what you wanted Ed," James said. Édouard gave the Englishman a vicious glare at this casual attitude and the shortening of his name. He looked at the notebook and flicked through the pages, the further he looked, more troubled his expression became.

"This is bad, very bad," he murmured.

"What do you mean?" asked James, suddenly concerned; this had to be the book. "What's wrong?"

"Nothing," said the French black-marketeer, "but he has much more information than I feared."

"You think someone spoke?" James lowered his voice.

"None of my men would break under torture. I am sure of it," insisted Édouard strongly, handing over the carton of cigarettes he had promised, without tearing his eyes from the small notebook, the black-marketeer was a man of his word.

"So how then?" inquired James taking the carton gratefully.

"A terrible conclusion," said the Frenchman quietly. "We have a traitor, a Nazi collaborator. I was suspicious before, but now I am sure beyond any doubt." The Frenchman hesitated. "Six months ago the Nazis burst into a house where we were hiding some escaped prisoners of war. They killed the whole family, the mother, the young son and daughter. They then easily found the escaped soldiers, they shot them all where they stood. Two English pilots, like you." James was about to interrupt to explain that he was not a pilot but thought better than to interrupt this Frenchman mid-speech. "An American airman, three Dutch soldiers and one Free French, all dead. They knew exactly where they were hiding. Someone betrayed us. They were to be smuggled into Spain and then back to your home, England." His voice had changed to one of sadness and James was in shock, that one man could cause such a massacre.

"You knew them?"

"The Free French soldier was my brother. Until eight months ago I was willing to sell my illegal things, to the resistance, to the French, to the Germans, I didn't care. When the resistance decides to help get my brother out of a Nazi prisoner of war camp, I stopped my men selling to Germans and joined the resistance and now I only sell my wares to the Maquis. I would never betray my brothers' memory." James understood this giant of a man that little bit more.

The two men looked around at the people milling around the underground base with scepticism, this Nazi spy could be anyone, they could trust no one and if a collaborator could give the enemy this much information, then how long would it be before they knew about him and his connection with the resistance and British military? Seeing James' concern, Édouard added, "This information would have taken many months to collect, so you are the only one I can truly trust."

"Do you have any suspicions?" asked James turning his voice to a whisper.

"Maybe but nothing for sure. But I will find out and when I do, you, my good man will eliminate this evil traitorous scum." Édouard had a hint of pride in his voice.

"I'll need a gun if I am going doing your dirty work for you," said James hoping for some hardware. Édouard smiled.

"Come, I shall give you a weapon. But when the time comes to take out this insect, I shall give you something more… more substantial. But for now, you would need something small and easy to conceal." He led James to a hidden door, identifiable by a padlock fitted on the wood panelled wall, where a man suffering from dwarfism, wearing short baggy trousers and a brown waistcoat which he had left open showing his plumpness, hairless body, sat smoking a cigarette, with a Luger revolver nestled in his lap. "This is Theo, he works for me, he guards our weapons, not really fair to put him on the street, it would draw the wrong kind of attention," he said introducing the small man who slipped of the stool and handed a large key to Édouard, which he had tied on some string around his neck, before trotting off from the immediate vicinity. After watching the small man disappear into the depth of the headquarters Édouard unlocked the heavy-duty padlock from the door and swung it open with great ease, he shone the flame lit lantern into the small neighbouring room, it was an 'Aladdin's cave' of weaponry. It was stacked with British Lee Enfield mark four bolt action rifles, American Thompson submachine guns and German MP-40 submachine guns, along with grates holding boxes containing hand grenades and three wooden plank shelves holding various handguns, loaded ammunition clips sat beside each weapon. Édouard considered carefully before picking one out, loaded a clip and handed it over to his English associate. It was a Walther PPK revolver with an attached suppressor, a favourite among the German Nazi officers. "I hear Herr Goebbels has a golden one. It is loaded, be careful, *mon amie*," he said patting James on his shoulder. "We shall talk again." With that, Édouard re-closed the door and fitted the large padlock back in place, he left James to admire his new weapon, as he gave Theo back the key. Theo slipped the key back over his neck and retook his stool, he sat back, lighting another hand-rolled cigarette which he took from the selection of ready rolled ones in a small gun metal box.

James spent the following hours meeting with fellow resistance members and ended having a beer at a bar, chatting with Constance, hearing about her and Pierre's upbringing. They had grown up in a picturesque town called Domme, in the Dordogne region of France and she would recollect how they would explore the extensive cave system beneath the town, swimming in the clear beautiful Dordogne river, she described the splendid and beautiful views from the high vantage points. She reminisced how as she grew older, she would spend many days with friends at the small local café in the town's main square, *Place de la Halle* and take midday walks along the original fortified walls and large gateway. All the streets were lined with a mixed array of houses and cottages in a lovely honey coloured stone which was distinctive to that region and the magnificent market day, every Thursday, Constance described in such detail that James could almost see it in his mind's eye, she made it sound like a far-off paradise. She described how difficult it was moving to Paris after their father had been shipped out and died in Africa and their mother had died of a flu virus soon after her husband's demise. She continued describing how things changed when the German army marched into Paris and took its occupation of the French city of light, Paris. James enjoyed just listening to her speak, her voice was calm and soothing that you could forget that there was ever a war happening. She explained how just after a few days the Nazis re-opened the many theatres, opera houses, cinemas and nightclubs, to distract the Parisians from the true nature of the Nazi occupation, even though they had banned all films produced before 1953 and all films made by Jewish directors were outlawed, resulting in many of them being destroyed. She and Pierre had not been so easily swayed and were firm supporters of *Charles de Gaulle*, even after he had escaped to Britain, which apparently Pierre assisted with.

The day spent with one another ended with the beautiful Constance taking James to a local undertakers, who happened to also be the resistance forger, he made fake identification papers for James, for a solid twenty-four carat sovereign coin, it took the forger just shy of five hours to make the illegal, legal papers, James was hugely impressed by the skill and accuracy, the identification papers had every detail up to and including the original looking eagle stamps, which he had made with just half a potato and a pot of blank ink.

That evening due to a close at the resistance headquarters with James playing craps with a group of resistance fighters, the translation was tricky but the rule was the same. That night not one of them could sleep, there were air raids in Germany and Paris' Nazi anti-aircraft heavy artillery fired rapidly at the British Lancaster Bombers flying overhead, supported by the greatly admired Spitfire fighter planes. The sound of the continuous weapon fire vibrated the ground violently, the walls of France shook with the artillery fire and the flaking ceilings rained down their rubble, littering the ground in debris. In the underground headquarters, they could only imagine the terror that was unveiling above ground.

Chapter 5

James had left early that morning. Even though the sound of the allied air raid had been muffled in the reinforced, confined underground base, the sounds of the ruinous explosions had kept everyone awake and on edge. It was clear by the shuddering of the ground and the raining of the dried-up plaster and peeling paint which fell off the walls, during the fearsome display of force, that the bombs had not fallen too far from the resistance headquarters. James had even shouted, at one point, over the cataclysmic din, "You bastards! You will kill us if you keep this shit up!" Not that it helped.

As he stepped out from the secure warehouse, as he breathed in the fresh air, glad to be out of that stuffy armoured cellar, he looked around surprised how unscathed the area seemed. Apart from a few tiles, which had been shaken loose, by the violent vibrations and shattered on the street below as they fell and the occasional cracked or pulverised window, there was little to no other damage, this was the last thing the Englishman had expected, obviously the 'glorious RAFs' bombardment was not as devastating as they were made to seem. This thought swam in James' mind as he wandered down the street.

Walking down the quiet street a French cyclist passed, wearing a common black and white jumper and a black beret, with a cheery '*Bonjour Gnar!*' (the French seemed to have trouble saying his name correctly). James just rose his hand with a smile, not that he recognised the man, but he was now well known by the Parisians, as he had been introduced to many people when he was out with resistance members, either going out for a drink or on some illicit activity, but he was never revealed as a member of the resistance.

He reached the end of the road where he was met with an utterly different scene, one of distress and despair. The whole single side of the street had been obliterated into a large single pile of rubble, the opposite side of the road, which consisted mostly of shops had been mainly spared apart from the window having been blown in and a few of the doors now hanging by their hinges from the force of the previous night's cataclysmic barrage. Yet this did not deter the resilient shopkeepers from moving their wares onto tables outside the shops, making the entire road look like a street market. James slowly walked down the road and watched with admiration as the French residents helped each other collect anything of value from what they had once called their homes and loaded them into horse-drawn carriages. James saw three young Nazi soldiers jeering and laughing as an elderly man fell over the debris to try and move a wooden table from beneath it. Without thinking, James clambered up the steep heap of rubble and went to the man's aid, after a few hard shoves the table came free and the two men carried it down to street level, lifting it into a wooden cart which already had a matching pair of chairs and a rolled-up rug loaded on it.

"*Merci, monsieur, merci,*" thanked the man; James gave him a friendly pat on the shoulder and said quietly:

"There are people fighting for you out there." James gave the once jeering soldiers a stern glare, their schoolboy like juvenile antics had now ceased to be replaced by sneering looks at the man who had just ruined their fun. James wanted to truly ruin the three soldier's day, which would have included a bullet for each of them, but even though he had a strong urge, he knew better, this area was swarming with Nazi soldiers and French police walking up and down the street on the lookout for looters. So James continued on his way, only stopping to help someone lift an item onto some sort of transportation. His mind still on the three German troops he had just seen, but his mind soon wandered back to his friend, Henry Farrows, his premature demise and the promise made by Pierre at their first meeting, to have the chance to avenge his comrades death, after all, this was why he had joined the French resistance in the first place. It was true that since joining he had helped with the assassination of the German ambassador and murdered a Gestapo officer, but these had all been 'favours' for the resistance or tasks given to him to earn their trust, none had been his choice or a chance for revenge. In his mind, a Nazi has to die... A Nazi officer, by his hand. So the Englishman went on the prowl, this was not the work of the Paris resistance, this was personal.

It had taken him a few hours to find the perfect target, a German Major who was standing on the banks of the Seine river, which divides the great city of Paris into two distinct halves, watching the barges float by as he smoked a cigarette. James casually walked up beside the man. He was a lean man who had a friendly look and could be seen as attractive. Unlike many of the German officers in Paris, who seem to forget themselves in the magical city, with their hygiene and smartness deteriorating, this man was very clean and smart, with a single gold wedding band being the only jewellery he wore. James removed a cigarette and then repeated what Carl Hurten, their team leader, had taught him. He had tried to teach his two comrades some useful German phrases on the plane flight, before his death. So asking for a lighter he said, "*Feuerzeug Bitte?*" The officer smiled nicely at, what he assumed, was a Frenchman trying to speak German.

"*Oui,*" the officer replied in French, his voice gave the impression that he was thrilled to have the interaction with a resident of Paris, as most of the French population kept their heads down to avoid any contact with the occupying forces, no matter if the Germans were trying to befriend them. The officer got out a black matchbook, James could hardly believe his eyes, he recognised the logo, it was from the La Belle de Nuit nightclub. This pristine soldier was one of the loud Nazi louts who frequented the club, where James had used to prop up the bar. The officer lit a match and held it low for James to light his cigarette, once the American brand cigarette had caught alight, the soldier froze, he dropped the match and his face turned white as all the blood drained from it. The German officer had a silenced Walther PPK revolver sticking in his gut.

"*Danke*, you a'hole!" James whispered into the man's ear. "This is for Henry," and with than he squeezed the trigger and watched the man fall to the pavement before him, without a sound. James instantly felt as if a huge weight had been lifted off his shoulders, the Englishman replaced his weapon and coolly, as if nothing had happened, strolled back towards the resistance underground headquarters, casually walking past German patrols, forcing himself not to smile, as he went along his way.

Arriving back to the subterranean base, he found it sparse, seemingly deserted and eerily quiet even though it was midday, he had never seen it this quiet and it put him on edge, he walked through the control centre, minding every step he made, not wanting to break the deafening silence, looking for any sign of life, the lack of anyone else made him more nervous by the second. A horrendous thought dawned on him, *the Nazis couldn't have found the headquarters, could they?* James heard a muffled cough, from behind a dirty curtain that led to an annexe. He stopped in his tracks as his blood ran cold. James instinctively reached around behind his back, gripping his revolver, ready for immediate use. He nervously approached the filthy tattered sheet and in one swift action, jerked it roughly aside, James dropped his hand from his gun sharply as he was met with a cry of "*Bon Anniversaire!*" from the three resistance members that he now knew the best. Constance, her brother and resistance leader Pierre, as well as the giant black-market dealer, Édouard, who met him with beaming smiles. He received a tender kiss on the cheek from his female comrade, who said in English, "Happy birthday, England." He then received a handshake from the two male comrades, who directed him to the old worn settee.

"How in the world did you know it was my birthday?" James said once he had recovered from the initial surprise. If he had been honest, he had actually forgotten himself.

"As I told you the first time, at our first meeting, my friend, we are big fans." Pierre laughed handing his comrade a wooden box of Havana cigars, Constance produced a Victoria sponge birthday cake that she had made herself and then Édouard pulled out a large flat package, wrapped in brown paper and tied together with string.

"*Bon Anniversaire, mon amie*," he said with a smile, handing it over to James. The Englishman pulled the Hitler youth knife from his boot, cut the cord and tore open the wrapping to reveal, to James' utter disbelief, a Vera Lynn 78 RPM shellack record. Vera Lynn was a favourite of the British soldiers and was known as 'The Forces' Sweetheart' as she would visit the troops in the trenches and sing for the brave allied soldiers, James had had the honour of seeing her sing live at Surrey Southwark music hall in London before the war.

"How on earth did you get this?" James asked, overjoyed by his new gift.

"I made a special request for it with the last delivery from your glorious RAF," replied Édouard. This really touched James, the thought that Édouard had contacted London and asked them to send a record meant a lot to him. "We play it, yes?" asked Édouard and without waiting for a reply, he disappeared into his own storage annexe. Meanwhile, Constance sliced her home-made cake and placed a slice on to four separate plates.

After a couple of minutes, Édouard returned carrying a phonograph in one arm and a couple of bottles under the other. He put down the large record player and produced a bottle of Johnnie Walker 'red label' (a favourite of the British prime minister, Winston Churchill) and a bottle of Russian vodka. He pulled out four mugs from beneath the table, poured whiskey in three and vodka in one for their female companion. Édouard took James' record, wound up the phonograph and the Angelic voice of Vera Lynn singing her newest song *'We'll Meet Again'* began playing. James offered his comrades a cigar each who all accepted, except for Constance, this was a surprise as he had only seen Édouard smoke his pipe and he had never seen Pierre smoke anything, but these were a rare luxury. They then all had a toast to their English comrades before digging into the home-made sponge cake, James considered that Constance must have used over a week's sugar ration to make this and then he remembered that their giant friend could get his hands on anything.

Before long the two bottles were near empty and the four friends had begun alcohol infused dancing, many resistance members had begun to turn up and investigated the noise that surrounded their underground headquarters, only to end up joining the party. James sat down on the settee, exhausted and staring into the bronze speaker horn, remembering his home, the sombre thought brought a tear to his eye and he fell to sleep where he sat.

Chapter 6

Over the month that had passed, the Paris resistance had done various minor operations, such as blowing up communication depots, cutting telegraph lines and felling trees across the roads to disrupt the enemies progress, James had helped with many of them, these were just standard everyday jobs of the French underground, the resistance work was endless.

James had just woken from a stuffy night's sleep in the headquarters when he searched out Pierre, he found his French associate with his sister, Constance, who both welcomed him in a friendly manner.

"Pierre, I need a wash old boy," he said in a quiet casual voice, he knew that hygiene was not the top priority for the resistance, but after a few weeks smelling your own musky body odour, there is only so much a man can stand.

"Of course, my friend, we may spend our life in hiding underground, but we are not animals," Pierre replied. "Constance here will take you to a... safe house," he said, making doubly sure that the final two words were in the correct order. "You can have a bath," he smiled broadly. Constance also had a sly smile on her face; they obviously found this situation quite amusing.

Constance rose from her seat and began to lead James out and in the tone she now used every time she spoke to James, which he always found slightly seductive, she said, "Come on, England."

As they passed through the depressing, damp, cobbled streets of the capital city, dark grey clouds grew in the sky and covered the sun, making the occupied city all the more gloomy. James and Constance travelled arm in arm to give the appearance of a standard Parisian couple and it seemed to work as they had hoped, as they were passed by more than half a dozen lone Nazi soldiers or the occasional guarded enemy tank parked by a bridge or on the side of the road and apart from a couple who gave Constance a quick once over, they were otherwise ignored. Constance led the way to a narrow blue door and up an uneven set of wooden stairs to a quaint second storey apartment, it was rather homely with black and white photographs of people he did not recognise, inexpensive china plates and a few pieces of worn-out furniture. The bath was situated behind a near transparent curtain in a connected room, down a short hallway. Constance filled it with hot water, which she heated in a pot on a hob and once James had undressed, he wallowed in the steaming water. He covered his privates from Constance; undeterred, she topped it up with warm water. James was relaxing when Constance handed him a cream coloured block; "Soap," she explained. James examined the wax-like block.

"What are these black bits?" he asked, concerned.

"From the fireplace," she tried to explain.

"Ash?" This was beginning to feel surreal.

"*Oui*, to kill the lice." This explanation surprised James, he had never heard of ash being mixed with soap at all, let alone to kill lice. But if they claim it works, who was he to argue? Constance left James to get cleaned up, he could not remember the last time he had felt so relaxed without the assistance of an excessive amount of alcohol, it must have been before the war, yes; since then he had relaxed but not to this extent. *If I had a glass of good whiskey and a Cuban cigar, I would be in heaven right now,* he thought to himself with a small smile, regretting that they had finished his new cigars two days before. His mind snapped back to reality when he heard the voice of Constance and the gruff voice of a man speaking French in the front room. James swiftly grabbed a towel and chucked it over his Walther PPK pistol which he had previously placed on top of his clothes, it was over a foot from the bath and if this was an enemy spot check, he and Constance would be shot if the Nazis found it. He heard heavy footsteps approach the bathroom door and James held his breath, the door opened and in strode the large silhouette of a man James couldn't make out any distinguishing features through the combination of the steam and the curtain. The figure closed the door behind him and pulled the curtains aside.

"*Mon amie*, we must talk." The giant figure looking down at him was Édouard. He pulled up a small wooden stool, not at all concerned that his comrade was laid in a bath naked. The large man sat on a puny, wooden stool which was a humorous display. He continued in a low voice, "We have found the spy. I had suspected him for a long time as being a member of the Vichy." The Vichy regime was a pro-German group of collaborators from the southern un-occupied zone of France, which also involved the majority of Frances' previous political figures who retreated south a matter of hours after the Nazi forces had marched on the grand capital city.

"Are you sure?" asked James in a hushed whisper, feeling a bit uncomfortable at the close proximity of this giant of a man to his nakedness, but the Frenchman did not seem the least bit disconcerted.

"*Oui*!" Édouard insisted. "I gave the man false information about a weapon delivery at the cathedral *Notre-Dame de Paris* the last night. My men followed him and he met a German colonel and after talking the German paid the traitor." James could tell Édouard was fuming with anger. "My men watched the Nazis set up a trap at the meeting point, but the truck never turned up."

"So what now?" James inquired, feeling a sense of excitement build inside him.

"Tomorrow, he will come to me and inform me that the truck never turned up." The large man gave a slight smile to himself. "I will say to him that the boat had some delays, so the truck will be there in two days' time, he will then go to inform the Nazi officer. And that is when you come in, *mon amie*." The Englishman was shocked, the large man had evidently given this a large amount of thought.

"*Me?*" James asked, no longer in a whisper.

"*Oui*. We shall plant a sniper rifle with a…" It was obvious that Édouard was unsure of the next words. "*Vue télescopique*? To shoot longs way?" he enquired, trying to explain what he meant.

"You mean a telescopic sight?"

"*Oui, oui* and then you shoot both the Nazi and the spy from a roof above the plaza where they will meet," he said excitedly, looking for any reaction in James' face, but the Englishman was too embarrassed by the situation to show any kind of a reaction. "I will give you a carton of Lucky Strike cigarettes for each dead man," he urged in a near pleading tone.

"No, it will be a pleasure to execute this scum, there will be no need to pay, just remember, I did you a favour," said James. Now Édouard would owe him. "What about me getting out of there? Shooting an officer will bring all the krauts down on me in seconds." Édouard smiled, he must have had this thought beforehand.

"You go along the roof and there is a balcony, it has a wooden hatch in the floor, you can hide in there for an hour or two and all will be okay," he assured him, James wasn't too sure.

"Who is the target? The traitor?" asked James, not too sure that he wanted to know, in case it was someone he had grown to know and like.

"You have met him," replied Édouard; this was not what James wanted to hear. "It is Luc." James recognised the name and then in his mind's eye he remembered the young man with the unnerving smile who had accompanied Pierre and Yosef to pick him up after his assassination of the Gestapo officer in the red-light district, he recalled how Luc was still just a kid, no older than nineteen years of age. But kid or not, he was a Nazi collaborator, a Vichy member, he had earned what was coming to him. With that, Édouard gave James a pat on his bare skinned back. "We will not meet again until it is over; I will send you a message when it is time. *Bon chance*." And with that, he left James to his bath. This sobering conversation had ruined James' relaxing bath, so minutes later James jumped out from the cast iron bathtub, dried himself with a brown moth-eaten towel and changed into some new clean clothes that Constance had laid out for him, identical to his previous clothes, except for the colour of the new Polo neck jumper which was now a dark cream (which James did not feel utterly comfortable with, he had become accustomed to his red one) and pocketed the bar of chocolate she had laid on top and retrieved his knuckle duster from his old trouser pocket.

The couple casually strolled back to the resistance headquarters, once again arm in arm. They were only stopped once when some over-enthusiastic patrolling Nazi private asked for their identification papers, which he glanced over before handing them back and sending them on their way, the forger had obviously done his job well.

Back at the hidden, cellar-like headquarters, the atmosphere was rather relaxed. A fellow resistance fighter handed him a metallic cup of a dark brown substance, claiming it to be coffee, James accepted it and downed the hot, thick liquid which had a strong flavour and a texture that nearly persuaded James to chew it. But it was coffee and that was all that mattered to him. James sank into a settee beside the beautiful Constance and snapping off half the bar of chocolate, they shared it between them; for the remainder of the night they talked. Pierre joined them for approximately twenty minutes, before leaving them alone. James and Constance eventually fell asleep together where they were sitting.

James awoke early the following morning, the headquarters were ghostly quiet. James wearily travelled up the narrow concrete stairway and stepped out into the fresh air where everyone was gazing up into the sky in silence. It looked like it was snowing, except it was too warm and there was not a single cloud in the sky. James was puzzled as he saw the white flakes hit the floor, without melting, James searched the crowd and approached his new acquaintance Pierre.

"A sad display, is it not, my friend?" James looked questioningly at him.

"It is ash, they are burning the executed Jews," explained the Frenchman. James' jaw dropped, it was raining the ash of murdered Jews over the city of Paris. He saw the German Jewish resistance member, Yosef, had tears streaming down his face, Pierre saw the man's reaction and acted immediately, if he were to be seen by any passing Nazi soldier he would draw suspicion to them immediately and it would draw them too close to the resistance headquarters when they went to investigate, why this man was weeping. Pierre put his arm around his friend's shoulder and directed him inside. James felt a deep feeling of sadness and a bitter hatred grow inside his chest. He had to walk off this feeling or he felt he would explode. The ash rained down for another hour until it finally ceased, the ash had dispersed so widely it had hardly littered the road. After this morning's horrific spectacle, no one could have expected the day become so clear and beautiful. The sun was beating down upon the capital city and the population, who had been in hiding, had once again come out to roam the cobbled streets.

A man ran in a beeline towards James, making him nervous, the man stopped directly in front of James and handed a folded piece of paper to the Englishman.

"I have a message for you, *monsieur*," he said in a hoarse voice. This took James back, how this man knew who he was, anyone's guess.

"Erm *Merci,*" James replied taking the note and the man vanished into the streets of Paris. James hastily slipped the note into his top shirt chest pocket, so as not to arouse anyone's suspicion and walked casually to the end of the block, he got out one of his American Lucky Strike cigarettes, then along with his newly received message, he pulled out his silver lighter, lit his cigarette, casually replaced the lighter in his pocket and read the note, it was written in a very messy, scratchy and nearly illegible handwriting and read,

'*Mon
amie,*

The spy is going to see the
German.

I have marked where with a cross on the
map below.

The gun will be on the roof for you.

Bon Chance!'

Beneath the short note was a roughly drawn map of the district around the resistance headquarters, James turned back to the man to ask for directions, but he had disappeared, the Englishman looked down the street but there was no sign of the messenger, it was as if he had just evaporated into thin air. It took James a good fifteen to twenty minutes to get his bearings, the map was very rough and not nearly to scale, the markings were also quite vague, he eventually found the building whose roof he needed to get to, where he hoped the scoped rifle would be waiting for him and would give him a clear overview of the aforementioned plaza.

After a while, James had got his bearings and found his way to the apartments. He tried the wooden door but it would not budge, it was securely locked, it would be simple enough to break down but even if he wasn't spotted and arrested by a Nazi patrol, the noise of the break-in would cause some much-unwanted attention from anyone in earshot. This relied on a substantial amount of stealth. The Englishman casually, as if he was waiting for a lady friend from one of the above compartments, examined the outside of the property. It was a narrow building five stories high and each floor had three windows, with curtains all drawn and open wooden shutters, to the left of the windows in a slight alcove, was a rusting metal drainpipe which went all the way up to the roof. Time was not on his side, every second that passed was another second the treacherous Luc got ever closer and James could not be seen or the whole operation would be a bust and the collaborator would be gone with the knowledge that he had been discovered and have a possible price on his life. The Englishman lit another cigarette as a pair of Nazi soldiers passed him. They walked directly past him and then stopped, one of the soldiers took a couple of steps towards him and in a high, but still manly voice asked in German,

"*Hast du ein Feuerzeug bitte?*" The soldier got out a cigarette and motioned so James would understand, blatantly he didn't know James' nationality and assumed even if he was French he most likely would not speak German. So the Englishman got out his silver lighter and lit the soldier's cigarette. "*Danke*," the German said and they then continued on their patrol. Once they had passed out of sight, James jumped into action. He made one last check of the streets and then a Nazi sentry tower, which the Nazis had erected around the city, James was clear to act. He took hold of the rusty drain pipe, gave it a hard yank to make sure it was securely fastened to the brick wall and with great agility, climbing hand over hand, he clambered up it, he used his legs, with his feet flat against the wall, to push himself up and his arms to pull him. Halfway up the flaking pipe, James' arms began to burn but he couldn't stop climbing, he had to continue on and after a few hard minutes climb he clambered onto the slate roof. He was obscured from the view of the guard tower by a large red brick chimney which contained the vent to the apartments below. James studied the so-called 'plaza' below, it was actually a paved courtyard with the only vegetation being four young apple trees placed in each corner and an ivy plant which had grown around the archway that was the only entrance and exit. Sitting on a ledge which came off the side of a roof was a Swiss made Schmidt Rubine M1931 carbine and as Édouard had promised, it had a telescopic scope, this was the perfect weapon for this operation, he had trained with one of these, back over the channel in England. Still hidden from view, James scanned the courtyard through the scope for either one of his targets, but there was only an elderly lady, clad in worn, moth-eaten clothing, with a bland grey scarf over her head, she looked tired and worn with her head to the ground, carrying a bag of groceries, which included what looked like a whole weeks meat ration. He could have no idea what time the contacts would be meeting and could not even be sure it was going to be today. James made himself comfortable, sat against the brick chimney overlooking the courtyard, he watched the very occasional person arrive or leave. He remembered that, in hindsight, Luc had been very relaxed and laid back when they had evacuated James. He looked through the rifle scope, for this balcony that had previously been mentioned to him, once again the translation was not accurate. There was a concrete seating area with a pair of deck chairs and a rotting wooden table, this must be the place that had been suggested to him. James was thinking about calling it a night, it was beginning to look that they would not be meeting this evening, the sun was beginning to set and the air was getting chilly at quite a pace. He decided to wait just a short time longer as he couldn't miss this chance, he would not have this opportunity again.

Fifteen minutes later a Nazi colonel arrived, he was in a grey dress uniform with a black iron cross on his left breast and a wreath cockade under the normal alloy eagle on his peaked unison cap. The officer stood in the centre of the courtyard and coolly looked around with his hands behind his back. James calmly took aim with his rifle and waited for the young Vichy collaborator, it was tempting just to assassinate this officer and cut the traitors throat, face to face, after all his dirty, evil business had caused the death of at least seven escaped soldiers and this did not include the innocent victims who had been hiding them and only God knows how many more people who had died due to this man's connection with the occupying Nazi invaders, it was even possible that he was involved in the hanging of Pierre's, potato farming friends, that they had seen on their return journey to Paris earlier, as James recalled, Luc did not seem surprised by their demise, but that was not the plan. It was obvious the German officer below was getting impatient, the officer had lit a cigarette he had in a short decorative amber cigarette holder and continually checked his watch, it was unmistakable he was waiting for someone. Then James spotted the officers contact, looking through the rifle's scope, he confirmed that it was the young Frenchman known as Luc. James watched intently as the resistance traitor gave the colonel a fascist salute, this made the English sniper sick to his stomach,

James took aim, as the two men spoke and the officer gave the young man a small wad of notes, the traitor flicked through the notes greedily, he must have blackmailed the soldier for more money, with an excuse such as, it was getting too risky for him or some other reason, as it was well known that these collaborators had a large imagination.

James took aim at the Nazi officer first and fired a single shot, which echoed around the courtyard, the bullet hit into the man's left breast, just to the right of the satanic cross for bravery, puncturing the man's heart, the soldier's still body dropped where he was stood. The French collaborator dropped his newly obtained Reichsmarks and headed at speed to the exit, the English agent was not going to let this man get away, he took aim and five shots rang out, emptying his magazine, each bullet powering into the young man's back, he crumbled to his knees before falling dead. James could not linger here. In a few moments time, the Nazi military police would be combing the area for him. The former British SOE slung the rifle to his back and clambered on his hands and feet across the rooftops, hanging from the ledge as he passed the large chimney which blocked his path to the concrete seating area. Once he reached the area, he clearly saw the trapdoor on the floor, it took him a couple of attempts before he was able to open the heavy trapdoor and jumped into the damp, hidden room which lay beneath. The hideout was no longer than a walk-in wardrobe or spacious larder. James dropped the sniper rifle into the room before lowering himself in and gently lowered the wooden hatch above him shut. James felt around and found a candle, fitted in a brass candle holder, along with a box of Vesta matches, he lit the candle which illuminated the space. Even though the room was constricted, it was clear that this was a hideout designed for someone to disappear, for hours or even days. There were supplies stacked on a single shelf, it was full of tinned fruit, beans and soup, as well as a mess tin and a small fire set to heat up the food. There was also a cushion and rough horsehair blanket, which was evidently there for anyone needing to spend the night in the confined space, James hoped he would only need to spend a few hours here.

The Englishman lit a cigarette and dug out of his pocket the remaining half bar of dark chocolate. He removed the remaining wrapping from the rare treat and enjoyed the bitter taste of the dark chocolate. He could hear the sirens of the Nazi police, the shouts of German soldiers' and the countless coming and going of vehicles outside. After an hour James settled down, he had no idea how long he would have to stay in hiding here, he had already been here longer than he had hoped, yet the noise outside had not yet ceased. The sky grew darker as night drew in, James snuggled back on the cushion, pulled back the blanket over him and settled down for the night as the fatigue suddenly hit him like a thunderbolt, he blew out the candle and fell asleep in the concrete hole.

Chapter 7

James awoke with a start, by the harsh sound of knocking. It took him a good thirty seconds to recollect where he was. James froze and carefully removed his silenced Walther PPK revolver, from his trousers and slipped off the safety catch with a click. He dared not move a muscle or even inhale too loudly, in case he may draw the attention of what he could only assume some overly noisy German soldier. He heard the distinct knocking on the wooden trap door above him. Two slow knocks, followed by three rapid ones. James recognised this hammering pattern, it was the 'code' to unlock the entrance of the Paris resistance headquarters, he had witnessed Constance use it not long after they had first met. He thought for a couple of minutes in silence before saying the only French word he could think of at that particular time.

"*Oui*?" he said, putting on what he hoped was a French accent, he spoke loudly enough to be heard outside the confined room but still quiet enough not to draw attention to his hiding spot.

"James, my friend, it is Pierre," came a reply, James hesitated. What was the resistance captain doing here? This was meant to be a secret operation, only between Édouard and himself. Édouard didn't trust anyone else, not even Pierre.

"Pierre? What the bloody hell are you doing here?" James called through the closed trap door.

"We were worried about you England," came the female voice, of Constance. James could not help but to crack a small smile and gave the wooden trap door a hard shove, the sun shone into the small room flooding it in light. It took the special operations executive a few moments for his eyes to adjust, the only light he had had was from a single candle, which had burnt out many hours ago. Along with Pierre and Constance were three other, armed resistance fighters, who had secured the area. Constance gave James a quick comforting embrace and Pierre shook his British acquaintance warmly by the hand.

"How in the world did you know I was here?" James asked, collapsing into one of the tattered deckchairs.

"We got worried when you did not return, by the nine o'clock curfew," Constance explained. Pierre then interrupted his sister.

"So we question Édouard, we know you spoke together when you had a bath." James knew precisely from who Pierre had heard that snippet of information from and Constance confirmed, by avoiding James' look and turning a radish red. The Englishman just gave a nod to Pierre showing that he understood as the story unfolded, urging him to continue "So, we expected you to return in the morning. After the curfew had ended, but when you did not return, we feared the worst. So we decided to come and find you." James looked at his wristwatch, it was ten o'clock, he had overslept, curfew had been over for just over three hours. He appreciated their concern.

The six-strong resistance group climbed down a rope into the stone courtyard, where James had assassinated the Nazi officer and the treacherous collaborator, Luc, the previous afternoon. Naturally, the bodies had, of course, been removed by the Germans that night and the courtyard was once again vacant. They split into two separate groups of three, any larger groups would arouse suspicion from the occupying forces.

Walking down the peaceful streets of Paris with Pierre and Constance, James felt awfully relaxed, even with a menacing enemy soldier on every street corner.

"Is it true about Luc?" Pierre asked in a whisper.

"Yes, but he got what was coming to him," replied James, getting a questioning look from Pierre, not understanding the English terminology. "I shot the bugger, five times in the back as the coward ran, trying to save his own skin."

"It is so hard to believe," said Constance. "He was not even twenty years of age and he was part of the Vichy regime?" James just nodded solemnly. The six resistance members walked down the thin concrete stairway of the industrial unit and through the reinforced door, into the underground headquarters.

Édouard greeted James as he entered, the bald, scared, giant of a man, was sitting by the door, on a rickety garden chair, waiting for their return as he smoked a small rustic wooden pipe.

"*Mon amie!*" he boomed. "We heard of your success on the wireless. The officer had just recently been promoted by the *Reichsführer of the Schutzstaffel, Heinrich Himmler*." Édouard laughed. "The Führer is not happy. I am pleased you are safe, *mon amie*. When you did not return, we were afraid you may have been captured or killed, by the Nazi military police."

"I am just fine, thank you for your concern." James smiled feebly; he needed a strong black coffee.

James spent the majority of the day in the underground headquarters, drinking the warm, hot, thick and flavourless liquid, eating the cardboard like biscuits and smoking more of the newly obtained American Lucky Strike cigarettes, than he should have done. He was getting tired of the constant congratulations by the many members of the resistance for his successful assassination of the one man who could have brought down the entire target for the liberation of France, or that was at least the claim.

Many evenings consisted of listening to the wireless radio. They would listen to the former member of *Oswald Mosley's, British Union of Fascists, William Joyce*, more commonly known as *Lord Haw-Haw*, spouting his Nazi propaganda, which they would jeer and laugh at. By day the resistance would collect thousands of flyers from secret print houses hidden around the city, entering the buildings with an empty suitcase and leaving with the same suitcase, now full of anti-Nazi propaganda and the demoralising of the German troops. At night they would leave piles of these leaflets in public phone booths, public toilets and plastering these resistance flyers on walls and advertising columns, the Nazis had erected hundreds of these cylindrical outdoor structures, with the sole purpose to promote the demonic Nazi regime, to no avail. The resistance made sure to tear down any Nazi propaganda, or at least cover them up with their own posters. What they were doing was highly illegal under Nazi rule and if caught they could be shot on the spot or worse be held and tortured by the ruthless, brutal Gestapo, many had been caught over the years, but this did not deter them from what they took as their duty. On countless times they had to dodge the Nazi troops, with a more than a couple of close calls, yet one advantage of being in the resistance is that you know how to quickly disappear. They also distributed illegally printed underground newspapers, from another clandestine press, called *'Défense De La France'*, which provided first-hand intelligence information on escape networks and helped any stranded allied forces trapped behind enemy lines, James could only hope that they spoke better French than he did.

After a couple of days rest, James became restless, there was not much glory in posting flyers. He saw a middle-aged woman sitting in the corner who had been never seen before, she was leaning over a large leather-bound book, scrawling ferociously with a wooded quill and a glass inkwell of black ink. James approached the lady, she had a dark bob haircut and a face of someone in her forties, someone who had seen more than her fair share, she was also wearing the officers' dress of the French military.

"Bonjour Monsieur Garner," said the women without looking up from her writing. James stopped in his tracks, taken aback.

"You know who I am?" James asked in shock, he was sure that they had never met in the past.

"Every resistance in France knows of the Englishman who helped rid us of the German ambassador, Otto Abetz, it has taken up a whole chapter in my book," she said with a feeble smile, finally looking up from her work. James had never thought much about the assassination of the Nazi ambassador since it had happened, but it must have been more important than he had previously anticipated.

"You are writing about the war?" This was quite a shock to James; who on earth would write about such a horrific time?

"Yes. In many years' time, our children and grandchildren will learn how the great people of France earned our liberty from the fascist oppressors." She had a hint of hostility in her voice. "I was a librarian in my previous life, before the war and now I help the Maquis as part of the French military, to get back the artwork stole by the Nazis, from places such as the Louvre, not to mention wealthy Jewish families. This is part of our heritage, our culture, the Nazis have already taken our glorious country, we cannot let them take our culture or we will have nothing left!" James was not entirely sure what she was talking about and was about to ask her what art she was talking about when his train of thought was interrupted.

"Ah, I see you have met our great resistance scholar," cried Pierre, coming over to the conversational couple.

"Well, actually, we have not officially met," commented James.

"My name is Rose Antonia Maria Valland," said the lady and then ignoring James turned to Pierre and began speaking in French.

"Pardon James, Rose and I must talk," said Pierre apolitically.

"Of course. Rose maybe you should have to translate that book of yours into English so I can have a read of it," said James, preparing to leave them.

"Or maybe you should learn French, my friend," chuckled Pierre as Rose continued talking to the resistance leader in French. As James, who this woman, who knew only too well wouldn't understand a single word that she said, wandered off thinking, *I have been thinking exactly the same thing myself for some time.* He had picked up a few of the basic words of French listening to resistance members, but not even near enough to hold any sort of real conversation and he found that many of the French spoke so fast he would not be able to understand a word anyway. So he eventually decided to act and walked behind a tattered curtain, which separated the rooms. Sitting on a multicoloured settee, recovered using second-hand curtains, was Constance reading a small notebook. James sank into the seat next to her. They had grown to be good friends and close companions, he guessed that she pitied him, there was only a little handful of resistance members who could speak more than a couple of sentences in English, even though others tried but didn't make much sense, plus he was positive that she had a soft spot for him, even though she tries, with not much success to hide it and had never actually confessed it in so many words. Once Constance noticed James approaching her, she closed the cardboard book cover and tucked it down the side of the settee.

"A diary?" asked James, sitting back in the settee, Constance gave her little schoolgirl giggle before replying,

"*Oui, mon journal*, I have kept one since I was eighteen. I started it in England as a holiday journal but never stopped writing it, it relaxes me."

"Well, that and your Russian vodka," joked James, she gave a small shrug of her elegant shoulders and another small giggle.

"It takes me back to a time of peace and makes me feel normal in this time of…" She hesitated, thinking of the word; this was the first time he had noticed her unsure of an English word, but James understood what she was trying to say.

"Time of chaos," James completed the sentence for her which made her smile and blush slightly from embarrassment. They got lost in each other's eyes for longer than either had previously intended. "I need to ask you a favour," the former SOE agent finally continued, tearing his eyes away from hers. "I was wondering if you could teach me French?" This request made the young *mademoiselle* smile broadly.

"Of course, I will." She laughed gently, resting her tender hand reassuringly on his rough hand as if she was not only relieved but also surprised that it had taken so long for him to ask for her help and for the next hour Constance began to teach her English comrade the basics of the French language. It was complex with the masculine, feminine and neutral versions of the words but he was picking it up quite easily. They continued until, as always, Pierre intervened.

James had to admit, he was beginning to wonder if Pierre was worried about him spending so much time with his younger sister or whether it was just dumb fate that every time he was in the company of Constance, he was summoned by the head of the Paris resistance cell.

"James, my friend. We are meeting tonight at the apartment of a Spanish artist. Rose needs our assistance."

"Is it safe?" James asked concerned.

"Yes, he gets harassed by the Gestapo. But he *has* helped hide people for us, mainly escaped prisoners of war and Jews," Pierre said encouragingly.

"Why the hell would the bloody Gestapo harass a simple artist?" James questioned, a bit concerned that they may be getting involved with the ruthless Nazi secret police, the Gestapo were quite simply Nazi thugs, they were not known for their kindness and were avid supporters of the Führer, Adolf Hitler, they found it enjoyable to hinder and harass locals of German-occupied areas.

"They do not agree with his type of art," explained Pierre. "They said it does not fit in with the 'Nazi idea of art'; when the German invaders outlawed bronze casting for the war effort, he came to me to ask if I can get him some bronze, so for his support I get him scrap bronze." This sounded somewhat familiar to James.

"What is this artists name?" he inquired. Pierre seemed to have unchallengeable faith in this man, which would normally be enough, but then he remembered how Pierre had trusted Luc and how quickly he himself had been trusted, so he was not going to be caught unprepared this time.

"Pablo Picasso." James had heard of this artist before, the artist was said to have started the cubism movement and his art had become one for collectors all over the world, including the National art gallery in London. James had heard that since the invasion it was officially illegal to display his artwork in public.

That evening a couple of hours before the curfew, eight resistance members, including James, Rose and Pierre, who carried some bronze piping for their host, disguised as firewood, left the hidden resistance complex in groups of two and three and took separate routes, all with different alibis, to the famous artists home.

They walked through a narrow, wooden, red door, which led to the equally narrow staircase of an apartment complex. Rose led the way up the stairs, on the second floor she knocked on a very plain plywood door. As they waited for an answer, they were joined by three other members of the group and the door opened to reveal a sixty-one-year-old man with a balding head and strong brown eyes, his gaze lingered on each of his visitors one at a time before he opened the door and led the way into the lounge of the small apartment. The man seemed spry and not at all as James had imagined. The man's eyes lit up when Pierre presented him with the salvaged metal.

Chapter 8

"Vino?" the artist asked, offering a clay cup of red wine to the Englishman who accepted it with a nod of thanks as he admired the simplicity of an unusual ornament hanging on the man's wall. It looked like the seat of a bicycle with two brass made horns adorning it on either side. The elderly artist stood beside James looking at his masterpiece with pride, he said something in French that James couldn't understand.

"He says it is his newest work, he calls it the 'Bulls Head,'" Rose translated, appearing on the other side of James, also looking up at the artwork.

The other members had all turned up at the apartment, accepting the beverages being offered by the Spanish artist and talking in hushed voices. The friendly man then returned to a worn, brown leather sofa, which was seated in one corner of the room and sank into it observing his guests as they made themselves comfortable around his home, leaning against walls and sideboards or perching on the corner of tables and chairs that were untidily displayed around the living room. There were expressionist paintings dotted all over including a pile of rolled up paper which James assumed were more of the art master's works. With these works of art, metal scraps and not to mention the dirty glasses, jars of paint mixed water and assortment of paintbrushes which were strewn around the room it was very busy and eclectic, to most this would seem a mess but to an artist, everything had its place.

Rose stood up and the room fell quiet, James did not have high expectations that he would understand anything the resistance scholar would say, as it was quite obvious she would be speaking in French and even with Constance's lesson he was only likely to understand a couple of words and that was only if she spoke slowly which he knew was highly unlikely. His fears were confirmed as she began speaking in a hushed voice, yet still loud enough that the whole room could hear. Pierre began to whisper a translation from behind him, which he truly appreciated.

"We are all here to discuss an attempt to reacquire items such as silver, clothing, crockery and many of the items stolen from arrested Jewish families, including the paintings on this sales sheet given to us by our good friend," the lady gave a small bow to the Spanish artist who lifted his own goblet of wine, she waited with a small smile for Pierre to finish his translation, before continuing, with Pierre still repeating in English. "There is a warehouse situated on the edge of the city guarded by the SS elite forces. As we witnessed a few days ago, the Nazi army is exterminating and burning the bodies of the helpless Jews which is just another step to their thousand-year Reich and final solution.

But this will mean that everything they owned, including the clothes on their back, were taken, catalogued and stored to be sold or used to fund the war effort, so I say we should take it back from the Germans and use them to help us." This was met by the entire room applauding her, which James joined in, it was an honourable plan. She then rose her clay mug and said,

"*Viva La France,*" which needed no translation and everybody stood, rose their own glasses and in unison replied,

"*Viva La France!*"

Then a second man rose to his feet, raised his glass and in great enthusiasm said, "*Viva DeGaulle!*" which everyone repeated with a small cheer.

"How many guards can we be expecting?" James asked, ignoring the second man's outburst. with Pierre translating for the benefit of the others present. Rose replied

"*Entre Vingt et trente.*" James had learnt numbers with Constance, so could roughly understand.

"Twenty or thirty?" he whispered to Pierre for confirmation. Pierre just nodded. James scanned the room to see if he was the only one perturbed by the overwhelming odds, to his surprise everyone seemed quite calm and relaxed about the whole situation.

The following couple of hours consisted of planning and questions being answered. The attack was to take place that night after dark, which meant that they would be out after curfew. The Spanish artist, with the help of Pierre, shifted the wooden coffee table and pried up a pair of wooden planks from the floor to reveal a secret weapon's cache hidden beneath, to James it seemed that Pablo Picasso was more associated with the French underground than Pierre had previously let on.

The troops left the artists to the solitude of his home at approximately half past eleven, by this time most residents would be in the sanctuary of their homes and the roaming military would be a little more relaxed. Heading Eastward the city was ghostly quiet and all eight soldiers of the resistance, now all armed with the very lethal guns, including a couple of Sten guns received from an airdrop by the British RAF, and knives. Of course, James still carried his silenced Walther which he had out and ready in case they ran into the path of a patrol. James had been given a vital task in this operation, which carrying a larger weapon would have hindered. Naturally, they wanted to as stealthy as possible, if the alarm was sounded, they would be facing more than just the Nazi 'elite' but as well as any nearby German military, which would then change the entire mission from bad odds to utterly impossible odds. The city was cold and the full moon glared down upon them. The light of the moon would be a disadvantage, but the cold would assist them, as James had been taught during his special operatives executive training, guards' concentration are more likely to lapse during cold weather and shift changes were more often.

The group made sure to keep in the shadows, anyone caught after curfew could be shot on sight, they walked away from the city of light, sticking to back alleyways as much as possible to avoid Nazi patrols and lone soldiers, ducking every time a German soldier was seen or the rumble of a military truck or Jeep was heard. They would have two lookouts, every time that they had to cross a road, one watching the road and the second watching the sentry in the towering guard towers or taller sniper posts. It was a long strenuous trek, as they continued moving away from the centre of the French capital the streets became darker and the enemy became less frequent. Ahead of them, they could see light illuminating a large complex with a giant, manned, watch tower overlooking it. Keeping low, the resistance quietly ran to cover. Discovery now would be a colossal failure and a real dent for the Paris resistance, not to mention the ideal publicity tool for the Nazi propaganda machine.

It took them another eighteen minutes to reach the mesh wire fencing that surrounded the immense building, it was decorated with the red Nazi banners, displaying the white circle and black swastika and overlooking the entire property. Looming over their heads stood the guard tower, with a soldier wandering back and forth in his bird nest to try and keep himself warm, he was unlikely to be relieved for a good few hours, unlike his two comrades standing by a large sliding door on the other side of the concrete courtyard. They were clearly SS soldiers, armed with MP35 submachine guns, a weapon favoured by the Schutzstaffel. They were wearing long, green waterproof overcoats, a red Nazi armband on their left upper arm and the Stahlhelm helmets, which on the right side of helmets bore the tricoloured shield of black, white and red stripes, the traditional national colours of Imperial Germany and on the left was the much-feared Armenian runic SS insignia. The courtyard was littered with clusters of red metal fuel barrels and crates around the side, but otherwise, it was deserted. Rose went to the corner of the fence and carefully pulled aside a rusty piece of corrugated iron to reveal a hole cut into the wire, James smiled, this had been the plan for a long time. Rose signalled to a young resistance member named Claude, his job was to take out the guard tower. He leopard crawled through the gap and waiting for the two guards to be facing away from him, with baited breath, he chose his moment and ran in complete silence to the bottom of the ladder, hiding with his back to one of the vision tower's legs, he checked the two guards who had now lit a pair of cigarettes and from the tone of their voices were talking intently about some French prostitutes in one of the many Parisian brothels. The troop watched as young Claude silently ascended the ladder up to the guarded platform, they saw the resistance fighter hesitate on the ladder before jumping up and cutting the guards' throat, then calmly lowering the body to the floor, he replaced his own navy mariners cap with the guards helmet, this would be his post during the covert operation, from his elevated position he could see the whole complex, any approaching reinforcements and assist with any defence, if needed. Claude lit a cigarette, this was his signal to the resistance member to enter the compound. One at a time the fighters slipped through the gap and lay flat against the ground, weapons at the ready. Watching the two guards, James was feeling anxious, these few guards were nowhere near the twenty or thirty they had expected and the collected information could not be that wrong… could it?

"Allemands!" came an urgent whisper from one of the French freedom fighters who was to guard their escape route from the opposite side of the fence, he then ran for cover in a crouched position to the opposite side of the road.

"Germans!" translated Pierre, the entire group split up to hide behind the barrels and crates or flat against the legs of the guard tower, they didn't have time to check the two guards, who were fortunately still deep in conversation. James and Pierre slid behind a group of red barrels, neither man was watching the courtyard, one of the soldiers was now lighting the others' second cigarette and only turned when they saw the torchlight of eight soldiers, one with a vicious Doberman tugging on a leather leash, wondering past the entrance of the complex, oblivious to the resistance fighters hiding in the shadows inside. Each resistance member held their breath as they watched the patrol pass on their routine guard duty around the high-profile Nazi storage facility. Once they had passed out of sight, James breathed a small sigh of relief, he could see the other members doing the same. The Englishman took a peek around the barrels to see the two guards, who seeing the patrol seemed even more relaxed, enjoying their cigarettes. "Shoot them," whispered Pierre, James removed his silenced pistol, which he had replaced in his trousers when he had slipped through the gap in the fence, he took aim, inhaled and whilst slowly exhaling fired two shots into the chest of each man, as he had been taught as SOE school to double tap with every shot. The two Nazi guards crumbled on the spot.

"Nice shooting," whispered Pierre as Rose whispered an order and two more resistance fighter ran across the courtyard and dressed in the long overcoats and helmets of the deceased soldiers, before waving over the others.

Pierre tried to pull open the door but it was locked. A forty-year-old female named Jeanne stepped forward, she had been a thief in her previous life before the resistance. She inspected the lock and got out a small black pouch of flat slithers of metal in various shapes, the other members looked on in anticipation as two men with Sten guns concealed themselves at the far end of the courtyard, with viewpoints to the entrance of the compound in case of reinforcements. There was a dull click as the door unlocked. Rose cautiously pulled at the door, opening a wide enough gap for the troop to enter through, two at a time, ready for anything the team entered the warehouse. It took them a couple of minutes for their eyes to adjust to the dim light inside. Encircling the inner walls of the massive warehouse was a metallic walkway which held four more Nazi guards, they seemed unaware of the band of armed newcomers. Rose silently motioned to three fellow resistance members and signalled to James to shoot the guard at the end of the large building by making a gun with her hand and pointing to the target, James gave a nod and took aim. From the corner of his eye he saw the three chosen resistance fighters stealthily move up the metal stairs, once they had reached the walkway, James took his silenced shot, the man collapsed with a clatter as his steel helmet and rifle hit the metal platform, this alerted the other three soldiers, but they did not have time to figure out what had happened as they were sprung upon by the three resistance members. There was a brief scuffle, the three guards were felled quickly with only a minor injury to a strong resistance fighter who had his arm slashed by a Nazi blade. His associates acted swiftly, they wrapped the wounded arm with a sleeve from one of the Nazi's coats and tied it tightly to stop the flow of blood. Meanwhile, Rose pulled sharply at the cord to a generator which sat to the left of the entrance, she had to tug at it multiple times before it growled to life. The large lights hanging from the high ceiling switched on one at a time and seemed never-ending, they illuminated the entire warehouse. The display that unfolded before them was both terrifying and heart wrenching, the entire group were dumbfounded. At the far end, beneath James' assassinated soldier, was a mountain of clothes which went as high as the walkway and covered the entire stretch of the back wall. Directly in front of them were countless wooden shelving units, each six stories high, each shelf was covered with silverware which included an unnaturally large collection of Jewish Shamash candelabrum's, there were piles of leather-bound books, most had gold leaf Hebrew lettering on the covers, these must have been Torahs. There were piles of empty suitcases, wooden furniture, there were tables in between each shelving unit covered in collections of crockery, combs, hairbrushes and glass bowls filled with multiple types of spectacles, jewellery and even boxes full of shaving brushes. James and Pierre walked over to a pair of large, wooden barrels and cracked off the top to reveal that they were filled to the top with small golden nuggets, James picked up a handful.

"Bloody hell, it is gold!" James laughed.

"*Mon Dieu*!" Pierre suddenly exclaimed examining a couple of nuggets. "They are teeth, my friend, gold teeth!"

"Good God!" James dropped the gold back into the open barrel with disgust. "These are all from Jews?" They were looking at what was left of Jewish lives under Nazi rule. Before Pierre could confirm there was a French call from the other end of the room, which attracted everyone's attention.

Everyone assembled to see Rose frantically tearing off dust covers, revealing countless paintings. This answered some of James' questions, this is why they had met at Picasso's home, it was more than a sales list he had given Rose, it was a list of Jewish customers and after the invasion, all the paintings would have been confiscated along with all their other possessions by the Nazi forces. Under the rules of their fascist regime, the Jewish people were not classed as human beings, so were not allowed to own their own private property. This building was a clear sign of the Nazi oppression towards other cultures and beliefs, James was finding it difficult how Hitler's minions could accept this horrendous treatment of other human beings as being the normal way of life.

All of a sudden the door slid open a fraction and a Nazi SS guard ran in, it was a disguised resistance member and he said something to Rose, who nodded in reply.

"What did he say?" James asked Pierre who he assumed was standing behind him, when he received no answer he turned to see that Pierre was nowhere to be seen. Instead he got an answer from Rose.

"He said that your time has come."

"What are you talking about?"

"Pierre said that you are a good driver…"

"Well, I don't know about that."

"Did you not escape the Nazis after the assassination of the German ambassador? And get Constance away safely?"

"Well yes, but—" started James before Rose interrupted.

"A German supplies' lorry has just parked outside, as it does every night at this time. We will be stealing it and drive these painting to a secure, secret place so they can be returned to the rightful owners after the war is over." There was such determination in her voice that James could do nothing but admire her.

Once they had been informed that they had taken out the German driver and the 'coast was clear', the resistance members formed a human chain, passing the large framed paintings along and loading them into the back of the dark grey Nazi lorry, marked with the white lined black cross. It was half full when a voice was heard which made everyone stop in their track and made their blood run cold as ice.

"*Halt! Nicht bewegen!*" The French and single Englishman turned to the road, where the sound had come from. Standing there at the entrance were the eight guards and the vicious dog with his ears back and his teeth bared snarling at the strangers, they had their MP35 machine guns aiming directly in the direction of the resistance thieves, for what felt like an hour but was only a minute, the two armies stared at each other, neither side wanting to make the fatal move. In a split second, the Nazi officer blew loudly on a small silver whistle, raising the alarm. Claude, up in the guard tower, was the first to react and let out a single volley blast of gunfire, which hit its mark and shot every soldier. James saw the soldier who had previously been restraining the bloodthirsty Doberman had fallen, yet the dog had survived the onslaught and was still pulling at his restraints to get to the men before him, the leash was still clasped in his now deceased master's hand. The animal was snarling and barking at them maliciously. James had heard enough, whilst the resistance members ran about in a frenzy, trying to load as much into the lorry as possible, he drew his silenced Walther PPK and fired a single shot into the base of the dogs' skull, he had always been more of a cat person anyway. He was sure the Germans whistled alarm, the rapid gunfire and the hysterical dogs barking would catch someone's unwanted attention. Rose walked past James and stopped briefly to turn to him and say bluntly,

"We need to go, get in the truck!"

"Are you mad?" James blurted. "That whistle was the alarm, we can't leave these guys here to die!"

"We will hold them off until you make your escape, my friend!" Pierre shouted. "We will meet you back at headquarters!"

"Non, I will drop off James, then I must get back to base," said Rose, James was sure Pierre hadn't been talking to her,

"Er I think he meant me."

"*Bon!*" Rose noted.

"Go! Quick!" prompted Pierre, his eyes no longer on his associates but past them, through the compounds large entrance and down a dark street, he had seen what they all had been dreading, the headlights, belonging to Nazi reinforcements, coming towards them at speed.

James jumped into the driver's side cab with Rose beside him. The low rumble of the approaching engines grew louder as James drove the large military lorry out of the Nazi compound and turned a sharp right. Both occupants looked in the wing mirror, to see lights pursuing them. The French woman smashed the window behind them with the butt of a Fallschirmjägergewehr 42, also known as 'paratrooper rifle 42', a malicious weapon of Nazi fire-power. Turning in her seat, she aimed her weapon through the smashed window, James checked his wing mirror, there were two bikes trailing them, one had a side cart carrying another armed soldier. Rose did not hesitate, she opened fire out the back window, deafening James and making his ears ring as the gun spat out its empty cartridges littering the cab. He watched, in the mirror, as the first bike swerved, crashing into a towering fir tree, turning into a fireball, moments later the driver of the second bike fell and the soldier in the side cart stretched over to try and keep control of the bike, he had no chance as Rose let out another volley and the bike swerved off the road. James could not help but give a sly smile, he could not believe it, they had just escaped Nazi bikes. James slowed as they approached a fork in the road. "Go south," instructed Rose.

"South? But that takes us into Vichy territory!" exclaimed James.

"Yes, I have friends; they run a resistance from *La Forêt des Landes*. It is the last place the German army or collaborating Vichy troops would look for the paintings and they will keep them safe," explained Rose. This made sense, people did not often find what was under their very noses and the enemy forces were less likely to expect the stolen paintings to be in their own territory. James had to admit that driving through the 'free zone' did not fill him with confidence and found himself checking his mirrors more than usual.

Rose directed James down a narrow mud path, which led them deep into the claustrophobic Landes forest. James suddenly stamped down hard on the brakes, stopping the lorry instantly. Standing directly in their path, with a malicious array of hostile weaponry, aiming at the pair, stood seven men all wearing matching dark corduroy trousers, wool jumpers and dark coats of various colours. The man in the centre of the assailants stood out from the others; he was six feet tall, with a tangled long brown goatee beard; he wore a black beret and dark green jacket, which had at one time belonged to a Nazi but now had all the insignia removed. He stepped to the drivers' side window and tapped on it with the barrel of an Astra 900, a powerful deadly automatic pistol, on a shoulder strap he carried an MP60 machine gun with a drum magazine. James slowly wound down the window and the man barked something in French.

"Just keep your hands up and do what they say," advised Rose.

"I don't speak French," James reminded her through clenched teeth, yet not taking his eyes off his aggressors for a second. The man barked something else,

"He is telling you to get out."

"I take it, these are *not* your friends?"

"I don't recognise them," she said looking at the men before them. *Great, bloody Vichy!* James thought to himself.

"*Silencieux!*" commanded the man, violently swinging open the drivers' side door and roughly dragging James from his seat, nearly dropping him to the floor, but he was able to regain himself and stop himself from toppling over. Whilst a couple of the mans' associates dragged Rose from the vehicle. The two were roughly put up against the side of the lorry and frisked, they had their weapons relinquished by the men. James' mind was racing, these men could be standard gangsters, members of the Vichy regime or members of the resistance, yet the final one was seeming less and less likely by the second, as none of them seemed to recognise Rose. The first man barked something, spitting as he spoke, directly into James' face, but of course he had no idea what the man had said, so he just kept the man's stare and stayed silent, for which the SOE received a punch to his stomach which dropped him to his knees, before he knew it, he had a second pistol, aptly named the Executioner (identifiable by the rings on the grip for the fingers), aimed at his temple, once fired it would easily remove half of James' skull at this range. The man looked at the man below him and once again spoke in French, James understood two words '*Vichy*' and '*Mort*', 'Vichy' and 'dead'. James just closed his eyes and waited for what he was sure would be his end.

Chapter 9

Rose was shouting so rapidly James could not pick up a single word, he was also rather preoccupied with his impending fate. The French would-be assassin lowered his weapon and gave the Englishman an order, James still did not understand.

"Get up," whispered Rose. "*Il ne comprend pas*," she explained, letting the man know that James did not understand him. James, a bit fed up with this, rose to his feet and once again raised his hands.

"*Rose, mon amour?*" came a loud booming voice, followed by the man whose voice matched his appearance. The man seemed overly relaxed. He was a skinny man with a neat thin beard, he wore a pair of dark green combat trousers and a black vest, he carried a Steiner rifle slung over his left shoulder and a Raum pistol stuffed in the front of his trousers. He casually walked over to the two prisoners and embraced the forty-year-old woman, giving her a kiss on each cheek. The woman spoke to the man in a friendly tone, calling him Jacques. James just stood still watching the two people, with his hands still in the air. Rose then introduced James, who was too nervous to lower his arms until Jacques offered him a hand and began speaking to him in French as he shook it warmly, Rose had to translate.

"He says, we are happy to welcome a brave English soldier here. We are sorry about the way we treated you, but the only people who usually are driving Nazi vehicles are part of the Vichy government." The man paused to let Rose catch up. "He wishes to know if you have come to train them?" she continued. James looked around at the seven rough men who were listening to the conversation closely.

"Tell him, I accept his apology and his caution is understandable." James chose his words carefully because he truly wanted to smack this guy around the face. He had nearly been obliterated because some uneducated Frenchman thought that a man who couldn't speak French was collaborating with the Vichy government. But James wanted to keep this civil considering his previous assailant was still staring daggers at him. James cautiously removed a cigarette from his jacket pocket, offered one to the apologetic man and lit them both before continuing. "I am afraid I am not here to train his men, I was sent here with two comrades to kill Dietrich Hugo Hermann Von Choltitz." He was surprised he still remembered the name, it had been drummed into him at the operation briefings. "Both of my comrades were wiped out. Since the British military can't get me out, I am now working for the French resistance." Once Rose had finished translating to the man, he smiled at the explanation.

"Welcome, friend," he said in broken English.

That night, James and Rose spent the night around the resistances campfire, under the heavy forest canopy. The man who had nearly assassinated James previously, just sat on a stump, all evening glaring at the English visitor maliciously. James decided to ignore the un-trusting Frenchman and try to understand the conversation between Rose and Jacques. The Frenchman was obviously asking for some assistance and Rose was refusing.

"What does he want?" James asked.

"There is a party, that the Nazis have arranged," she explained. "There will be many members of the Vichy regime and they are asking for our assistance." James looked at the man, who looked back hopefully. It would be a bold mission, if the Nazi forces were holding a party for the Vichy, it would only be for high ranking members in the Vichy governments and rich families, not to mention the high-ranking Nazi officers. Also, they could not rely on the local population to help them, if they needed a quick escape or hideout, in the so-called free-zone, most of them were Nazi sympathisers.

"We can't, Pierre will need you back," said Rose sternly. "This is not your mission!" James considered the proposal, she was right of course, this did seem like a bit of a suicide mission.

Before they left the lorry of paintings with the Southern French resistance, Rose and James were given a matt black Kaiser limousine, it had once been a Vichy politicians car. The men claimed to have assassinated the politician, stolen the car and repainted it to disguise its previous occupants. It was a beautiful car, even with its un-tasteful paint job. At first light, they left their new acquaintances and travelled back into occupied Paris where they could both breath that little bit lighter.

"Last night when they asked for our help, I thought for a moment you would accept," Rose said.

"So did I," replied James.

Chapter 10

It was past midday by the time the two counterparts had got back to the large building where the resistance headquarters hid beneath. James stopped the car outside the entrance of the metallic building.

"Please tell our brave comrades that I must return to the French military base and do my reports," Rose said calmly. "Pierre was right, you *are* a good driver. The British Maquis." She smiled. James could only give a faint smile back before disembarking the luxury vehicle. He watched as the car disappeared in the distance, walked casually into the cast iron building, giving the guards in the rafters a wave before descending the narrow, brick steps. Knocking the code on the door, he waited but received no response, he knocked louder a second time, making doubly sure he was using the correct code, it took a full minute before someone opened the door without even checking the identity of the caller. Walking into the basement command post, it looked more like a war zone hospital, people were strewn on stretchers and collapsible bunks with various wounds and injuries, there was a strong metallic smell of blood in the air. James could discern by the looks he received that he had not been blamed for leaving before the perilous battle had ensued.

James threw off his leather coat revealing his tight fitted maroon woollen jumper and threw his grey flat cap onto the side of an old wooden crate. He wandered throughout the subterranean resistance base of operations until he saw his compatriot, Pierre, laid on a stretcher in one of the annexes with his younger sister kneeling beside him, there was a blood-stained bandage around his neck.

"James, my friend!" Pierre croaked, giving a faint smile, Constance tipped a glass of water to the French leaders' lips.

"You're looking gay old chum," started James, then seeing the bandage he instantly regretted it. "Jesus, are you all right?" Seeing the concerned look on his English allies faces, he said:

"Do not worry, it missed my throat."

"If it had been shot another two centimetres to the right, it would have hit your air pipe," complained Constance, both speaking in English for James' benefit, which was becoming the normal routine when in his presence.

"Do not worry, my dear," dismissed Pierre. "I am still alive and will be back fighting for the liberation of our beloved France very soon. Until then, James, Édouard needs you to help him," with that Pierre flopped back hard onto the stretcher; it was clear to James that even though his French associate was talking tough, he was still very feeble and exhausted from his ordeal.

"Sleep brother," said Constance calmly. "I will come back later." She rose, took James' hand and led him away.

Once they were alone, Constance looked James in the eyes and spoke quietly so as not to be overheard. "Many people got hurt and some have died, please be careful when you are working with Édouard, some of his men have families who have died in the fight. You cannot rely on them. You can trust Édouard, but not his men."

"You think they blame me?" James whispered, appalled by the thought. "But why?" Constance looked around before saying in a reassuring tone,

"Non, not blame you but do not trust you." James could see in her face that she was concerned and full of conviction. The Englishman took note of the French maidens dire warning and gave her bare arm a reassuring stroke before turning, in search of the black-market dealer. Constance words lingered with him as he walked to Édouard's storage room annexe and threw aside the curtain.

"*Ah, mon amie*! I am glad to see you are well." The large man was sat behind his wooden desk. Before him, he had many metallic pieces of a disassembled revolver and a basic weapons cleaning kit. He began to reconstruct the firearm, lubricating each piece with gun grease from an aluminium tin on the table behind him. "I have an easy job for you to assist me with." James did not have high hopes, Édouard definition of an easy job was usually anything but easy. "We need more supplies," he said without looking up from his weapon assembly. "This last attack has made us short of morphine and other helpful supplies, such as weapons. I must go to the office at *La Belle de Nuit* and make a call to your army on the secret radio and ask for an airdrop. You and three of my men must stand guard, so the radio will not be discovered!" he said, slamming a loaded magazine into his now assembled Colt .45 revolver and looked up for his partners' response.

"Okay, it seems simple enough, but before we go, I need some more rounds for my Walther." Édouard opened his desk drawer and dropped a handful of bullets onto the table, James gave a small chuckle and began refilling his magazines. "When are we going?" The plan seemed like a straightforward and uncomplicated plan. It was true they would be in a place often frequented by the Nazis but all they had to do was ensure the enemy forces did not enter the office whilst Édouard was on the radio to Britain. The Germans were usually too interested by what was on stage than investigating anything, especially whilst on leave.

"Now." The large man rose and led James up the stairs where three men were waiting, smoking hand-rolled cigarettes, their conversation ceased when they saw the two men appear from the stairwell. The group all had concealed pistols with fitted silencers and without a word they left the security of the resistance-controlled building and walked down the cobbled street towards the Jewish owned nightclub, *La Belle de Nuit*.

The journey had been uneventful apart one very keen Nazi soldier asking for their papers which they calmly handed over, he scanned the documents before handing them back. James wondered why they had been targeted but came to the conclusion that he must have been bored, the soldier had no idea how close he was to being killed.

Once at the club they left one man outside the main door as the other four entered. One of the men went up the stairs to the balcony and walked around so he could see the door to the office, the second leaned against the bar. After paying the checkout girl with some Francs, Édouard entered the office and James stood guard outside the door watching the intoxicated Germans whooping and whistling at the dancing burlesque girls on the stage. James felt sorry for the young French girls who had to accept these leering, drawling, drunk Nazi soldiers. James grabbed a match-book from the check-in counter and lit a cigarette as he waited for the seven-foot black-marketeer to complete his communication with James' homeland.

Watching the on-stage show James was entranced but was snapped back to reality when he heard his full name being said, James Garner. Not wanting to give himself away he looked from the corner of his eye and saw a woman talking to the young girl at the counter. This was no ordinary French female, it was a ravishing blonde beauty with wavy long locks which dropped just past her shoulders, she wore a bright orange scarf which looked out of place against her pale white skin. She had a slim fit, tanned and suede driving jacket which showed off her slender figure, it was only done halfway up showing a bleach white low-cut top which revealing her impressive bust, she wore tight mustard yellow trousers and knee-high brown leather boots. The innocent check out girl pointed out James, who was now staring at the women as she approached him.

"James Garner? My name is Olivia Hayhurst," the lady stated in a very posh English accent. "I am with British military intelligence, I think we need to talk." James looked at this British bombshell in shock, he couldn't quite believe what he was hearing. It took him a good few seconds to absorb this new information.

"I am a bit busy right now," he said, looking around nervously. "Maybe we can talk a bit later," he said in an attempt to dismiss her.

"Fine, I will wait in your room and we can share a bottle of this," she opened her coat to show a bottle of twelve-year-old Vat 69 blended scotch whiskey, a sly alluring smile formed on her lush red lips as she saw James' eyes light up. He had only had German or French whiskey since he had been deployed here, he would be willing to pay handsomely for this American beverage, even back home in England, a bottle of this whiskey brand would set him back a few 'bob' and she was offering it freely, she had got his attention. "I take it your silence is a yes," she said and as he watched her walk down the side hallway, James could not deny that he was checking out her pert behind. The Englishman couldn't believe it, what the hell was military intelligence doing here in occupied Paris? What the hell did they want with him? James took another deep drag of his cigarette when he heard the door behind him unlock and open.

"*Any trouble, mon amie?*" asked Édouard stepping out from the office, he looked around and closed the door quietly behind him. James had to think quick, he would need a plausible excuse to meet this apparent British spy, he didn't know enough to inform his counterpart and he knew how touchy these government spooks could be about their identities being revealed.

"No, it is all quiet," James lied, his mind was running in overdrive. "Hey Ed, you mind if I don't go back with you guys? There is a nice young dancing girl who I have had a bit of fun with. I think might stay and see if I can get a bit of action." James had no idea what he was talking about. "Just keep it quiet from the guys back at base," he didn't want it getting back to Constance, he was not quite sure why not, it was not like they were an item, but he knew she liked him and he liked her but did not want to hurt her feelings.

Édouard nodded and said "Be sure you are back for tomorrow night, *mon amie*." He looked around before saying, "We will be getting our delivery." James was relieved that no other questions were asked and Édouard reached into his coat pocket and handed James a British military regulation Prophylactic Kit which was for genital cleaning. It contained ointment, a soap saturated cloth, cleaning tissue, and a condom. James just laughed as he tucked it into his trouser pocket.

"Thanks, I will see you tomorrow," smiled James as he watched his three comrades leave through the front door.

Looking around the room full of Nazis, James' head was spinning. He strode with determination to the backstage changing area, grabbed his silenced Walther PPK revolver from the back of his trousers, flipped off the safety catch and cocked it, he got some unsure looks from some of the changing performers, he gave them a reassuring wink and opened the secret door into his previous accommodation. He did not see the attractive, curious women at first until he looked to the settee where she was sat with her coat laid beside her and an Enfield no.2, six shot service revolvers laid on top of her legs. She had a glass of whiskey in her hand and had poured a second which sat on the table awaiting James' arrival.

"So Olivia, or should I call you Agent Hayhurst?" he asked, standing in front of her, making no secret of his gun.

"Olivia is fine," she said. She had a posh, almost musical voice. "And you are James Garner, the only surviving member of a three-man SOE team dropped behind enemy lines and you are now working for the French resistance." As she spoke she noticed James' weapon and with a smile added, "You won't need that; if I wanted you dead, you would be."

"Is this about my extraction?" questioned James, not moving.

"We can talk about that. Please, it is not polite to let a woman drink alone," she urged, gesturing to the sofa. James hesitated, placed the revolver on the armrest of the sofa, before taking a seat and picking up the spare glass; raising it he toasted:

"Bottoms up!"

"Cheers!" she retorted. James downed the glass in one swig, he closed his eyes as he felt the alcoholic beverage fill him up. He had not tasted anything as nice as this for a long time. Olivia smiled and refilled his glass from the black glass bottle she had nestled next to her, James decided to take his time with this second glass, the first seemed to have gone straight to his head. His vision had become impaired and his head felt woolly. He tried to speak but he could not manage any sound to escape his mouth.

"Are you feeling okay?" asked the woman. "Feeling a bit sleepy?" She smiled. James felt the whole room spin before everything went dark and he slumped back on the sofa.

Chapter 11

"Good morning, Corporal Garner," said the voice of a Scottish male, the voice was once again very posh and instantly James thought, *this guy is a Rupert,* meaning an officer. His head was still cloudy and his eyes were heavy yet he was able to force them open, it took him a couple of seconds to take in his surroundings. He was in a one room, studio apartment, which was much cleaner than his secret room at *La Belle de Nuit,* but no larger. He found himself bound with rope to a wooden chair and was unable to move a single muscle even if he had wanted to. The windows were boarded up and the morning light seeped through the gaps. There was a single table which the lavish female agent, Olivia, was leaning against, beside her was a British issue ham radio. Standing directly in front of James was a lean man wearing a white shirt open to the chest, a black waistcoat and matching trousers, two steps behind him, to his right, was a stocky, muscle-bound man, with a face like a boxer. James recognised the second man, they had gone through the SOE training together, though they had never got along. He was a Cockney, previously a jeweller, they were always competing to outdo each other during training.

"Sampson," James greeted him dryly.

"Garner," came an equally dry reply.

"I am glad to see that you are all acquainted," said the first man, obviously not happy with the interruption. "I am known as 'The Fisherman'. Do not worry about your eyesight, the drugs will wear off soon enough," he said coolly.

"My eyesight is just fine," James said bluntly. "Who the hell are you anyway, Fisherman?"

"We are part of the British Military, His Majesty's Military Intelligence. And it is your duty to help us," the posh man demanded.

"Begging your pardon sir, but fuck you! You left me to rot! I don't owe you a damn thing! I work for the French resistance now, my duty is done!" spat James.

"I am The Fisherman and you are my bait and need I remind you that you are still a corporal in the British Special Operations Executive, who is currently working alongside the French Resistance. You owe us your allegiance!" The man's voice grew louder and stronger with each word.

"Bullshit! You think you can abandon me and then use me as you want?"

"In a word, yes." Olivia smiled.

"Go to hell!" James said, not tearing his eyes off the Fisherman. The man took a single step towards the helplessly bound Englishman and with a black leather-clad hand reached into his trouser pocket and slipped a nickel covered knuckle duster over his gloved fingers, before James could register what was happening, with built up aggression he punched James in his stomach. This show of violence made the Fisherman's associates both wince as if they could feel James' pain, giving the impression that they had both, at some time in the past, been on the receiving side. The force of the iron fist made James cough and splutter. This man was stronger than he looked.

"What exactly do you want?" asked James, knowing that any further resistance would be futile and was likely to result in more pain, after all the man was right, he was one of over nine thousand SOE agents dropped behind enemy lines and he was not the only one without an exit strategy, it was his duty to assist anyone fighting the Nazi hoards.

"You will meet a contact of ours in three days' time at the church *Saint Julian Le Pauvre*, on the Rue Galande street. He is one of our men and has been acting as the churches priest since the invasion. Do this to our satisfaction and we can see about getting you home." James raised his head and looked for the sincerity in the man's face but it was blank. "He will brief you on your mission. And this meeting is not to be shared with your resistance buddies," the man said sternly. "Do you understand, Corporal Garner?"

"Yes," said James, he hated spies, they were always vague and never gave a straight answer. "What is this all bloody about?"

"That does not concern you," Sampson almost growled.

"Agent Hayhurst will be assisting you." The man was judging James intently. Observing his reaction and reading his body language. "Good, now this location is classified. So we will have to blindfold you and will take you back to that nightclub." With that he nodded to his associates and Sampson roughly put a black fabric bag over James' head, he and Olivia then helped James to his feet and dumped him in the back seat of a car and set off.

It took well over half an hour to get them back to la Belle de Nuit nightclub, they dragged him through the back-door and only removing his hood once they were back in the hidden room. The first thing James saw once the dark bag was torn from his head was the ex-SOE, Sampson and Agent Hayhurst leaving his room by the secret door. James sat on the collapsing settee that they had placed him on and thought about the previous conversations as if in a loop. This was totally surreal, just as he had accepted that he was part of the French resistance and that the British military, who had now abandoned him, they now wanted him back.

As James eventually walked back to headquarters, his head was a daze, he was walking like a zombie trying to register what had just happened.

Once he was back in the basement control room of the resistance, he purchased a large bottle of Johnnie Walker Red Label whiskey on credit from Édouard. He had to act naturally, any deviation from his normal routine would raise red flags but the alcohol would help calm his nerves, which at this time were shot.

James spent the remainder of the day learning French from Constance and sipping from his new bottle of whiskey. James and Constance were enjoying their time together and were flirting a bit more openly when Pierre was not around to intervene, which was not a rare occurrence. The two of them had grown greatly fond of each other, yet neither of them had the nerve to share their feelings. Every time James had built up the courage to act, Pierre would appear out of nowhere, as if he had been watching the two of them and would ignore the evil look he would get from his younger sibling. Pierre had long recovered from his injury, even though he still wore a bandage around his neck which he hid with his assortment of various coloured polo-neck jumpers. James had not seen him since his return and happily, he had remained vacant.

By eight that afternoon he was collected by Édouard to pick up the Royal Air force drop which was planned for the following morning. The head of the Paris black-market ring led James up the narrow stairway where three men, all Édouards' men James assumed, were waiting. Two men were smoking rolled cigarettes, the third was smoking a cigarillo, they stopped speaking and dropped their tobacco products, stamping them out when they saw the two men appear from the narrow stairway. Without a word they followed the two men to a wooden out-building and slid open the shed door to reveal an old vegetable delivery pick-up truck, identifiable by the faded logo of fruit on the side of the rust covered vehicle. Édouard said something in French, when all the other Frenchmen acted, James just stood there.

"What?" the Englishman asked.

"He told us to get into the back of the truck," came a reply before Édouard could react. The man had a strong American accent, he had been the one smoking the cigarillo earlier. He was a rough looking square-jawed man with a thin beard and a head of short cut hair.

"You are a Yank?" James questioned, he was sure he had never met this man before.

"That's right bud," the man smiled, giving James his hand and helping him into the back of the pick-up. "The names Draven, from El Paso, Texas," he said this in a tone as if he was reminiscing back to his time at home, James would soon learn that this was his normal tone. James seated himself opposite the American, there was a crate of root vegetables between them, to most people it would look like they were just farm hands coming from a day in the fields.

"So, what the hell are you doing here?" asked James, this man seemed pleasant enough but the Americans weren't in the war, or at least as far as he had heard. In the back of his mind, James just hoped that this man turning up had nothing to do with his previous run-in with the British Intelligence, but in all honesty, he was hoping that the run-in with Military Intelligence had just been a bad dream.

"I am a US ranger helping you Brits, I got caught and escaped a POW camp in Germany, officer impersonation, just walked out the front gate." The American chortled. "Got a lift in the back of a crate train, then I got recaptured trying to cross the border into Spain, I had hoped to make my way back to England and then to the good old United States. I was caught again when we were betrayed. So them bastards were taking me to Gestapo headquarters to be questioned. Luckily for me, the Germans were not the only ones looking for me. The resistance had me on their radar, they ambushed the convoy and here I am." Draven just gave a small shrug.

"And Ed trusts you?" questioned James, he knew Édouard was not the trusting type. The American gave a sly smile at James' nickname for the giant man.

"I knew his brother, we were locked up together, I assisted in his escape, caused a diversion whilst he got through the fence." James couldn't deny he was impressed; it was understandable why Édouard trusted him.

As they drove through the occupied city of Paris they saw a couple of Nazis putting up some red and white striped speakers onto a wall by a crossroads. "Jesus, they have really taken over, haven't they?" said Draven.

"What the hell do you mean?" James questioned angrily, appalled at the thought that the Nazis had taken anything.

"Those are propaganda speakers, I saw them all over Germany. You take my word, in a few weeks' time you'll hear their leader talking all over the city," the American replied. This made James feel sick to his stomach as they saw more speakers, exactly the same, being erected as they travelled through the city.

"You want some gum, partner?" Draven asked, passing around a packet of chewing gum. It was eleven o'clock by this time, they had travelled for the majority of that evening, to a forest outside of the city of light. They had driven cross country for the best part of an hour and parked the truck only forty feet from where the supply drop would be delivered, which was a clearing in the woods before them. They dug a small hole, they sat around it, beneath the canopy of the forest and lit a small camp-fire inside. This kept them warm during the crisp night and enabled them to cook a pot of 'acorn coffee' which was not as bad as James had expected, without showing too much light, which could give away their position to any enemy troops or aerial surveillance.

The group were sat against fallen logs and tree stumps, they were all smoking cigarettes, except for Draven who had got out another cigarillo and Édouard who was smoking his pipe. It was quite relaxing being out of the city, this deep in the woods, the chance of bumping into any Nazi patrols was near impossible. There was not a sign of life and the peace was blissful.

They eventually heard some twigs snap from behind them which made them all spin round with their weapons at the ready. Out of the darkness stepped two men, aiming their own rifles at the small company. One of the men had black hair slicked back, with a short beard, his companion was noticeably younger, both were filthy and looked tired. The older of the two barked something at them in French.

"What did he say?" asked James, Draven replied,

"He asked who we are."

"You are English?" the assailant asked, lowering his weapon slightly, whilst the other man was utterly oblivious to what was being said.

"Yes," replied James

"American," Draven added.

"Français," continued Édouard, who was looking at the two men suspiciously.

"Resistance?"

"You got it," Draven replied.

"We are Jews, Jewish partisans, from Poland," the man replied, lowering the barrel of his partners' weapon and slinging his own over his shoulder. "We were once forty strong, but me and my brother are all that are left."

"Dead?" questioned James.

"Dead, captured or missing," replied the man sole fully.

"You're Jews?" asked Draven, as if it had only just registered with him.

"Yes, you want to check our cocks?" The self-confident Jew made James smirk.

"What are your names?" Draven continued his interrogation, undeterred.

"I am Isaac and this is my younger brother Tobias," the young man nodded nervously but politely, which the American and Englishman responded to with a nod. "May we join you?" The group looked to Édouard for permission. He was not so trusting and insisted on a physical examination, before buying their story and allowing them to join the group. As they sat around the campfire they continued to question the newcomers.

"You are a long way from home," stated Draven.

"Yes, we used to live in a Jewish community in a forest in Poland but the Germans located us and marched into the woods, shooting anyone they saw, we had to flee to live. We decided to head for Spain."

"You would have to get through Vichy territory first and believe me that is not easy." Draven chuckled at the man's ignorance.

"Collaborators," explained James. "They catch you and you won't be any better off than with the Nazis."

"We join you," the younger man, Tobias, piped up. James looked at Édouard, who gave a tired shrug in agreement.

"Welcome to the resistance," said Draven. James hadn't finished his questioning.

"Your English is good."

"I was a teacher before the war. I taught English and mathematics." The men continued to quiz the new Jewish recruits and shared what little food and tobacco they had with them.

It was another hour before they heard the low rumble of the Merlin engine of planes flying above them. Édouard emptied his pipe on a hollowed tree stump and nodded to his comrades who poured dirt into the hole snuffing out the fire, it was time. The leader of the black-marketeers stepped out into the clearing with a special lantern which had a shutter by the spotlight hole, a device often used to send coded messages, by Morse code. The men watched as the giant man gave three quick flashes and one longer flash, spelling 'V' for victory, after a couple of moments he repeated the sequence.

Whilst watching this display, James heard the mechanical clicking of a revolver cocking behind him. He turned and was greeted by one of the French black-marketeers aiming a Luger directly at his head. He said something in his home language, French, the man was quite literally seething as he spoke.

"What? I don't speak bloody French!" said James raising his arms.

"He said you killed his brother," translated Isaac, looking from one to the other.

"What? When?" James couldn't believe what he was hearing. "Draven! Ask him, I don't know what he is talking about, I haven't killed anyone... except krauts!" The American translated and without a second's hesitation, the Frenchman replied; Draven hesitated before giving James the response.

"He says at the warehouse attack. He says you ran off and left his brother to die against the Nazi reinforcements." This infuriated James, he was never going to be called a coward.

"You tell him." James was incensed by this accusation and was finding it hard to keep his composure. "You tell him, I was just following orders. I am sorry about his brother, but it wasn't my fault and if he wants to blame someone, he should blame the Nazis! It was not even my goddamn plan!" As he spoke he took a couple of steps towards his aggressor until the barrel of the gun was touching his temple, the American translated frantically, James was getting tired of French men aiming guns at him. The Frenchman looked a Draven, then to James and finally at the witness' all watching the altercation, stunned, before he gently lowered his weapon. James nodded sympathetically to let the man know that he understood and offered him his hand, he shook it roughly yet it did not feel sincere, they suddenly broke off when they got a call from Édouard. The men all rushed to the edge of the forest to see a swarm of Spitfire fighter planes flying overhead. One began to fly lower than the others, Édouard was flashing his handheld lantern continuously. The roar of the unmistakable Rolls Royce Merlin engine became louder as the plane flew over the trees, making everyone instinctively duck and Édouard threw himself flat on the ground. As the mighty plane passed by Édouard it dropped a metallic cylinder, the size of a water heater to the ground and pulled up sharply before reaching the other end of the clearing, the drop had been delivered. The four resistance members ran into the clearing with their flash-lights, directly to the cylinder, the two Jews just watched from the tree line as Édouard rose from the ground and brushed himself down.

The Frenchman who had previously threatened James removed a leather pouch from his back pocket and got out a Philips screwdriver, he began undoing the screws on the top of the metallic case using his torchlight to see and pulled of the panel to reveal the inside loaded with hand grenades, weapons ammunition, countless L'Éspadon tinned sardines, half a dozen bottles of Highland scotch, a couple dozen cases of cigarettes, twenty mini medical packs, four gold watches (this was not unusual for gold bars, jewellery or watches to be added to the air drops to be used by the resistance as bribes or for trade) and five Lee Enfield rifles, to add to Édouards already massive armoury stockpile. Everyone grabbed as much as they could carry and hauled it over to the truck, where they piled it on the ground, except for Édouard who dragged the metallic cylinder to one side and dumped the container into a ready dug ditch then covered it with twigs and fern to hide it from view. Everyone moved in complete silence and with a determined purpose. Draven stood guard at the front of the vehicle with his head darting around as if on a swivel as James stood guard at the back, anyone may have heard or seen that low flying spitfire. James looked into the darkness, the quiet that at one point had been blissful was now eerie and menacing.

He watched as the remaining Frenchmen passed down the dozen or more boxes of vegetables to the two Jews, who in turn piled them on the floor beside them. The Frenchmen then pried up three planks from the bottom of the truck to reveal a hidden compartment beneath and filled it with the newly acquired wares before replacing the planks and the boxes on top.

Édouard jumped back up into the cab as everyone else clambered back into the rear, each member had their weapons concealed but ready to use in an instant, including the two newcomers who had their rifles at their feet. Their position may have been compromised by the delivery of illegal products. They stayed on guard in the back of the truck as Édouard left off to another remote area in the forest where the group took turns standing guard as the others slept in their seats.

The following morning James was awoken by a jolt as the truck took off to continue its journey. After half an hour, James noticed, alarmingly, that they were travelling in the totally wrong direction to return to the headquarters of the Paris resistance.

"Where are we going?" James voiced his thoughts out loud.

"*Le Harvre,*" replied the Frenchman who had accosted him the night before, revealing that he understood more English than he had let on.

"*Le Harvre*? You mean the bloody harbour? Why?" questioned James. the man just stayed silent giving James an intent stare. "Draven, translate for me old boy?" he requested and the American did as his comrade had bid. The Frenchman replied to him not taking his eyes off James for a second.

"He says that there is a resistance cell there and the tinned food needs to be hidden," Draven explained. James had not expected this answer but accepted it, he had little other choices. They passed many personnel carriers, many of them were empty, just after dropping off the soldiers or supplies they had been carrying. They entered the small village, made up of a single pub, a chapel and between twenty or thirty small flints-built cottages, they were surprised by the lack of occupying forces, all they saw was a single lone soldier patrolling the vacant streets with no indication of any others.

"Where the hell is everyone?" James asked in a whisper, Draven just shrugged. Édouard backed the truck into an open wooden structure which neighboured the church. James watched as, without a word, their giant captain jumped from the cab and walked along some stepping stones to a Gothic style wooden side door of the chapel and knocked, two slow and three in quick succession. James was stunned, he recognised this knock, it was the coded knock of the resistance, the resistance cell was housed in the place of worship.

A scrawny man with an unlit cigarette hanging from his mouth opened the door and scanned around before shaking Édouards hand and inviting him in, closing the door. A Frenchman stood guard at the front of the truck, watching the streets, a couple more Nazi lorries rumbled past, throwing up dust from the dirty streets.

"Okay, that is thirteen now!" exclaimed James.

"Thirteen what?" Draven asked getting out another stick of gum.

"Trucks. So where are all the bloody soldiers?"

"Well this is the harbour, maybe they are all down the front," suggested the American, only just noting that it was all a bit strange. James got out his silver cigarette case, took out a German cigarette and lit it with his decorated lighter, his eyes locked on the side door waiting for Édouard to return. Draven moaned. "So, what are we meant to be doing here?" James grunted in agreement with his counterpart. Then the sound of voices at the front of the truck drew their attention. The duo turned to see their French associate wailing in his native tongue to an olive-skinned youth wearing a black norgi jumper, black trousers and a black fez supporting an embroidered faeces, the ancient Roman weapon and national symbol of fascism, this stranger was an Italian Blackshirt. Draven approached the two men, James took hold of his silenced pistol that was tucked in the back of his trousers, this could be trouble. "*Buongiorno,*" Draven said in a pleasant, fluent Italian tone, the rest of the language was inaudible and ended with Draven giving a fascist salute which the Blackshirt returned and carried along on his way. Once Draven re-joined James, the Englishman piped up,

"What the hell was that all about?"

"He just wanted to know where the harbour was,"

"So you speak Italian now?"

"I am fluent in Italian, German and French, my Spanish isn't too bad either," the American replied with a smile and a hint of boasting, it was now clear to James why this American had been chosen to be dropped behind enemy lines.

"What did you tell the wop?" James queried.

"I took an educated guess, this is the main street, so it has to lead somewhere and if we are right about the Nazis being dropped off there and that it is the direction the lorries are coming from." James looked at him in disbelief, it was quite a gamble. But he had no time to worry about that. The side door of the chapel had opened and Édouard was on his way back down towards them. When he reached them he directed his orders to the two English speaking members in a whisper.

"Okay, you need to help get the guns and ammunition into the church," he said handing the two men a couple of brown horse haired blankets each. They unloaded the boxes of vegetables from the truck before removing the weapons and wrapping them in the blankets to obscure them from view, they even included the two Jewish rifles, they then replaced the boxes and Édouard led them up the path to the side door and once again gave the coded knock. The same man opened the door, took a look around and ushered them inside. "Put them on the table," Édouard directed. James gladly dumped them on the table and Draven dropped the box of ammunition next to them as if they were a ton of bricks. There were three other men in the room and whilst they unwrapped the wares, the newcomers took in the small room. It looked more like a command centre than the larger headquarters deep in the Paris central. There was a single Gothic style window, which, as many windows in war-torn France were, was boarded up. There were maps of the city and surrounding area, on the walls, with Nazi restricted zones marked clearly in red and hundreds of black and white surveillance photos of enemy fuel depots, radio stations, spotlights as well as prominent members of the Nazi regime and high-ranking Vichy members. It all had a disorganised order to it. On the single empty wall hung the red, white and blue French flag with the duo cross of the Maquis in red at the centre. Apart from the wooden table, three wooden garden chairs and a good number of sleeping bags piled high in one corner, the room was rather sparse. Édouard was jabbering in French to his three colleagues but even with his constant lessons of the French language with Constance, they were talking at such speed that James was unable to keep up with their conversation, no matter how hard he tried. Édouard eventually turned to James.

"Go into the church, *mon amie,*" directing them to a second door, James accepted this dismissal, he was not able to keep up with what was being said here anyhow. He walked through the second wooden door, followed by Draven, the scene before them was surreal. There were about twenty men and women milling about all wearing an armband showing the French tricolour flag with the double cross. In one corner was a tubby middle-aged man stirring a couple of boiling pots over a small inside fire, they were filled with a thick brown stew, it had a terrible aroma. James went to inspect the food as the rumbling in his stomach reminded him that he had not eaten for twenty-four hours. He looked into the bubbling pots, he was sure that he could see some potatoes and beans floating near the top, James instantly lost his appetite, the mixture looked worse than it smelled.

The Frenchman took a spoon and tried his recipe. "*Bon,*" he said, obviously pleased with the result. He offered the spoon to James, who with a forced smile, waved his hand, refusing the offer; he would take the man's word for it. He joined his American comrade in the centre of the church's aisle. Every member either had a rifle slung on their backs or a pistol sticking from their waistband, these people would not be caught off guard, even the Padre wore a colt .45 revolver in a brown leather holster around his waist and kept a Sten gun with a side magazine behind the altar, unlike the others he wore a resistance pin, much like Pierre's, on his black robes. Near the giant reinforced doors was a small cut off area which James recognised, it had an uncanny resemblance to Édouards' annexe at the main headquarters, yet with less stock and as expected the dealer wore the black armband, signifying him as a black-marketeer so people would know that he could get them whatever they needed through his illegal trade. These religious surroundings delivered James a sombre reminder of his meeting tomorrow with an undercover member of British military intelligence disguised as a priest in a church, which he assumed would be much like this.

"I know what you are thinking. But it is not sacrilegious if we are doing God's work, my children," said a voice in a strong French accent, the two visitors turned to see the soft-faced elderly Padre.

"You speak English?" James was surprised. He had noticed that many of the people were too engrossed in whatever they were doing to even notice them let alone strike up a conversation.

"I worked for many years as a missionary and English is spoken all over the world," smiled the man. He had a comfortable, soothing voice which seemed out of place with the weapon strapped to his waist, in his hand he was fingering a set of rosewood rosary beads.

"Isn't this all a bit open and in plain sight to be a resistance stronghold?" asked Draven, looking around the church.

"People often miss what is under the nose, don't you find? Germans spend most of the time down at the harbour, I do give a small service on the church steps every Sunday, but the presence of any Nazis are rare. I keep the door locked just in case," said the man of God, showing a big heavy key on a cord around his neck the man chuckled to himself. Movement behind the priest caught James' attention, Édouard had just entered the church. The massive figure walked towards the trio with a sense of purpose.

"We must talk," said Édouard. He looked around for any eavesdroppers before continuing. "In private!"

"You can speak in my quarters," offered the Padre, Édouard nodded his thanks and the elderly man led his three comrades to a room opposite the one they had entered through, it was a small door to the left of the altar. It was a small room, the same size as they had been in when they first entered. It had a standard cot at one end, a clothes rack, a stool by a writing desk with a stack of various books beside it and a small altar at the opposite end, the only decoration was a single wooden cross and a painting of the Virgin Mary on the whitewashed walls. The Padre closed the door leaving the three men to conduct their business alone.

"I have another job for you, *mon amie*," Édouard said to the pair, in a low tone. Even though they knew that he was speaking like that to assure they were not overheard it made the whole situation all the more ominous. "The tins of fish need to be hidden in a cool place, we have a stash. It is by the train tracks. One of my men will take them and hide them, two resistance soldiers will be going with him but I do not trust them. They could kill him and take the fish, they are worth twenty francs a tin on the black market."

"Bloody hell!" blurted James. "That is a lot for a tin of sardines." Ignoring this outburst Édouard continued.

"I want you two to go with him and make sure they do not try anything."

"You really think they will?" asked Draven. "After all, they are resistance." If James had not been a witness to the operations of Luc, he may have agreed with the American, but he knew better.

"Greed is always a risk during wartime," said James. "As they say: 'Greed is the root of all evil.'" Draven shrugged in agreement.

"Indeed, I have two men who watch train movements and can observe the stash, you will not see them but they will see you, they know you are coming, I have radi—" A knocking interrupted Édouard mid-sentence. "*Qu'est-ce?*"

"Maurice," came a voice from the other side of the door, Édouard seemed gleeful by this response. He opened the door and a man in his thirties entered. He was no taller than five foot, eight inches, his head was unnaturally spherical, he had sleek oil black hair in a side parting, a thin black moustache which looked like it could have been drawn on with a pen and overly large ears, which looked like handles of a trophy cup. This stranger wore a tweed jacket over a collarless white shirt and brown corduroy trousers, and as expected a black armband on his upper right arm. Once Édouard had closed the door he embraced the man warmly.

"This is my oldest friend, Maurice," explained Édouard, James shook the man's hand introducing themselves while Draven just settled with a single strong nod.

"My English not good," said the man. "You keep me…" He closed his eyes trying to find the word. "Safe? Yes?"

"Yes, we will protect you, old chap," James said in a tone he hoped inspired confidence; he appreciated the man trying to speak in English.

"You have a gun?" he asked the duo. James withdrew his Walther with the suppressor still fitted and showed it to the Frenchman before replacing it. Draven withdrew a dull black Wembley Mark IV service revolver, it was an impressive wheel gun which looked like it had come from an old western movie.

"A real cowboy!" joked James, seeing the American's choice of side-arm.

"Yeah, except that horses scare the crap out of me." James looked at the man with a raised eyebrow, that was the last thing he expected. The Frenchman had even informed James that he had come from Texas, 'horse country'. Draven looked at his English comrade and laughed "Yeah, I get that look a lot as well."

"Right, Maurice is in charge," Édouard commanded. "You do everything he says and protect my friend."

"We've got it bud," confirmed Draven, James nodded in agreement.

"I will get you when it is time," said Édouard, "and this conversation must stay private." With that the two black-marketeers left the room. James and Draven both gave a heavy sigh.

The two men decided to go across the road to the local pub. Walking down they stopped at a large tree where five women were seen hung by the neck, their heads were shaven and they had a black swastika drawn on their foreheads. Each had a wooden placard hung around their necks with some cord, on each there was French writing.

"What does it say?" asked James, looking at the depressing scene.

"It says they slept with the Germans," translated Draven.

"Kraut-bags! They bloody deserve what they got," spat James. "Come on, I need a beer." The pub was an old timber building and the inside was just like an old-fashioned tavern with an old gramophone playing '*Beethoven*' in one corner, half a dozen beer stained wooden tables, which looked like they hadn't been cleaned in a decade. Supporting her weight on the bar was an overly heavy-set woman with a sour face, looking like she had been sucking on a lemon. She wore a ghastly blue floral dress and had a hand-rolled cigarette hanging from the corner of her mouth. They assumed she was the Landlady and apart from her there were few people in the bar. There was a group of five men with long grey beards, wearing dungarees and mud-covered Wellington boots, giving the impression that they had just finished a long day work on the field, playing a game of dominoes. Another man was strewn across the bar passed out, this looked like his normal state and in a dark corner, in full black dress uniform, smoking a lavish Calabash pipe sat an SS officer. The two men had expected some Germans, but the impression the Padre gave they had expected more.

The two men had enjoyed a few beers, Draven had just started to explain how his wife in America was pregnant, when a man entered the pub, he strode over to the two foreign resistance fighters and whispered something to them in French. Draven turned to James. "It is time."

Chapter 12

Édouard seemed a lot sterner once the two men had re-entered the building of worship through the side entrance, it was evident that he was uncomfortable with the entire situation.

"I will introduce you to the men who you are going with," he said gloomily, leading the men into the chapel to the front pew where two men were sat. The first was rough looking, with a pockmarked face, a crooked nose and thin lips, he had a Vesta match sticking from his mouth and wore a dirty black with an ammunition belt wrapped diagonally across his body. The second man was younger, he wore a white short sleeved shirt with a navy criss-cross pattern, he had his head down as if in prayer. They both had the normal resistance armbands but theirs had a subtle difference, the clear bold letters FFI.

"What is FFI?" asked James.

"It stands for *Forces Françaises de l'Itérieur,*" replied Édouard.

"French forces of the interior," translated Draven. Édouard gave the American a hard stare for the interruption.

"Because we are the liberators of France," grunted the first man with a genuine hostility in his voice, he stood to face the three men, James noted for the first time that this man had cold, dead eyes as if there was no life behind them. "My name is Jean-Paul and this is Claude," the man looked up from his prayers. He had a plump innocent looking face and gave the guests a polite nod without rising from his hard wooden seat.

"When do we leave?" asked Draven, ignoring the French freedom fighters.

"Soon, you must wait for Maurice," said Édouard pulling out a pair of light canvas bags with shoulder straps and handing them to his English-speaking associates, they took a look into each and saw multiple cans of sardines. Édouard then handed each man a black armband. "We must identify you for my lookout men," explained Édouard as the four men put them on their upper right arms with the French resistance men removing their FFI armbands and placing them into their trouser pockets. They looked towards the altar as the door to the Padre's quarters opened and out walked the black-marketeer, Édouards good friend Maurice. The five men had to use every part of their energy to hold in their laughter. The plump man was wearing a Norgi jumper which was two sizes too small and matching black trousers which were too long, he looked comical. Maurice approached the group and looked at each one before saying in his strong French accent and broken English:

"We be going!" James gave a nod in agreement, Jean-Paul picked up a dark overcoat and pulled out a giant German MG34 machine gun, Claude hastily rose and picked up a Lee-Enfield rifle.

"Wow, wait guys!" said Draven. "This is stealth, the Jerries will see them from miles away, pistols only!" he demanded, James stood beside him for support. They looked at Édouard who confirmed in French. They reluctantly put down their weapons on the pews and revealed that each of them had a Nazi Luger in the back of their trousers. Claude kissed a silver crucifix which he had around his neck before they left.

The five men crept from the side door and began to trek over the grass-covered hills in total silence with James and Draven carrying the satchels full of sardines. The only light they had to guide them was the full moon, like a spotlight in the dark sky. It took them twenty minutes to reach the train tracks, running through a valley. They turned left, walking beside it and continued for another eight minutes until their French expedition leader, Maurice, put up his hand. The four men behind him stopped instantly. Maurice then motioned to drop down flat and without hesitation the men fell down, taking cover in the overgrown grass. James instantly regretted not looking before lying down as he had just put his left knee straight into a muddy, wet puddle, he closed his eyes with discomfort as his trousers absorbed the liquid and cursed under his breath.

Keeping low, the troop looked along the train tracks, through the darkness they could see a torchlight going from side to side as it approached their position. They could make out the outline of a Nazi soldier through the moonlight, it was too late for them to move. Jean-Paul whispered, getting out his Luger,

"*Laisse le tuer.*" James only understood one word; '*tuer*' meant kill. James put out a hand and lowered the pistol the Frenchman was now aiming at the patrolling soldier, Jean-Paul looked at him angrily. James knew what this soldier was doing. A soldier would check the tracks for obstructions or sabotage on a five mile of train track, at the end he would trade places with another guard who would check the next five miles. If he did not turn up the alarm would be sounded and bring the whole army down on them and a gunshot would be heard for miles down this valley, the sound would ricochet from wall to wall and alert the Germans with the same result.

The troop lay still and flat on the grass as the patrolling man got ever closer. The enemy soldier passed the group who were now holding their breaths, he flashed his torch from one track to the next and continued on his way without a moment's hesitation, there was not a sound except for the crunch of the gravel that held the tracks in place, under the Nazi jackboots, the group remained stock still. James could hear his heart racing in his ears, it was so loud like a jungle bongo drum, subconsciously James was worried it was so loud the soldier would hear it.

Maurice eventually checked behind them and decided that the patrolling soldier was far enough away for them to continue their mission. Each man rose to a crouched position and the five-man team, keeping to the grass to muffle the sound of their steps, took off at a crouched run towards their objective. After passing a white painted rock along the tracks, which looked out of place, Maurice counted the wooden sleepers quietly in French, he reached the twenty-first cross bar, crouched down and began brushing the gravel away between the twenty-first and twenty-second sleepers to reveal a heavy wooden box concealed beneath, locked with a rusting old padlock. The French black-marketeer handed Claude a torch and removed a brass key from his pocket. Using the torchlight that Claude directed to the box, Maurice unlocked the case and opened it revealing its contents. Inside the wooden box, there were over a hundred tins of sardines, half a dozen bottles of whiskey and bags of sugar. "Why the hell would they need all these?" Draven whispered as he and James opened their satchels and began stacking the contents inside.

"Germans buy many," replied Maurice in his broken English, "for parties."

"Édouard said you don't deal with the krauts anymore," James interjected.

"*He* does not, but many of them still do," Jean-Paul commented. "Money is still money." James could understand this but was pretty sure his good friend, Édouard, would have a few things to say if he found that his own men were still selling wares to the enemy.

They had emptied the satchel's contents into the box, Maurice relocked it and they once again covered it with stones, hiding it from view. Out of the darkness the five men became illuminated in light, they then heard a low rumbling sound. They turned to see a dark grey Sturmwagen armoured car coming to a halt directly in front of them, they must have noticed the light from the flash-light Claude was still holding. Four armed Nazi soldiers jumped from the back, aiming their menacing guns at the five resistance fighters. They watched a German officer in a long overcoat and peaked hat got out from the passenger side, lit a cigarette and casually strolled past his men he walked along the line of captured men, looking at each man in turn. He stopped in front of James and asked him something in German, James was at a loss.

"Any of you chaps speak the lingo?" he asked out loud to his comrades.

"Ah, English, yes?" said the officer, throwing James off guard. "And you?" He turned his head to Draven, to James' right.

"American," he answered dryly.

"And you?" he asked Jean-Paul, at James' left, who did not reply and just spat onto the Nazi's black boots; the officer smacked the man across the jaw. "Where are you from?"

"France," replied Jean-Paul clutching his face. Maurice stayed silent, nervously shuffling from one foot to the other, he may be a black-market trader but was obviously nervous when being confronted by a Nazi officer, or it may have been the weapons aiming at them.

"You are under arrest!" he continued in his strong German accent. "What do you being here?" James looked at his comrades and saw Draven slowing moving his arm around his back for his revolver, so, to keep the officer's attention on him, James replied,

"We are just out for a moonlit walk on this beautiful night. You had the same idea, did you?" His voice came out a bit more sarcastic than he had intended and for his snide comment he received a punch in his stomach, exactly in the same place he had been struck by the Fisherman. James' knees buckled as he grabbed his abdomen and he fell to his knees.

"Obviously not," he spluttered. Refusing to give the officer the satisfaction of breaking him, James rose back to his feet and stared back into the officers dark blue eyes.

"Why do you help these French terrorists? Who murder our troops and disrupt our great occupation? You were blowing up the railway lines!" snarled the Nazi officer.

"Wrong! Anyway ,you know what they say, the enemy of my enemy and all that," replied James, his sarcasm was back at full swing.

"I am not familiar with this saying," the officer said, perplexed. He looked down the line for an explanation, with no success.

The next scenario happened as if in slow motion. A shot rang out and smashed through the windscreen of the Nazi vehicle, killing the driver. The Nazi soldiers began waving their machine guns frantically, looking for the shooter, the officer was fumbling with his pistol holster but it was too little too late, Draven had drawn his own gun and removed half the officers face with a single shot at point blank range. James and the two resistance fighters hastily drew their own weapons and rapidly shot at the remaining four soldiers, dropping them in quick succession.

"Someone's going to have heard that chaps!" said James, talking normally as there was no point of whispering now, he stared into the darkness for German reinforcements. Jean-Paul walked over to each fallen soldier and fired a single shot into the soldiers' head for good measure, this did not make James feel any more relaxed. He then pried open each deceased Nazis mouth and with a pair of pliers from his back pocket withdrew any of the Nazis gold teeth, putting them into a small pouch attached to his belt. After a hasty deliberation the group stripped the Nazi soldiers and dressed them in their own clothing, so it gave the impression that they were resistance members that had just been executed, they bundled into the Germans vehicle and drove at full speed back towards the church headquarters. Only returning after disposing the vehicle over the side of a cliff.

Chapter 13

It was midday by the time Édouard and James got back to the Paris resistance subterranean headquarters, Draven remained in the secondary church headquarters along with their new Jewish comrades, pending his escape across the Pyrenees into Spain and then across to British controlled Gibraltar. James was offered the same opportunity, but he was a member of the French resistance now and even though he did not want to openly admit it, he was pretty sure that he would most likely never see England again and would be arrested and shot the second he arrived on English territory if he did not complete the task given to him by military intelligence. The Englishman was given an FFI armband by the padre out of respect for his decision to stay and fight for the liberation of France.

The British Special Operations Executive was restless, the thought of the impending meeting with the military intelligence agent at the church was weighing heavy on his mind, he was dying to tell someone, absolutely anybody about the overly ambitious military intelligence recruitment, the pressure was overwhelming. James spent a couple of hours pacing, building up his courage before leaving for Saint Julian L Pauvre church. He walked down the cobbled streets, passing German patrols, he kept his head down deep in thought.

James entered the picturesque place of worship by three o'clock that very afternoon. He saw a priest in his mid to late fifties with short cropped silver hair and stubble covered chin, which was not normal for a man of the cloth, consoling an elderly lady at the front of the line of pews. James walked over to the decorative column and witnessed this interaction. The priest looked up and saw James observing them, he held James' eye contact, bent over and whispered something to the old women, whilst keeping his eyes on James, James returned this, keeping his eyes on the undercover British agent. The priest then strolled down a narrow hallway beside the altar. James hesitated, he took a glance around the small church, the only other person in the building was the weeping widow. James followed the old priest, he followed the narrow path to a back room of the church, unless you knew the plans you would have never known this room was here. The inside of the room was lit by a dozen candles, there were no windows and the only furniture was a low hardwood coffee table with large multi-coloured cushions surrounding it, otherwise, the room was spartan.

"Garner?" the priest asked in a very posh, stiff-upper-lip accent seeing James standing in the doorway. James nodded calmly. "I thought so, you couldn't look more like a British agent." He chuckled. "Well, don't just stand there. Come in sir, close the door and take a seat." The undercover military agent took a seat on a cushion at one end of the table facing the door. James did as he was bid and took a seat opposite the ageing man. "You have met the Fisherman I take it?" James just gave another nod, he had decided not to speak unless he felt he had to. "Drink?" asked the priest getting out a pair of crystal engraved whiskey tumblers and a bottle of Vat 69, pouring a generous amount into each glass, he passed it along the table to James, who gave the man a nod of thanks. The Englishman lifted the glass and put it to his lips but stopped before drinking, the last time he was offered a drink, this exact drink, it was doped. The priest understood James' hesitation and took the glass from James' hand with a crooked smile, downed the contents in one, refilled the drained glass and returned it to James. James shook his head with a snigger and thankfully drank the rare beverage, he felt the liquid relax him and made him feel comfortable enough to finally speak.

"So what is this important operation that I have the *honour* to be chosen for?" asked James, his voice full of sarcasm. The priest did not react to James' attitude as if he had expected it.

"My superiors in Whitehall, in all their almighty wisdom, need you to retrieve a file from a Jerry control station," the priest paused and took a sip of his own alcoholic beverage. "These files are of top importance to our success in this war. This is the file," said the man, tossing over a black and white picture of a file with a swastika and eagle in the centre and a stamp in the elaborate German writing saying '*Nur Führeraugen*'.

"What's that say?"

"For the Führers eyes only," said the spy soulfully.

"Now, I understand why you want to get your hands on it. What is in it?"

"You are not permitted to know," the priest said sharply. "If you look into the file, your life will be forfeit." The man looked uncomfortable saying this but he leant over the table and looked deep into James' eyes; without blinking, he said with all sincerity for confirmation, "Do you understand? You are not to look inside the file."

"Okay, okay. I understand," confirmed James. "Where is this thing?" The priest passed over another two photos. One was of a heavy cast iron safe and the second was of a wooden building, what caught James' attention was the six German soldiers which could clearly be seen around the building in the photos.

"I understand you were the best in your class at lock picking—" the priest started, but James interrupted:

"Second best. Donald Jeffries was best."

"Yes, Donald Jeffries was dropped into Poland, he was caught and executed last week, so that position now falls to you." James had never been too fond of the man, Jeffries had aced every challenge at SOE training school which made him a bit big headed and overconfident. "The documents we require are locked in this safe, situated in this cabin. There are many of these kinds of buildings hidden all over the occupied area, no one would expect secret files to be kept in such places." James stared at his objectives.

"What kind of resistance can I expect?" quizzed James.

"There are no more than ten Jerry guards outside at any one time, we expect half as many in the guard room on the inside of the building, plus between three and five non-military personnel, you will require some stealth and secrecy to infiltrate the property."

"What about my ex-filtration?" asked James.

"Your escape is down to you," the priest said. "Agent Hayhurst will meet to a Café Noir in the village of Senlis, she will take you back to meet the Fisherman with the documents."

"I guess you want this done without raising any attention."

"Indeed."

"And when is this all meant to take place?" asked James growing less confident by the moment.

"We recommend tomorrow at daybreak, the soldiers will be less alert and it will still be dark enough to make your approach undetected." James accepted this, it seemed the only reasonable thing to do in this whole operation. After another half an hour of discussion, James rose to leave. "I have left you some items you may find useful, at a dead drop."

"Where?"

"The first bridge you get to, go beneath it and there you'll find a brick marked with a 'V'; once you remove it, you will find a hidden space, it is one of our usual dead drops," the priest said. "God be with you, my son." This remark was hugely surprising to James; after all, being a priest was just this agent's cover story. The priest chuckled seeing James' surprise. "I often thought whilst I was growing up that I would either be a priest or a secret agent."

"So you decided to become a spook?" questioned James, feeling his dislike for spies rise.

"When my parish closed back home, I was recruited. I guess being fluent in French and having knowledge of the German language made me the ideal candidate and once we learnt of Herr Hitlers plans, I was placed here to report on the jerry occupation of Paris."

"Rather you than me," joked James, taking his leave.

The Englishman wandered the streets heading in the general direction of the woods, where the secret Nazi base of occupation was situated. James began walking over to a red brick bridge, he stopped in his tracks as he recalled the dead drop the priest had mentioned. He looked around to make sure he was not being watched, the streets were clear so he climbed down the side into the creek below. James looked around frantically when he saw the letter 'V' engraved into a brick. James went to work removing the brick from the wall with a knife, chipping away at the cement. Behind it James found a suede bag, he checked inside to find a couple of steel rods which had at some time in the past been bicycle spokes, these were ideal for lock picking, and a McLaglen Peskett close combat weapon, the bag was common enough and the ideal size to carry the files secretly. He replaced the brick and continued on his way, away from the city. All of a sudden, the air around him was filled with the sound of the German führers voice spouting from a pair of propaganda speakers attached to the corner of a farmhouse. James slowly shook his head in disbelief as he continued his slow trek, even if he could understand what the leader of the Nazi hoards was ranting about he wouldn't listen, he had to make it to the forest before the start of the curfew, at nine o'clock, which was only in half an hour.

James had found the log cabin, he viewed the restricted area from behind a large tree, it was exactly as described, totally secluded with exactly ten sentries surrounding it, all wearing long water-resistant overcoats and their coal scuttle like helmets. There were seven ZP750 motorcycles, two with side carts, sitting by a side-door to the property and a single square soldiered guard. James had made a simple single bushwhack shelter with fern branches against a tree in a teepee tent style, a mile from the cabin in the forest, this would be a great place to hide from the Nazis. He would stay here, in the woods that night and head for the Nazi post at sunrise. He watched the place intently for any deviation in their routine, there was none. From behind a prickly shrub he watched and hatched his plan of attack.

James crept, watching his every step to assure he did not step on a twig or fir cone, alerting the guard to his presence and ducked behind a bramble bush just two feet from the Nazi sentry. James removed his close combat weapon, the guard had his back to him, James took one final check, all clear. James acted, he pounced towards the soldier in total silence and slipped the blade into the nape of the man's neck, paralysing him instantly and without a seconds pause dragged the disabled human body behind the foliage and looked down at the soldier. He grabbed the man's head with both hands, twisting it sharply to the right, killing him instantly. James undressed himself, packed the clothes in the bag and dressed in the heavy Nazi uniform, he could not believe how uncomfortable these uniforms were, not to mention he must have killed the only soldier in the entire German army with a shoe size smaller than his mothers, yet he had to squeeze his feet into the Nazi jackboots to complete his disguise, there was no room for half measures. He rose out from behind the bush wielding the common MP40 machine gun the guard had been armed with and the suede bag containing his clothes. He placed the two steel rods into the pocket of the large dark green overcoat, dumped his bag into one of the side carts and with the blade of his SOE weapon pierced the rubber tyres on the other six motorbikes. James then took a deep breath and as bold as brass strode through the wooden door to find himself in a pine wood-panelled corridor, he walked to the end to find another matching corridor leading from left to right with numerous doors leading to separate rooms on either side. Which of these rooms, was the one that contained the safe with the desired confidential file? A door opened to James' right and out came a slender girl in her twenties with a blonde barrel curl ponytail, wearing a rose red blouse, black coat, a matching black skirt which dropped just below her knees and a clear red swastika armband on her upper right arm. She gave the soldier, James, a small smile as she passed him and walked through a door in a neighbouring corridor. James then noticed that none of the doors had locks, the priest had told James that the office he was looking for was secured and locked, he was sure of it. James turned to the left, his eyes darting from door to door as he walked past them, not one had a lock, he then turned one hundred and eighty degrees and strode in the opposite direction, the third door down was the only door which could be locked, this had to be the door, there was no other option. He checked the corridor, it was all quiet. He tried the door, if it was unlocked it would likely be occupied, which meant he would have to act fast and disable the occupant. It was locked. The disguised Englishman removed the steel rods from his pocket and gave a last quick glance around. He got to work picking the heavy lock, the pressure was on now. There was no way to know how long he had before someone exited one of the many doors and caught him in the act, he had one chance to get this right, his training came streaming back, he heard a dull click from the keyhole, he had done it. He removed the steel rods, checked the hallway and entered the room, closing the door behind him quietly.

Even though the room James found himself in was small, it was intimidating. The single window had a blackout blind down, in the centre of the room sat a single wooden table with a typewriter, on the right-hand wall hung an A2 sized painting of Adolf Hitler and beneath it sat the heavy duty green safe. James lay the machine gun down onto the desk and once again stuck the metal rods into a keyhole and began moving them as he had been taught at SOE training, of course, there was more pressure now and he was beginning to feel it, if someone walked in on him now his cover would be blown and there was no escape from this room. He wished he could have some of his resistance friends to cause a distraction right now. James froze, he could hear the unmistakable sound of jackboots walking on the wooden floorboards along the corridor in the direction of the room, he grabbed his close combat weapon and put his back against the wall to the right of the door, hiding him when it opened. He looked into the room, the machine rifle was still on the desk and two rods sticking from the safe's lock but it was too late to remove them. He remained stock still and listened as the footsteps strode past the room, without slowing, he gave a huge sigh of relief and relaxed his shoulders, he then turned his attention back to the safe. What could be so important that the British were willing to risk his life for? James had heard rumours about how Nazi scientists were trying to make some kind of super soldier, stronger, faster, almost bulletproof, but this was just fantasy, Whitehall wouldn't send him to get something based on a purely absurd rumour would they? Then again he was a deniable asset so anything was possible. These thoughts were racing through James' head as he struggled to unlock the safe, it was proving to be much harder than the door had been. Finally, his ears picked up the long-awaited clunk of the safe door unlocking as he gave his lock picking tool a decisive push to the right. He felt his muscles relax as he turned the brass handle and the heavy door opened to show a stack of brown files. James hastily flicked through the pile of documents until he saw a file he recognised, a brown file with a thick black swastika, an eagle and a red stamp with the German wording '*Nur Führeraugen*', James gave a sly smile, he could hardly believe that he had got this far. He tucked the file into the back of his trousers and closed the safe, so at first glance, everything would look normal. He picked up the German gun from the table and put the misshaped bicycle spokes in the overcoats pocket.

He stood for a moment with his ear against the door, listening for any sound from the other side, a soldier being seen leaving a locked room would only arouse suspicion, which was the last thing he needed at this stage. There was an eerie silence from the opposite side of the door, but even the stillness was unnerving, it was what James had hoped for though. He carefully opened the door and took a stealthy look along the corridor before stepping out, without turning he closed the office door behind him and made his way back to the previously guarded side door, that he had entered through.

James stepped out into the cool morning air, the absence of the guard James had assassinated had not been noticed by the other Nazi sentries. James looked around, he saw a squirrel scurry up a tree and couldn't help thinking how much easier it would be to be a squirrel right now. He slipped the stolen file into his bag along with his clothes which were still lying in the sidecar of a motorbike. He mounted the motorcycle and kick-started the engine, the roar of the revving engine attracted the attention of the other sentry's. There were at least seven armed Nazi soldiers shouting and aiming their guns at him as they appeared from the sides of the cabin. One of the guards blew an alarm whistle and that was enough for James, he released the throttle and took off down the dirt road at immense speed, he heard multiple engines rev up behind him and then more hysterical shouting, he turned a corner in the road and slowed the bike, he had escaped the hornets' nest, James could not help but laugh with relief, he could hardly believe how easily he had completed his mission and escaped.

This sense of relief was short lived. It did not take long for him to hear the monstrous grumbling of a half-track tank, it was an open top armoured vehicle which could seat up to eight fully armed soldiers, not including the gunner that operated the MG 42 machine gun and the driver. The front of the vehicle had a pair of wheels with thick rubber tyres while the back had caterpillar tracks. This menacing vehicle must have been hidden on the other side of the building. It was not the fastest of vehicles but James was not willing to put it to the test so he sped up to full speed, he had not yet escaped.

The pursuit continued for another half an hour, every time James thought he had escaped, he soon heard the rumbling, alerting him that the Germans were still coming up behind him. By this time they had reached the outskirts of the mighty city of lights. The bike would tip perilously around every corner because of the speed of the driver. James spotted his escape, a public toilet. These were dark green with a small tower in the centre surrounded by a metallic wall that hid the indiscretion as the men relieved themselves in the open air. James turned a sharp right and parked the bike in a small alleyway, grabbed his suede bag and replacing it with his Nazi helmet. He ran his hand through his hair before trotting across the road and into the dark green cylindrical cubical, in total haste he walked around the inner centrepiece until he found the grating in the floor, he removed his McLaglen Peskett and slipped the blade in between the metal of the grate and the surrounding concrete, with a twist of the blade the grating rose and the Englishman was able to lift it from its place, he then took a deep breath and jumped into the stench of the sewer below. James carefully replaced the grating as he heard the rumbling of the half-track pass by. James took off the Nazi overcoat and wrapped his suede bag in the water-resistant clothing. The stench of human waste turned his stomach and made him yack. He waded through the brown, liquid which measured just above his shins, he never thought he would be so pleased to wear the Nazi Jackboots which was now holding back the pungent contents from soaking into his clothing. He could see the light at the end of the sewer and headed directly for it, he had to get out of here, he had to try and hold his breath as long as possible.

He stepped out of the sewer by the riverbed and took a few deep breaths of the clear air, compared to the sewer the air was sweet. Secluding himself beside the sewage pipe exit he undressed and changed into the clean clothes from the bag, dumping the dirty Nazi clothing into the pipe and clambered up a steal ladder fitted on the river bed wall and back onto the streets of Paris. He flung the strap of the bag over his shoulder and began to make his way to the quaint village of Senlis and Café Noir, for his meeting with agent Olivia Hayhurst. The army had obviously been made aware of James' escapades as many soldiers were searching the city suspiciously as the Englishman held onto the bag ever tighter. As he walked casually further out of the city, the Nazi presence dissipated slightly and James could breathe a little lighter, yet knowing better than to drop his guard completely.

The village of Senlis was more of a large hamlet so the café was easy enough to find. As he strode into the coffee shop the beautiful smell of the warm beverage flooded his nostrils. The Englishman scanned the room. It was full of couples, too busy looking longingly into each other eyes to notice the newcomer and not a single German to be seen. James took a seat at a small corner table, the young French serving maid approached him, it took James a couple of minutes to remember the words, Constance had recently taught him a few useful sentences.

"*Café s'il vous plait,*" he smiled in what he hoped gave the impression that he was relaxed and comfortable. The waitress left and returned swiftly with a steaming cup of dark liquid. "*Merci.*"

Once James was sure he was oblivious to everyone he dug into his bag and withdrew the brown file, the temptation was too much, he had to know what he had just risked his life for and why this file was so important to the British military intelligence. He opened the file. There was a map of the military installation on the beaches of Normandy along with black and white Ariel photographs and pages of German text. Why the hell was Whitehall interested in where the Nazis had their beachside armaments? How would these documents assist them?

"I think you were told not to look in the file," said a female in a posh English accent, James looked up from the file and standing over him with a raised eyebrow stood his model like contact, Olivia. James blushed, closed the file and slipped it back into the satchel.

"I had to know what exactly was so important," he tried to explain, embarrassed that he had been so careless to be caught doing exactly what he had been told not to, the words of the priest ringing in his ears, his life would be forfeit. Olivia's stern face turned to a smile, she was obviously amused by James' discomfort. She took the seat opposite him at the table and said in a low voice, "You are lucky I am not the Fisherman or he would tear your head off and it would be such a shame to ruin such a handsome face." She gave a small smile and took a sip of the beverage from James' mug. It was said in a way that even the threat was seductive. James was hoping she was just being herself, being a spy, she had to be charming and even flirtatious to get past Nazi or French police checkpoints, but she could at least dial it down when she talked to him. It was hard to hate her when she spoke like this, but then again it was her profession he hated more than the women.

"So when are we going to meet the all high and mighty?" James asked sarcastically.

"Now." The luscious agent rose from her seat. "And I would not let the Fisherman know that you looked in the file," she advised. James chucked down a five-Reichsmark note onto the table, grabbed his brown bag and followed Olivia out of Café Noir. He saw a mustard yellow Palomino Sedanca car sitting on the street outside, it was not the kind of car you would hide in but that was spooks for you, hiding in plain sight. "You can drive," she chucked James a set of keys and got into the passengers' side seat.

"Great, where to?" He was glad that he did not have to wear a blindfold this time, he may find out where the military intelligence were hiding out. Not that it would help him much.

"*La Belle de Nuit,*" she replied, making James look at her in shock, a gaze she refused to return. So James set off and even though he was pretty sure he knew the directions Olivia had to correct him a couple of time along the way.

It took them a good hour before he pulled up at the front of the nightclub and Olivia led the way through the club to James' secret room where the Fisherman and his muscle Sampson were waiting for them. Olivia walked directly behind the Fisherman and turned so all three were facing James.

"Mr Garner, I understand you were successful," said the Fisherman. James dug his hand in his bag and produced the file. Sampson stepped forward, took the file and flipped it open, after a quick scan of the documents to confirm it was the file they wanted he nodded to his boss.

"This is it."

"Good. Did you see the contents?" the Fisherman interrogated, his accent stronger than ever. James saw Olivia behind the man shake her hand subtly.

"I was told, it was none of my business," James said calmly. "So when do you get me home?"

"Ah, yes, well, I made some calls and it does not look like it will be possible any time soon, I am afraid." There was not a sound of regret in his voice and James was not in the least surprised, he was fairly sure that the Fisherman had never even intended to get him back to England and was pretty sure that the Fisherman had not made any calls. "Sorry," the man added and led his two fellow spies out of the nightclub without another word.

Sampson stopped beside James and without looking at him said in a quiet tone, "*Pucker* job Garner." James was surprised; he would never have expected such a compliment from him.

"*Ta!*" he said in shock. As Olivia passed him, she touched his arm affectionately and with a smile, left James to his thoughts.

Chapter 14

"Where have you been?" asked Constance in a worried tone as James re-entered the resistance headquarters, greeting her with a peck on each cheek.

"Around, just clearing my head," explained James, this was the end of the interrogation. He looked around the underground base, the mood was sombre and quiet, everyone was looking towards a sealed off annexe where faint voices could be heard. "What's going on?" he whispered into Constance's ear. Before she could reply they were interrupted by a tremendous roar making the room jump with shock. It was as if some wild animal had escaped, they watched as they heard a table being thrown over and saw Édouard tear down a curtain in rage and aggressively stride into his own black-market annexe. James began to wonder how long he had been gone for, what on earth had he missed? James stepped forward to speak to his giant friend but Constance put a slender hand to his chest stopping him.

"Leave him," she said tenderly. Pierre followed the large man out of the annexe and walked over to the couple.

"I just told him about Maurice," he said.

"What about Maurice?"

"He has been killed," Pierre said, looking at his English comrade closely. James was in shock, he had seen this man only yesterday. This really brought the reality of war home, one day you could meet someone for the first time and the next day they are dead.

"What? When? How?" spluttered James, confused.

"After your fight with the Nazis, the Germans burst into every home looking for the resistance members involved." Pierre's voice was one of sorrow. "They went into the church, killed everyone, even the padre. They lined the bodies on the street as a warning. Maurice was one of them."

"What about Draven and the Jews?" asked James.

"None were left alive." Pierre shook his head sadly. James felt a wave of anger build up inside him, most of the people he had met there were just trying to survive and were no real threat to the occupying forces. He strode to a red brick wall and slammed his fist against it, his rage was so intense he did not feel the pain as his flesh hit the solid wall. Pierre placed his hand on his friend's shoulder, feeling the man's anger, he turned and looked into the Frenchman's eyes.

"We will show them that we will not give in, that for every one of ours that they kill, we will kill ten of theirs!" Pierre had a glint if menace in his eyes that James had never seen before. The Englishman nodded slowly in thought and without a seconds hesitation pulled the French resistance 'FFI' armband from his pocket and tugged it up to his right upper arm, then turning to the Paris resistance commander and his attractive sister with a face of pure determination and strength he said three words which told them all they needed to know.

"Let's do this!"

Over the following week Pierre, James and two other resistance lieutenants spent all day and night browsing through maps and marking Nazi guard posts and strongholds, which they got from resistance spies who were coming and going at all hours. Many were just children, but Pierre explained it best. "No one would suspect a child and they do not yet know the meaning of betrayal." Édouard had retired to a safe house, to gather his thoughts, with half a dozen bottles of whiskey. The four men only took a few hours kip, when Constance strongly insisted after they had been awake for over forty-eight hours straight, she was tougher than she looked.

James was laid on a settee having a much-needed sleep with Pierre on the floor beside him. He was abruptly shaken awake by a young resistance fighter.

"*Monsieur*, please wake," said the lad. "It is Édouard!" This snapped James awake, instantly sitting up and kicking the snoring, wheezing body of Pierre to wake him. The Frenchman wearily looked up at the two men above him and tiredly shuffled to an upright position.

"Go on kid, what's happened," urged James.

"I go to see Édouard and he has been arrested," explained the young man.

"Gestapo?" asked James

"Non. Police," the lad answered. James couldn't deny that he was relieved to hear this. If his friend had been arrested by the Nazi secret police it would most likely end in his demise, but the French police (even though most were collaborators) did not perform torture or executions. "I found six empty bottles of whiskey on the floor at the apartment," the boy continued. "The people in the building say he was singing *La Marseillaise* loudly and the police arrested him." The boy was frantic.

"Merde," blurted Pierre, "the idiot! Our great anthem is illegal under German law!"

"Bloody fool," agreed James.

"He was arrested for being… ivre," explained the boy. James looked to Pierre for a translation, even though he could probably guess.

"Drunk," explained Pierre after a brief pause, recalling his friend only had limited understanding of the French language.

"We have to get him out," prompted James concerned for his friends well fair.

"*Oui,*" Pierre agreed, "of course." This was the last thing they needed right now. James got out his packet of cigarettes, it was empty. He rose from his settee and strode to Édouard's stash, took a single pack of Lucky Strike cigarettes and put a ten-Reichsmark note on the table along with a small pile of notes and coins that people had left for Édouards return, he then wrote on a sheet of paper what he had taken as the previous people had, trust was of the utmost importance at these times.

The two men collected three other resistance fighters and made their way through the darkness of the streets towards the police jail, the night had a chill which sank deep into their skin down to their bones. They had each grabbed a Sten gun on their way out of the hidden headquarters, the route to the police jail was down dark side roads and unlike the police station, they were not lit up so thankfully the operation would be done under the cover of darkness. With James and Pierre was a brunette women in her mid-twenties, she wore a black beret, navy blue blouse with white spots and beige shorts, a blonde haired man in his late forties wearing a white collarless shirt with the sleeves rolled up topped by a grey waistcoat and the third man was the young man who had woken them previously, he was still in his late teenage years and was wearing a Nazi top with the emblems torn off with dark brown trousers.

The Police jail was separate from the station in a dark area on the outskirts of the Nazi-occupied capital city. German soldiers rarely, if ever, frequented this area and at night they could only expect a couple of police guards at the very most. This was the smaller of the city jails, used primarily for people arrested by the police, the larger jails had been taken over by the Gestapo and Nazi military police for the detainment of resistance fighters, Jews and anyone else who was considered undesirable under the Third Reich.

It took them little more than twenty minutes to reach the grey brick building of the city jail, it was an intimidating property. The flame of a candle or lantern could be seen flickering from inside through a small window, this was the only light that could be seen.

"James, my friend, you and Madeleine stay guard. Watch out for Germans, we will find out where they are holding Édouard and get him out," commanded Pierre in a whisper.

"Wait," came a whispered reply from James. "We will need a car."

"The police keep some out back, when we get Édouard we will take one and pick you up on the way out," replied Pierre and patted his friend on the shoulder.

"Okay," agreed James and then for some reason believed this was a good time to try out some of his new French and said, *"Bon Chance!"*

James took up a post beside a flint-built barn by a rustic waist-high wall which enclosed the prisons forecourt, it reminded him of the walls back home in Yorkshire, Madeline took a post behind a tree at the opposite end of the forecourt. James had a perfect sight down the north leading road whilst Madeline kept watch on the mud track that led easterly. James watched as Pierre stealthily led the two fellow resistance members into the quiet jailhouse and closed the door securely behind them.

James had to confess he was getting bored after being stood here for fifteen minutes looking at nothing but into the deep black abyss of the night. When he looked behind him for his friends' return, all that could be seen through the blinds of the jail was the occasional movement when someone passed in front of the candlelight. It was tempting to light a cigarette to help pass the time, but he remembered from basic training that the light from a cigarette could be seen for twenty miles when dark. In the distance he could hear a low rumbling, he was unsure whether it was thunder, heavy arms fire or the air force bombing Nazi military positions until he saw the magnificent fork lightning display. He put out a hand, it was not raining, the flashes gave him a clear view down the quiet road. A couple of minutes later he and Madeline were ducking as the thunder erupted directly above their heads, but as quickly as it had come, the tremendous weather display dissipated. Just then Madeline ran, in a crouched position, along the wall to where James was based.

"*Allemands!*" she whispered harshly, James knew this word, it was one of the first words Constance had taught him for this exact eventuality. It meant Germans. James took a moment to think, if these soldiers decided to check in at the prison for some reason or other, even though James could not think of a plausible reason why they would, James and Madeline's positions would be compromised. He considered his option, he could see the torchlight of the approaching patrol now and could hear some talking and laughing. There was only one option and not much time.

"Follow me!" prompted James, he knew she wouldn't understand but when he motioned by waving his hand and then he ran to the jailhouse door and waved her over she understood. She ran across the paved forecourt as the Englishman knocked in code on the door, the small Judas hole slid open, seeing his comrades who were looking nervously over their shoulders, the forty-year-old resistance fighter unlocked the heavy-duty lock with a sense of urgency and opened the door to allow his comrades to enter. The two members raced through the doorway and their comrade secured the door behind them. The prison's reception was as morbid as the outside of the building. It was a cracking concrete room with a pair of worm-eaten desks, a couple of filing cabinets. There was also a large heavy-duty safe sat in one corner and on the wall hung a calendar showing various photos and drawings of Adolf Hitler, showing that these officers were genuine Nazi sympathisers even though they would never confess to being such and unlike some police officers, who would turn a blind eye to resistance activity, it was quite clear that these men would not. This was worrying, if they had known Édouards true identity he would have been handed straight over to the Gestapo and then a rescue would have been impossible. On a pair of wooden rotating office chairs, sat bound and gagged, were the two French police officers who had the unfortunate task of being on duty on that particular night.

"Pierre?" James asked the man, who pointed down a flight of concrete stairs, through an open metallic bar gate.

"*Là-bas la cellule Treize.*" James did not have a clue what the man had said but got the concept. He rushed down the cold stairway. From the bottom of the stairs finding his friend was easy enough, he could hear Édouard making an uproarious display. James entered the small cell where the giant Édouard was sitting on a mattress, dripping wet, the young fighter was holding an empty wooden bucket the contents of which was now thrown over Édouard in an unsuccessful attempt to sober him up. Pierre was clearly stressed out by his counterparts intoxicated state, but James had to ignore his drunk friend.

"Pierre, *Krauts!*" Édouard looked up at James and cried:

"*Antoine! Tu es lá!*"

"Who is Antoine?" James whispered to Pierre.

"Antoine was his brother," replied the resistance leader looking at his large friend in pity. "He died more than eighteen months ago." They could hear the Germans outside the jailhouse, Pierre attempted to cover Édouards mouth to silence him to no avail as the large man was too strong and flung Pierre off him with a single wave of his arm. James looked for something to silence this colossal man with and hanging on a leather cord, just outside the cell in the narrow hall was a wooden baton.

"Sorry about this old boy," said James and with a swift swing smacked his friend around the top of the head with the club, knocking him out cold. The other resistance members stood stock still, listening to the enemy soldiers, they were standing directly outside Édouard's jails slit window, smoking and laughing. James thought they all sounded a bit drunk themselves. They were most likely coming back from a late-night party and were keeping out of view from any of their strict superiors, which would most likely result in them going straight to the Russian front. They were defiantly not a Nazi patrol, they were being too conspicuous and loud for that.

The resistance barely dared to breathe until the soldiers continued their travels.

"We must go!" urged Pierre, James nodded, he couldn't agree more. So with James and Pierre putting an arm over each shoulder they lifted the large lifeless body of their friend to his feet and dragged him down the corridor and up the stairs, with the youngest member of the troop carrying their weapons behind them. The two men dropped Édouard on the floor in the prisons reception area, relieving themselves of the extreme weight. Pierre, taking back his weapon carefully, opened a side door to assure that the enemy soldiers had left the vicinity. He then strode over to the bound guards and pointing his gun at them barked a single word "*Clés?*" James made an educated guess what his friend was asking for, the keys to the vehicles they had spoken about before. The bound guard twisted his head to the left and nodded towards one of the desks. Madeline opened the single draw in the centre of the desk and for a few minutes she rummaged through the various paperwork, including blank Jewish identification papers and armbands to be issued to any Jew who followed Nazi law and registered themselves with the local police, there was also an assortment of stationery which she chucked onto the desk until she found a ring of six keys.

The troop piled into an old confiscated Renoir Clunker which sat out the back of the prison and drove, cross country, into the night.

Chapter 15

Over the next few weeks the same four men poured over plans, the attack was to be aimed at a secluded train station, this is where the enemy forces loaded supplies they did not want seized by resistance forces. Reports were in that a train would be in the station, planning to transport supplies, troops or both, the true reason for the train being there was sketchy at best and everyone had their own theory but why it was there was not important. The chosen station also had a spot light situated by it and a large broadcast tower which sent its signal to the array of speakers, placed around the city and further. Its destruction would be a cataclysmic blow to German defence and regime. There was only one evident problem.

"We need more men!" blurted James slamming his fist down on the map covered table as the plan was being discussed. "Without more men we will be torn to shreds!"

"Oui," the other men agreed.

"There is a communist resistance cell to the west of us," said Pierre, his mind deep in thought and weariness. "Go to them, *mon amie*, James. Take Constance to translate and give you introductions, she has had some dealings with them. They may need some convincing. They are run by… by erm… un comte… an earl."

"Blimey! An earl!" exclaimed James. "I better work on my manners then," he joked half-heartedly. "How will I find them?"

"They are hidden in a cellar at a vineyard," explained Pierre. "Take your armband, Constance will show you the way." He took James' hand. "Good luck, my friend, I know we can rely on you."

James and Constance had stolen an abandoned Pegasus, it was a beautiful vehicle, its only reason for being abandoned was that it drank more fuel than it did miles and fuel was a scarcity. Much of the available fuel was requisitioned by the Nazi army for their use on tanks and other military vehicles but the resistance had their own sources, often syphoned from the pre-mentioned Nazi tools of war.

The matt black leather seats made them feel like they were driving in luxury, the ride was comfortable and they passed through Nazi military roadblocks with relative ease after flashing their forged identity cards. The ride was entirely uneventful and James casually followed Constance's instructions while she explained about the resistance cell they were visiting.

They would receive air drops from the Russian military, so Constance who only drank Vodka and wine had traded a lot with them, and if James was honest he was hoping to get his hands on some genuine Beluga caviar. Constance explained to him that the earl had a single weakness, it seemed that the aristocrat had an extreme addiction to morphine.

Just as James was sure they must be getting close to their destination, it was confirmed when he saw, chalked on walls, the hammer crossed with a sickle out of support for the communist Red Army of Russia. "Pull over, just here," said Constance as they passed a fenced off park supporting a radar van, guarded by half a dozen heavily armed elite guards and a single soldier wearing a gas canister strapped to his back, brandishing a deadly flame-thrower, the Nazi *'Kriegsmarine'* flame-thrower troopers always wore a gas mask to protect their faces from the heat when using their weapon, it made them look all the more menacing. If children were to have a nightmare about a Nazi soldier, which wasn't uncommon, it would most likely be about one of these. James looked around, he couldn't see anything out of the ordinary, apart from the cobbled streets it looked like any other street in any national socialist occupied city in the world.

"Are you sure that we are in the correct place?" queried James as they exited the vehicle.

"Yes, of course." Constance smiled. "Look." She pointed to a wooden hanging sign over a stone archway, displaying grapes and in lavish lettering saying *'Vignable'*, translated as vineyard, but James could see nothing out of the ordinary. He looked quizzically at his female resistance comrade, who gave a small laugh. "Look at how the grapes are placed," she prompted. James looked at the sign a little closer and to his utter astonishment, the grapes made the symbol of the resistance, hiding in plain sight, but unnoticeable to anyone not looking out for it. James could hardly believe his eyes.

The couple walked calmly and casually, arm in arm, through the brick archway, the other side was as if stepping into another world, without war, tyranny and oppression of the fascist jackboot. The hills were lined with vine canopy's, giving the image of true tranquillity and peace. There was a small red-brick bridge, which went over a small creek and led to a shed housing an open-topped workhorse truck and neighboured by a log cabin with smoke coming from a stone-built chimney, there was such a sense of purity that you could truly forget the terror just a stone's throw away. James had to pinch himself to make sure he had not drifted into a dream world. Constance boldly led the way and knocked on the door, James could hear a gramophone playing on the other side. James looked around disconcerted, even though he was in these relaxed surroundings, a log cabin was a bit too open to be an effective headquarters to hold a French resistance force, even a small communist one. The female rapped once again on the door, louder and with growing impatience. The door swung open and showed a stocky man with a bald head and short white stubble on his chin. He was wearing a net vest and a pair of dark green corduroy trousers, held up with a red pair of shoulder braces.

"Bonjour Constance, ça va?" the man said cheerily, giving her a hug.

"Rémy." Constance smiled fondly. "*C'est James, il Anglais.*" The man shook James' hand vigorously his hand was rough with short plump sausage-like fingers.

"Welcome James," he said in a fluent tone without a hint of an accent, James was taken back, this was the last thing he expected from such a man.

"Er… thank you. I understand that this is the resistance headquarters?" The man looked somewhat amused by this enquiry.

"*Oui, oui,*" said the man grabbing a dirty red chequered shirt and slipping it on yet leaving it unbuttoned, he led the two newcomers around the back of his home. The back of his log cabin differed hugely from the front, it was littered with empty, rotten, broken barrels, planks of worn insect bitten wood and some rusting woodwork tools such as saws and iron jacks. Rémy led them to a light blue painted basement hatch and descended the steps, it couldn't be this simple, could it?

The basement was less than half the size of the garage, this was obviously not the resistance headquarters, with five large barrels along one stone-built wall, the others were all panelled.

"Do you like wine?" Rémy asked James, he had to confess that he had enjoyed the occasional glass in the past and he did not want to offend this new acquaintance.

"Yes, sure sometimes," said James slightly reluctantly, hoping that this was not about to turn into a wine tasting session.

"Then I think you will appreciate this," the Frenchman smiled, showing a set of uneven yellow teeth. This unusual man went to one of the wood panelled walls and removed a single panel, he then removed the remaining panels from the wall which were all joined together, revealing a large wine rack hidden behind, it covered the entire stretch of wall and had around two hundred various wine bottles. "My grandfather and father were both winemakers before me, we have been making wine here for over one hundred and fifty years." The man was evidently proud of this fact, so James just nodded and gave the impression that he was finding all this of great interest. The man went onto his tiptoes and stretched to the top left corner of the rack and pulled out a dust-covered bottle. "This is the first bottle we ever made, it is priceless," he said, handing the bottle to James. The Englishman partially rubbed off the dust, it had a worn brown label dated 1789.

"That is impressive," said James, trying to sound convincing, but to be honest he was finding this quite tiresome. Constance obviously felt the same way and said something in French to the vintner. The man gave an understanding nod, replaced the bottle carefully and replaced the panels. He then quite coolly walked to the centre of the large barrels and with a hard tug, pulled the front open, it was a hidden doorway.

"I am not permitted to enter," said Rémy, holding the door open, allowing his friend and new acquaintance to enter with a smile and shut the secret hatch behind them. They walked through the circular tunnel until it opened out, they once again found themselves in yet another surreal environment that could only be called an underground wonderland. They were in a cave by a waterfall which flowed over the entrance into an angelic deep blue lake, James was sure it would be teaming with fish, he had enjoyed carp fishing before the war and had a sudden urge to get a fishing rod. The damp cave had many Gothic arched piscinas carved into the walls with melting wax candles, giving the area a fluorescent orange glow. Resistance guards walked around, displaying blue armbands with the bold black image of the resistance cross, or as he had come to know it as, the cross of Lorraine. There were a couple of tunnels leading away from this single complex, each patrolled by a smoking resistance fighter or a guard sitting at its entrance, drinking a steaming hot drink from a metallic mug. James knew what had to happen here and removed his own red, white and blue, FFI armband and slid it up his right arm. He received a couple of inquisitive looks from some of the French freedom fighters, which if he had been honest, he had partial expected. On one of the stone walls hung a red flag with a yellow hammer crossed with a yellow sickle, this was the Russian flag of the Red Army, they were certainly in the correct place.

A tall man walked towards them, he was wearing a black and white pinstriped suit, a black bolo tie and a silver clasp with the cross of Lorraine engraved on it. He had medium length, gloss brown hair in a side parting, without a single hair out of place and brown bloodshot eyes. He was carrying a Russian Tokarev SVT-38 semi-automatic rifle slung over his shoulder and sticking from his waistband at the front was a German Mauser C69 semi-automatic pistol. Even though he wore the same blue armband as the other soldiers, he had a sense of authority about him, not to mention receiving the occasional nod or salute from the other men.

"Constance?" the man asked politely.

"*Comte de Beauregard,*" she replied giving a small nod, "may I introduce the British SOE, James Garner, who helped rid us of Otto Abetz?"

James gave the man in front of them a half bow and said "*M'lord,*" the man gave the Englishman a once over as if judging him, it took him a few minutes before finally offering James a soft, well-manicured hand.

"*Monsieur* Garner, welcome to the western resistance." The man cracked a small smile. "You have served France well by getting rid of Abetz."

"Well," James started; he was getting embarrassed by all the praise. "I was just the getaway driver and that was nearly a year ago now."

"Your reputation proceeds you, I think you underestimate yourself, my good man." James could sense the last three words had been forced out to try and sound more English. "We have heard of many of your exploits, you are thought to be some kind of super hero to many of these men, you are a symbol of our grand fight, a real hero." The man looked at James proudly, then a change came over the aristocrat's face. "Come, we shall talk," said Earl de Beauregard, leading the way down an adjoining pathway.

"What is this place?" whispered James, it was bigger than just a dugout cave, this place had a history.

"It was a hiding place for the French aristocrats during the French revolution," said the earl without turning. He led them to where a heavy-duty wooden crate and four cushioned stools sat. The Frenchman took one seat for himself and invited his two guests to join him. "So what can I do for you? I get the feeling you have come for more than just vodka, this time?" he said, producing three glasses, pouring an overly generous amount of vodka into each and served them to his associates.

"I am afraid you are correct *m'lord*," started James, taking a sip from his glass. "We are planning a large attack against the Nazi forces, it will cause them major trouble and disruption, we just need more men to assist with the attack, we need your help," James pleaded, seeing the stony, emotionless gaze from their host.

"You are not from this country so I shall forgive you. Favours are earnt my good man," said the Earl after an unbearable five minutes of silence. James was getting used to the French Maquis asking for his assistance, he could have kicked himself for not seeing this coming. He was getting tired of constantly risking his neck just to please people.

"So what exactly are you wanting?" asked James, downing the remainder of the glass, which the Earl refilled before replying.

"We have an issue that we could use your expertise with." The Earl was obviously choosing each word with care. "We were making plans to do this ourselves but I think it would be, as you English say, right up your street." James listened to this resistance cells leader intently, if they were planning to do it themselves it must be of some importance. "There is a Nazi general who for the führers birthday has decided to have a book burning for his fascist troops on the first of the month, under the *Arc de Triomphe*, he calls it a righteous pursuit but they are destroying our culture and our heritage and must be stopped!" This is not the first time the French were worried about their culture and made him think that they cared more about their so-called culture more than the Nazi occupation.

"So let me guess, you want me to grab your books from the flames?" asked James full of sarcasm. The Earl rose abruptly and stood over James, saying in a near shout,

"Do not be so impotent when speaking to me! Do you forget who you are talking to?"

"Forgive me, *m'lord*," James apologised. The Earl sat back down and continued talking in his normal tone.

"I have heard you are a good shooter, is this true?" asked the man.

"Well, I have never missed my target, if that is what you are asking."

"Good, we wish you to execute this man as he gives a speech to his men, and if you complete this mission for us, then you will have earnt our help," the well-spoken noble man leant back in his stool and crossed his arms waiting for the Englishman's response. James considered the man's proposal, he looked at Constance who was keeping her eyes on the floor, avoiding eye contact with anyone. James knew why he had come here and couldn't leave without it. He downed his second glass of vodka and nodded lightly.

"Okay, I'll do it, but I need your word that you will assist us," demanded James, offering the Earl de Beauregard his hand, the Earl looked a bit taken back by the Englishman's attitude and he was obviously not a custom to people dictating their terms to him. Eventually, he shook the man's hand, sealing the agreement. "The first? That is today!"

"*Oui*," the earl commented. "The burning will start at seven o'clock tonight. I will send two of my most trusted men to accompany you and we shall give you a car so you can get close enough without causing too much suspicion. I will leave the planning to you. You may choose any weapon at our disposal," the man then rose, nodded to his guests and took his leave. James and Constance sat in silence until it became unbearable for the French maiden, she finally spoke

"Why did you agree? There must be another way."

"I need to do this, we can't do this without his help. Pierre is counting on us," James replied with determination. "It won't be the first Nazi officer I have killed, I will be fine," he smiled reassuringly.

"But this is a general!" she blurted, looking deep into James' eyes. "They will not stop hunting for you!"

"It is true, but I have to do this."

"What if they kill you?"

"That is a risk we take every day that this war continues. Relax, it will all be over by the morning." James smiled, rising from his seat. He had to arrange the operation for that afternoon, he only had five hours to plan this mission and arrange his escape.

Chapter 16

James had spent his time trawling through the countless weapons the resistance had to offer, the room which stored the armament was down a second adjacent tunnel. The underground armoury had wooden panelled walls and had the greatest variate of firearms fitted on the walls that he had ever seen, they were from England, America, Russia and Germany. From small pistols to monstrous rocket launchers, as well as American pineapple grenades, German stick grenades, even a mortar and a Nazi flame-thrower, it was an assassin's dream. At one end of the room stood four straw-filled dummies dressed in tattered Nazi uniforms and James enjoyed himself testing the weapons one at a time, maybe he enjoyed himself a bit too much, but he finally settled on the heavy perilous German MG 42. These guns were used primarily at the Nazi sandbag bunkers that littered the streets of Paris, often seen at high-profile Nazi areas, as well as the front battle lines. After eventfully choosing his weapons for his dark deed, he went to the top and strode to the side of the shed that housed the workhorse truck, where there was a Frenchman, known as the western resistance mechanic. He was removing a camouflage net that had a dozen various cars hidden beneath, including a black Mercedes Kaiser, it was a six-wheeled car often used by the Nazi high class, it had an eagle above a swastika on the front grill and in theory it was widely said that Adolf Hitler and other high ranking members of the Third Reich Nazi party such as Joseph Goebbels, Hermann Göring and Heinrich Himmler, all travelled in bulletproof versions of this very car. This was the ideal car for the job, no one dared to look through the windows of such a car and it would be able to get them as close to the Nazi function as they wanted. His final task was to meet up with the two trusted resistance members who would be assisting him with his mission. The earl introduced him to the two men who had mainly been chosen because they had a good understanding of the English language and could hold a suitable conversation, they had apparently both volunteered to aid James in whatever he needed. They were both in their thirties, like James and there was a sense that they would hinder the Nazi occupation, in any way they could, yet neither looked as withered as you would expect from resistance fighter, they were true French patriots. The trio walked deep into the vineyard and sat under a large elm tree, surrounded by vines, here they would not be interrupted and could talk secretly and discuss their plan of attack. Once they had discussed the plan down to the finest detail and verified that they all knew what part they would be playing, they went to get prepared, they were to leave in thirty minutes time, giving them ten minutes to get into place and five minutes to prepare for the launch of the attack, timing was everything. James went to Constance to once again reassure her that every possible detail had been assessed and he was sure his two comrades would have his back. He had full confidence that this operation would be a total success.

The trio met outside by the car that the mechanic had been checking over making sure it was in good working order, the last thing they needed was for it to break down half way there. One of his associates, Philippe, was dressed in a chauffeurs uniform and carried a small satchel, disguised as a gas mask case, which contained his everyday Parisian clothing for their escape. James was told he used to be an amateur racing driver, he was the perfect person to be their getaway driver. James was wearing his natural clothing, he fitted the heavy artillery weapon, wrapped in a tanned blanket down in the footwell, in to the back of the car and the third man, known as Albert, was also dressed in his everyday clothing, except for carrying a couple of American pineapple grenades, one in each of his trouser pockets.

The car set off on time, the three men stayed in utter silence with their minds lingering on what had to happen, but before they knew it, the historic monument, *Arc de Triomphe*, loomed up ahead.

Philippe parked the car along a road where they had a clear view of the ancient monument. Albert put on his black fedora hat and jumped from the back passenger-side seat with his hands dug in his pockets to obscure the fact that he was carrying a pair of pineapple hand grenades. James and Phillippe watched an assembly of soldiers form in ranks by a pile of what James assumed were the books. The still air around them was suddenly disrupted by a gramophone playing the German national anthem. From their viewpoint, they could see the soldiers giving the fascist salute and crying in unison three times: "*Sieg Heil!*" The inside of the arched monument became illuminated in an orange glow as the book barbecue was lit and the silhouette of a man could be seen stepping up onto a large platform facing the mass of Nazi troops before him.

"That is him," Philippe said without turning, to James who was sat behind him.

"Okay," replied James, tapping the man on the shoulder, this was the signal to approach the famous arc at a steady pace, which the Frenchman did.

As they approached, the car slowed to a crawling speed, the sight they had been observing became clearer. The flames that were lighting up the monument were not produced just by the smouldering books, but by two menacing Nazi flamethrower soldiers, continuously licking the bonfire with their flames to keep it alight. The Germans had decorated the structures with long Nazi swastika banners which hung the full length of the building on each of the four corners.

James directed the driver around the *Arc de Triomphe* so he could view it from each angle for the best shot. As Philippe drove around James unwrapped his weapon from the blanket, loaded the magazine and cocked the gun. Each entrance to the bonfire had a pair of heavy-duty, elite guards who turned away anyone they believed to be too close and gave them a beating for good measure. Each point of attack was the same as the first. From the different points of view, they could see the horn gramophone that played the German national anthem and even more soldiers than they had seen at first.

Once they had circled the monument once, James signalled to his counterpart to stop at the front, so Phillippe parked side on to the structure.

"Look!" Philippe motioned urgently. Albert was standing by the fence that surrounded the structure, smoking a cigarette and looking around as if he was waiting for a date, one of the guards was approaching him.

"Shit!" blurted James, if they had worked out that the bulge in the Frenchman's pockets were, in fact, hand grenades, the whole operation would be forfeited, Albert would be executed on the spot, reinforcements would then be called and they would scour the whole area for any other so-called 'traitors of the Third Reich'. No one, not even themselves, even though they were in a vehicle only driven by true Nazis, would be safe of the sudden wrath that would befall them. James withdrew his silenced pistol, if he could stealthily take out this soldier then they still had a chance of success, it was a risk, the probability was that he would be seen and if that happened they would need to make a quick getaway. "Keep the engine running," commanded James, reaching to open his side door.

"Non, wait, look!" prompted Phillippe, James looked towards their loan comrade. The Nazi sentry had got out a cigarette and requested a flame from Albert who was now lighting it with a Zippo lighter. James could not believe it, the one soldier who could have foiled their plans, just wanted a light for his smoke. James couldn't help give a little chuckle as he sat back in his chair and relaxed for a brief moment as he watched the lone soldier return to his post. They could clearly hear the fascist officer spouting his Nazi propaganda to his troops in German.

"He sounds like that fascist fanatic in Berlin," James jeered.

"A tyrant in the making," replied the getaway driver.

"Not for much longer." James gave a crooked smirk as he picked up the large gun. He could see Albert watching the car, getting ready for his move. James took a deep breath to try and calm his nerves, if it went wrong it would prematurely end the mission and more than likely their lives.

James steadily wound down his window, he could feel the heat of the bonfire drift through the open window. Some of the guards had also noticed the car and the man sitting in the back seat, who they could now see through the open window was most definitely not a high-ranking member of the Nazi party, but it was all too late.

With one strong swift movement, James raised the large weapon, rested the weight of the barrel on the door and took aim at his target, the general, who was totally unaware of the peril he was in. Before any of the enemy soldier could react, the Englishman let out a short burst of gunfire which tore apart the officer's chest, the force of the weapon's fire sent the generals body flying back from his platform.

"Happy Birthday Adolf!" James yelled over the din as he continued to open fire into the occupying soldiers who were frantically getting their weapons and diving for cover. Albert pulled the pins of his grenades and threw them into two groups of soldiers, sending them flying from the explosion. James clocked one of the soldiers with a flame-thrower taking aim at his comrade, without a seconds hesitation he aimed at the assailant and shot at the man, hitting his tank, blowing up the soldier with three others who were hiding behind the pillar and setting alight one of the banners. This close call seemed to awaken Albert to the danger he was in and he ran to the assaulting car, James gave him covering fire to assure the enemy would be keeping their heads down instead of returning fire. Albert had hardly entered the vehicle when the driver, Philippe, did his job and put his foot down hard on the accelerator, jolting them forward, James continued firing, assuring that the deluded enemy soldiers stayed in their hiding spots until they turned a corner away from the *Arc de Triomphe*. James retracted his weapon back into the car and sat back in his seat. The Englishman got out three cigarettes, lit them and passed them to these two comrades, who accepted them gratefully. But their victory was short-lived.

Before they had the time to enjoy their cigarettes, a sudden volley of gunfire made the car swerve violently. "*Merde!*" Philippe cursed. James and Albert looked through the rear window to see three Nazi bikes, two with armed side cars, pursuing their vehicle. James chucked the unarmed Albert his Walther PPK revolver and moved so he was now kneeling on the chair, once again raising the menacing MG 42 from his window and began firing at the motorcycles behind them. At the same time, Albert had wound down his window and was firing at them with James' revolver. The Frenchman hit the single motorbike in its front tyre which made the bike flip forward and crash into one of the ones with a sidecar, engulfing them in a cataclysmic fireball which spread the entire width of the street. Yet this did not deter the second bike who continued the chase, the man in the sidecar penetrating the chassis of the car with bullets from his constant weapon fire. Phillippe did everything he could think of, swerving the car, showing his expert driving skills, yet whatever he did to break off the pursuers, they kept right on their tail.

"Smash the back window!" ordered James. Albert looked at James as if he had lost his mind. "The rear window! Bloody smash it!" The Frenchman decided against arguing and holding the pistol by the barrel, he broke a hole into the back windscreen. James then awkwardly manoeuvred his weapon from the side window to the open rear window and fired rapidly at their pursuer. The bike tried to swerve to avoid the gunfire but the sidecar limited its manoeuvrability and it inevitably moved into the weapons line of fire. James hit his target and the bike swerved off the road into a carpenters lorry. James slid his machine gun back into the car and sat back with a laugh of relief, which his two comrades joined in.

Philippe parked the car down a secluded side street, James removed the firing pin from his weapon, rendering it useless, it was too large to take it with them. Phillippe changed out of his chauffeurs uniform into the clothes he had brought with him and from the glove compartment he pulled out a grey cylinder with a piece of string hanging from it. "Explosive. We must destroy the car," he explained, James nodded, he was not too sure a stick of dynamite was the way to go, but this was not his country and assumed they would know what was best. So he lit the fuse with his cigarette and the trio ran, they were over a block away when they heard the vehicle erupt behind them.

After the busy afternoon, the three men took their time returning to the headquarters where they were greeted with thunderous applause and James even received a long-awaited peck on the cheek from Constance. After James had pulled himself together from the surprising sign of affection from the French maiden, he asked her

"Where is the Earl?"

"He went upstairs not long after you left and I have not seen him since," explained Constance. "He did say he did not want to be disturbed."

"Really? Well, whether he wants it or not we had a deal and I need to make sure that he will honour it," insisted James. "And only then can we head for home." The resistance members here seemed more pleasant and relaxed which possibly had to do with their surroundings, but it made James more wary and unsettled, he had to get back the resistance he knew and trusted. James left and Constance followed closely behind, they walked through the hidden barrel entrance, up the wooden ladder into the open air. It was only then that James noticed the sweet fruity aroma in the evening air. The couple walked to the front door of the property with a sense of business in their stride, they could see the light of a fire through the window so it was clear that someone was still awake. It was only nine o'clock, yet the resistance activities could take it out of you.

James knocked loudly on the front door of the house, the pair waited but there was no response of any kind, James knocked once again, louder this time, he did not have time for this. They heard some kind of sound from within. Eventually the door opened and Rèmy, wearing the same attire that he had worn before and armed with a sawn down shotgun, opened the front door. He stood in the door and tiredly looked at the two of them, he took a look behind them before lowering his weapon.

"Did we wake you?" asked James, he didn't really care but he thought he would be polite enough to ask. "Were you expecting someone else?"

"No, I was just trying a new vintage of wine. I was worried you may be the Gestapo, they have been going crazy since you shot that general," he gave a toothy grin, he had obviously had more than a couple of glasses. "The weather has not been the best for the grape this year but it still had good potential."

"Who will help you pick them?" asked the Englishman. "I don't see any farm hands," he said, turning to view the vast vineyard in the dim evening light.

"It is part of a deal I have with the resistance. I allow them to hide their headquarters in my basement and they give me free labour." Everybody seemed to be making deals with the resistance, James guessed that it made them feel safer than being directly involved, but to the Gestapo it did not matter how involved you were, if you had any contact or involvement with any resistance, you were considered just as guilty and considered a traitor which meant you would either be hung or lined against a wall and shot.

"Where is the earl de Beauregard?" asked James. Rémy glanced behind him into the cabin, before turning back and replying to his new acquaintance.

"He cannot be disturbed."

"We do not have time for this!" demanded James, barging past the Frenchman into his home. The cabin was decorated with photos of the beautiful French countryside, the mountainous Alps and Paris from a distance with the towering Eiffel Tower high over the skyline of the loved city of light. There was a fire smouldering away in a brick fireplace and there were three open bottles of wine on a wooden rustic table, surrounded with six wood and woven twine chairs. James saw a flickering flame in the next room, without asking for permission he strode directly into the neighbouring room and saw the earl lying asleep in a cot. On the side table sat a candle in a clay candle holder, a small bottle of a milky amber liquid with a Russian label on the outside and beside it sat a metallic syringe. James gave a distinct clearing of his throat but the French aristocrat did not stir. "Excuse me *m'lord*," he said loudly, with still no response, James repeated himself louder, he was almost shouting now and still nothing. James took to shaking the comatose man who did not react except for a nearly inaudible grunt, James was fed up with this and responded by giving the earl a slap around the face with the back of his hand, turning the man's cheek red, but still, the man hardly moved.

"He is in a morphine coma," explained Rémy with a horrified look on his face, he had obviously never imagined anyone would do that to a member of the aristocracy, let alone a resistance leader. He and Constance had appeared at the door and witnessed the whole event. "He will not wake until around three o'clock in the morning when he will wake for his second fix and then sleep until eleven." James looked around the small room, the only other furniture was a single rocking chair and a decorative side table beside it in the opposite corner of the room. The Englishman picked up the small bottle of the drug and the syringe, placed them on the far table, he placed his revolver beside them and then he nestled into the rocking chair.

"Constance," he said loudly, in a hope it would stir the earl. "Why don't you go and try some of Rémy's wine, I am sure he would appreciate your thoughts on it, while I wait for our host to stir." James had an expression which told her that she should trust his decision.

Once the duo had left him to watch over the resistance leader James spent the majority of the night leisurely rocking in the chair. It was long past dark and James was beginning to nod off when the earl finally stirred and without noticing James who was now observing him from the corner of the room, he felt around on his bedside desk aimlessly. Not finding his drugs he wearily rose his head and saw his guest watching him closely.

"Where is morphine?" he asked sternly.

"I killed the general, now are you going to keep to your end of the bargain?"

"Give me morphine!" the Earl shouted.

"You can have your dope when you agree with our arrangement!" said James calmly. "Are you going to honour the agreement?"

"Yes, yes, honour agreement. Now give Morphine!" James turned to see Constance and Rémy standing in the doorway, roused by the aristocrats' uproarious behaviour.

"Did you hear that?" The French duo nodded. James slowly rose and casually placed the metal syringe and bottle of drugs on the bedside table. "Good, when he wakes again remind him of the deal and tell him we will contact him when it is time to carry out our plan." Rémy nodded frantically. With James satisfied that the Frenchman understood he led Constance back down to the communist resistance headquarters to get a couple hours sleep before they returned back to inner Paris.

Chapter 17

James and Constance left early that morning in the same Pegasus that they had arrived in. James had decided that they should have a couple of drinks at *La Belle de Nuit nightclub* before returning to the dreary resistance headquarters but Constance insisted that she had to check in with her brother, Pierre, first and would join him there afterwards.

James entered the club, turned to the bar and froze in his tracks. There, sitting at the bar, sipping on a glass of whiskey, was the British military intelligence agent, the luscious Olivia Hayhurst, smiling alluringly at him. James slowly walked up to the bar and took the stool beside her, without turning to her, he growled: "I don't care what the Fisherman wants, he can chuck me in the slammer for all I care, I am not doing it!" The barman poured James a glass of whiskey and put it in front of him. "Give me a beer," James said, pushing the glass back to the barman.

"The Fisherman does not know I am here. In fact, he has an affair in Poland to deal with. No, I am here to offer you a way out!" she replied with a smile.

"Way out?"

"I am going back to England, a plane is picking me up at an abandoned airfield tonight, there is room for one more person," she smiled the fetching smile that had attracted James to her in the first place. James had to consider this offer, but then full of reluctance replied,

"I appreciate the offer, but I am…" He looked around for any eavesdroppers. "French resistance now." As the barman passed James a cold beer, Olivia passed the barman a ten Franc note. "He will just stick it on my tab, you know," explained James.

"Your tab has been paid in full. Just a small thank you from British intelligence." The English agent laughed at James' surprise and then her face turned stern and she spoke in complete serenity. "Do you know who that general you killed was? He wasn't just another Nazi thug!"

"He was just some book burning, goose-stepping, jackbooted moron." James replied, sipping on his glass of beer. "Wait, how did you know about that?"

"It is my job to know, plus the Fisherman has a soft spot for Beluga caviar and your name came up during negotiations with the western resistance."

"You mean the Communist resistance. Great, well thanks for the help," James said sarcastically.

"We cannot get involved. That goose-stepping moron as you called him called Ernst Hermann Himmler." James just gave her a blank look. "He was the youngest brother of the head of the SS, Heinrich Himmler!" James could not believe what he was hearing, no wonder those communist fighters were so eager to give him the job. "The Nazis have put a price on your head. Seven hundred and fifty thousand Reichsmarks, dead or alive; you are not safe here anymore!" Olivia urged.

"I never was," James replied dolefully, looking at the female, trying to absorb the fact that he was now a wanted man.

"Well, if you change your mind, I leave at eleven o'clock tonight from an abandoned airfield just south of Beauvais." Olivia gave a discreet nod behind James, he turned to see Constance approaching them. "She is pretty," whispered Olivia, raising from her stool.

"Who is she?" the French maiden asked with a distinct tone of jealousy in her voice. James was not sure how he was going to talk his way out of this one when the British agent began speaking to Constance in fluent French and took her leave. Once Olivia Hayhurst had left the club, after giving a brief subtle glance to James, Constance took the English agent's seat. James asked her:

"What did she say?"

"She said she was asking you to buy her a drink," replied Constance, content with the explanation.

"Oh, that is what she wanted, I couldn't understand a word she was saying," replied James, relieved. He was sure Olivia would not have told the truth; after all, it was a spy's job to keep her cover.

"The general you killed, that was Heinrich Himmler's brother! The Führer has offered a reward for your capture. They are dropping flyer all over the city by plane!" she said, looking around at the German soldiers who were spending their free time and hard earnt money at this joint. "We should leave," she urged. James reluctantly agreed, with a seven-hundred-and-fifty-thousand-Reichsmarks price on his head, being in a place frequented by Nazi soldiers was most probably not the brightest idea. James downed the remainder of his cool beverage in one and the duo left together.

Upon entering the underground resistance headquarters, the Englishman was met with a response of cheering and applause. He had, at last, earnt his place in the French Maquis and more than he thought he could, he felt that he finally belonged in France.

Chapter 18

After shaking hands, receiving pats on the back and getting congratulations from most of the resistance fighters, James met back up with Pierre and the other two resistance lieutenants who all shook his hand warmly and looked at him in a more respectable light.

"The attack has been planned for tomorrow," stated Pierre. "Our contacts tell us that there will be a train at the station at seven o'clock in the morning."

"Tomorrow," James repeated, he had to admit, fighting in the resistance was non-stop action, there was little time for a break, but then he remembered the reason for this offensive. He took a glance around the headquarters, someone was still absent. "What about Édouard, after all, Maurice was his best friend, he should be involved!" insisted James, having the rage and the monster of the man on their side could only be an advantage.

"I understand your concern but I am afraid Édouard is still not in the correct state of mind to assist us, he may cause us more trouble and he may risk his own life in the attack," Pierre said soulfully. "But we have sent word to our new allies, thanks to you, my friend."

"I wouldn't count on that communist druggie aristocrat if I were you," advised James.

"He may have a vice of being addicted to the morphine, but I know him well," said one of the lieutenants. He was a stocky fellow with bulldog-like features, a paintbrush moustache and blading mousey hair, he never spoke much and mostly communicated with grunts or gestures, but when he did speak he was always polite and to the point, his name was André. "He is passionate about the freedom of our great nation. He can be trusted to keep his word, I assure you," insisted André strongly. James gave a small bow in understanding and apology for any offence.

"Any idea of what they may be transporting?" inquired James.

"We cannot find out, no one seems to know," Pierre replied. "Could be guns, troops or anything. It is very strange that our contact was not able to find out. The Nazis are, how do you saying? Playing their cards close to their shirt?"

"Chest," corrected James. "Playing their cards close to their chest."

"Ah, yes chest."

"Well, it has to be something of some importance if the krauts aren't willing to talk about it."

"*Exactement,*" said Pierre, in French.

"What kind of resistance can we expect?"

"Resistance?" inquired Pierre, blatantly confused by the context.

"Enemy soldiers," James explained. "How many enemy soldiers can we expect?" Pierre looked slightly embarrassed by his confusion.

"Sixty or seventy, Germans we think. But if it is a troop transport, there is no idea, it could be over one hundred." This made James cautious, last time they faced a large number of troops their casualties were immense, which included Pierre, but it was an expense every man and women among them were willing to pay.

That night everyone got their sleep, they needed their rest for the next days' task. That was everyone except for James, the offer he had been given only hours before at the night club by the British bombshell, Olivia, plagued his mind, his decision to remain was haunting him. At this very moment he could be returning to England's green and pleasant lands but had decided to remain here and fight with a civilian army, for a country which was not even his, he couldn't even understand the language, mostly. It would be too late to change his mind now, even if he wanted to. With this mournful thought churning through his mind, he finally drifted into a restful sleep.

James awoke to the hum of activity in the underground base of operations, the headquarters was at full capacity. Many of the resistance members who used this as their base resided at their own quarters around the city and some even had jobs. But they were all here today, it seemed somehow strange, how these men and women, who were all dressed in everyday Parisian clothing, were now all armed to the teeth with automatic weapons, pistols, rifles and knives, some had even strapped ammunition belts across their chests. A young Spanish resistance fighter named Manuel had fitted a resistance flag to a large pole. This was going to be a full head-on battle, relying more on distraction than the usual stealth.

James pulled himself up, he felt unusually drained this morning, he walked over to a water bowl which was filled with cold water, he splashed it in his face to wake himself up and was handed a towel, which he accepted and, after wiping the water from his eyes, looked to see who the helpful stranger was. Standing there with a beaming smile which lit up the room, wearing a black beret, a single ammunition belt strapped tightly across their body, a carbine rifle on a sling on their back and in a holster around their waist a Colt Commando pistol was Constance. Seeing her armed for war took James by surprise, he had to remind himself that she was also a resistance fighter, just like the rest of them, just like him.

"Are you ready, England?" She used the term as a sign of affection and had started saying it in the flirtatious tone that James was so fond of. She reached in her pocket and removed a resistance armband, identical to his own, which he always wore when in a secure area, and slipped it onto her upper right arm.

"Wow, you look ready for a battle." James smiled as he pulled his pistol from under his pillow and grabbed his knuckle duster off an uneven shelf, the dampness of the headquarters made them cold in his hand, but once he had slipped them onto his fingers they would soon warm up. He slammed a loaded magazine into his MP35, which he then slung over his shoulder. "Let's kick some krauts butt!" And the duo joined the line to leave the underground base. Everyone in the queue was being issued with extra full magazines for the fighters chosen weapon by some junior resistance members. At the top of the steps were four disguised personnel transport lorries with the backs covered to obscure its contents from view. James, Pierre and Constance jumped into the back of the first lorry with twenty others so that every last inch of space was taken up. James got out his cigarettes and passed them around to the other fighters which frequented the lorry. The engine roared to life and they set off. The atmosphere inside was sombre, no one spoke, they were preparing themselves in their own way for the battle as every person had to, James liked to think about the battle of Rorke's Drift of 1879, where 150 British troops successfully defended a garrison against an intense assault by 4,000 Zulu warriors, this made him remember that no matter the odds one could always prevail victoriously. Everyone was wearing their resistance armbands on their upper right arms. The Lorries would take separate routes so as not to arouse suspicion and would assemble at the bottom of a slope where the highly defended train station was situated with the valley on the opposite side. James and Constance were to fit explosives to the communications tower, on timers, which would cause a distraction for them to go over the ridge and take cover positions on the opposite side of the station, around a small work shed and rusty mechanics, which included redundant engines that littered the side of the tracks. The lorry came to an abrupt stop.

"Checkpoint," whispered Pierre. James drew his pistol and in complete silence screwed the suppressor on the end of it. Everyone held their breath. It would all depend if the driver could convince his way through the roadblock well enough so that the soldier did not feel it necessary to look in the back of the lorry, the lightest sound could warrant a check and if that was the case the whole operation would be over, along, most likely, with their lives. The two minutes felt like a lifetime, but once again the vehicle's engine rumbled loudly and they continued on its voyage towards the target of their assault as it was waved through the guard post. Everyone was slightly relieved and gave a sigh as they relaxed slightly, they had overcome the first obstacle, this could only be a good sign.

It was another hour until the lorry stopped again and the flap was thrown up, the sunlight flooded the inside with the morning light and the civilian army disembarked. One of the lorries had already arrived and the remaining two followed shortly after.

"The station is over that hill," whispered Pierre as the two lieutenants joined them. "The radio tower is set back away from the station and should only have one or two guards, they do not expect an attack on it." His focus was now set upon his sister and English friend. "The distraction is essential or we could all be seen and shot as we go over the hill so you must disable the guards quickly and quietly, set the explosives and then re-join your comrades back here. Our men on the MG30s," these were heavy machine guns supported with a bipod and often used by the Nazi occupying forces, "will support us from the hilltop. *Bon Chance!*" James nodded his thanks and waited for the brother and sister to embrace before the duo set off.

Constance carried a black satchel that contained the explosives for the sabotage of their target. They had left their heavier weapons back by the trucks and only carried their pistols and James' knuckle duster for support. They kept close to the tree line as they moved with stealth and determination. They walked, at speed, the long way around the train station until they were in the perfect position to observe their objective. From this secluded position, they could see both sides of the valley as they prepared to perform their assault on the giant radio tower.

The duo sat crouched, watching the guards at the large transmissions tower, they had to put the railway station out of their mind for now. The Nazi guards were casually talking and smoking, they were paying little or no attention to their surroundings, they never had had any trouble here, no one would be stupid enough to attack such a fortified area.

James glanced towards the station, the base of the radio tower which was now towering in front of them would be obscured by the low, waist-high wall and the row for bushes that surrounded the Nazi crowded platform. Pierre had been overly optimistic with his assumption of sixty soldiers, there were at the very least eighty or ninety and those were only the ones they could see. The train was obscured from his view but the plumes of smoke told James that his French friend's contact had been correct, there was indeed a train at the station, but this was not their concern yet.

James removed his silenced Walther and made his move, firing two muffled shot into the head of the first soldier. His brother in arms ran to his fallen comrade, James took aim and fired another two shots, felling the second soldier in an instant. Constance ran to the two fallen men and dragged each back behind the tree line, James fitted their coal scuttle helmets over their own hats, so that if a soldier from the train station happened to glance in their direction they would be dismissed as the guards they had just assassinated. The duo then began fitting the explosive charges on the inside of each metallic leg and set the timers to ignite the dynamite for eight minutes time. If any of the explosives failed to go off then the force of the other devices' explosion would detonate the other, with the same result, bringing down the tower. Once the explosives were fitted and the timers set, the comrades threw aside the German helmets and ran back to where their resistance army was waiting patiently on the adjacent side of the verge. James took a single look back to the tree line, somewhere in that forest the Communist resistance would be hiding, or so he hoped.

Panting and out of breath, they reconvened with Pierre, James checked his watch.

"Five minutes mate," he panted.

"*Bon*," replied the French leader. "Comte de Beauregard will attack from the other side and look who also turned up to help fight the upcoming battle," with a smile Pierre stepped aside to present an unnaturally clean Édouard.

"Ed!" cried James, overjoyed to see his old comrade. The large man produced a giant hand which James shook happily.

"I am here for Maurice, *mon amie.*" James nodded his approval.

"I am glad you are with us old chap," he replied. With that, the black-marketeer turned and pulled out a German made Bergmann MP 18 submachine gun, it had a drum magazine fitted horizontally on the top and carried fifty rounds, the monster of a gun was capable of firing five hundred rounds a minute. It was a giant of a gun, even in the hands of Édouard, the weapon was often fired with the support of sandbags or a windowsill but it looked quite normal for the large Frenchman who carried it with great ease as if it was a simple Carbine rifle. James couldn't help but smirk at this sight, it would put the jeepers up anyone and combined with the man's rage for the loss of his friend, Édouard would be a challenge to be reckoned with. This did not stop the Englishman from exclaiming, "Good God!"

"It is good he is on our side," Constance whispered into James' ear; he had to agree.

"Deux minutes, cite!" whispered Pierre harshly.

"Right, let's get the fascist bastards!" said James to no one in particular. They took up their positions lying flat against the grassy dew-covered slope, their firearms beside them. The young flag bearer, Manuel, handed James and Constance their assault weapons, pistols were not going to be of much use in this attack. James looked beside him to Constance.

"Bon chance, England," she whispered, James forced a confident smile, he had to admit that the chances of surviving this bold attack were slim, yet this was not going to stop him doing his best.

"Good luck," he retorted. Pierre looked at the two of them, it was obvious he was not comfortable having his sister risk her life, yet he never discussed the fact, with the knowledge that it would both anger and upset her. James watched as the seconds ticked by on his wristwatch, only one minute to go. The tension was unbearable and everyone could feel it. Over this ridge was a large count of armed Jerry soldiers and they had to rely on the Communist resistance to aid them, in James' eyes they were not much better than the fascists, but if they helped them win this war, then that was all that mattered.

James held his breath as he watched the second had sweep past twelve. He looked at Constance and behind her Pierre, in disbelief, they had planted the charges, he had set two of them himself and Constance had set the other two, they had both confirmed the amount of time, eight minutes. James leopard crawled to the top of the ridge and with great caution, not to be noticed by any of the enemy soldiers occupying the station opposite. He could see the train below, it was a matt black steam engine, the first carriage looked like a small armoured castle with heavy artillery guns. These were often used on the trains mostly used by the Nazi forces to defend the railway tracks from any opposing army troops. The remaining five carriages were cattle carts, mainly used for transporting prisoners of war or moving Jews to concentration camps or death camps. The carriages would hide their approach but what had happened to the explosives charges? Why had they not gone off? James looked towards the radio tower, there was no sign of any troop movement in that direct vicinity so they could not have found the explosive devices, otherwise, the entire area would be swarming with German forces trying to find the would-be saboteurs.

The still air was broken by a cataclysmic eruption and the radio tower went up into an inferno before collapsing into a pile of twisted metal and sending up a dirt cloud. They must have got the timing wrong, that was the only explanation. James looked down to the train's platform, the plan had worked, the enemy forces were in uproar and distracted by the explosion. James looked behind him to Pierre and nodded, he, in turn, waved to his resistance troops to advance. In total silence, like a still, silent wave against a shoreline, the French civilian army crept up and over the ridge and down the other side, not daring to make a sound which may alert the opposition of their presence. James took refuge behind a wooden mechanic's shed, along with five other resistance members, including Constance, Pierre and Édouard. Other members hid behind the rusting engines and other abandoned mechanical machinery, including a collapsing, rusting, moulding carriage. Above them on the ridge of the slope, for support, were twelve to sixteen men, each two-man team manning a heavy machine gun, such as MG 42s and MG 15, that had most likely been salvaged from downed German Luftwaffe aircraft. Once the attack had begun, these would fire continuous suppressing assistance to the ground troops.

James peeked around from the side of the shed, the carriages had completely obscured them from the Nazi forces on the platform. At the far end, he could see the large Nazi searchlight that looked like a giant cauldron, guarded by a single guard who seemed perplexed by the catastrophic sabotage of one of their most essential propaganda tools. If this lone soldier turned around he would see the whole resistance army ready to unleash justice on his comrades, even though they were hidden from view, taking cover, they were not entirely concealed.

"Pierre!" whispered James pointing out the man, Pierre went down on his hands and knees and crept to James' position on all four, observing the sentry, he could read James' mind.

"Take him out, my friend," agreed the Frenchman. James handed Constance his MG 42 machine gun to hold and removed his silenced pistol which he had been carrying in his trouser waistband. He took careful aim, steadying his hand by resting it on the forearm of the second. He steadied his breathing to a slow pace. The Englishman squeezed the trigger, he saw as a spark as the bullet missed his target and hit the metallic casing of the enemy's searchlight.

"Goddamn it!" the English SOE cursed under his breath. The German soldier had awoken from his hypnotic gaze and turned, to the dismay of the observing enemy, the young sentry's eyes met the eyes of his would-be assassin, James, Without a moment's hesitation, the Nazi put a silver tube whistle to his lips and blew on it loudly before James could get off a second shot which hit its targets, through the sentry's left eye, the whistle stopped as the man slumped on top of the large lamp, stone dead, but it was all too late, the alarm had been sounded, they no longer had the advantage of surprise.

The train began to lurch forward violently, pulling the carriages behind it from their stationary position as the drivers panicked. The soldiers from the platform began approaching from the side as they saw the onslaught of resistance fighters and were instantly taken down by the resistances supporting machine guns. James replaced the pistol into the waistband of his trousers and hastily retrieved the machine gun from his young maiden counterpart who still had hold of it. A sudden loud whirring aloud, identical to an air raid warning siren out. "They will reveal us to their entire force! That train is our only cover!" James shouted over the commotion of the alarm and supporting gunfire.

"You are correct!" replied Pierre loudly, over the din of the siren. "Thomas, Jean-Claude, *arrête le train!*" he directed to a couple of soldiers who were hiding behind the shed with them. Using the cattle carts as cover the two men took off in a crouched run towards the locomotive.

"Why are those bloody cannons not firing?" James asked.

"The troops get out for as long as they can!" Pierre answered. "It is hot inside and they only have limited air! They will still be at the station!" James was slightly relieved that they did not have to face that mobile fortress but it would mean they would have to face more military personnel on the opposing platform, whose attention had now turned to the attacking force. The train was still moving forward, opening the Nazis field of fire. James from the side of the shed was firing at the Nazi troops, along with the majority of the Paris resistance army, returning the Germans fire, supported by the heavy machine gun fire above them, sending the Germans diving for cover. They watched as their fire-power sent the enemy darting behind pillars, metallic benches, dustbins and notice boards. Both armies were firing at each other with zero remorse or regret. Édouard moved from his secluded space and stood out in the open as his rage took over and he fired his menacing weapon at any adversary he had in his sight. James watched his friend in amazement, then watched as the giant man got shot in his left shoulder, yet this did not deter the Frenchman from delivering his continues barrage of relentless fire. James watched on as he saw two of his comrades fall to the enemy's gunfire, yet the resistance continued to fire back.

Pierre's two men had made it to the locomotive and had halted the large machine, leaving half of the German-occupied platform obscured from the resistance rampage. James looked past the 'insane' Édouard and saw two men throw the French train driver and his assistant from the cab of the machine.

"Édouard!" yelled James. "Get those men over the other side of the verge! But do not kill them!" he shouted, it was the only thing James could think of to get his friend out of harm's way, he was sure if he had done nothing his friend would have fallen.

"Why do not kill them? Why do we need them?" asked Constance.

"They may be able to give us information," responded James.

"And they are still French, even if they work with the enemy," added Pierre, firing blindly from the opposite side of the shed to James. There were numerous explosions as resistance members threw hand grenades over the tracks onto the platform.

"Where is the bloody communist resistance?" James asked, turning to Pierre, then as if in response, from the tree line behind the platform, the sound of a bugle, sounding a cavalry charge, could be heard and a line of men firing their weapons idly came out from the forest.

"Better late than never," shrugged Constance as James took her rifle from her and handed her his empty weapon, which she hastily reloaded.

"Manuel? Where is Manuel?" Pierre asked. "We must mark our position so our comrades know not to fire at us. We must raise the *Drapeau Français* (the French tricolour)!" The three comrades began calling the young Spanish resistance fighters name in unison. Finally, the young man ran down the slope and appeared among them.

"*Oui?*" he asked, with his back flat to the shed.

"Raise the bloody flag kid!" shouted James. The boy nodded and lifted the long pole over his head and waved it from left to right, signalling their position to their communist allies.

The ruckus continued as the two resistance groups advanced closer against the dwindling group of Nazis. The pursuing battle deafened its competitors with constant weapons fire, the drone of the alarm siren had long dissipated.

James had exhausted his machine guns ammunition as well as Constance's rifle rounds and had resorted to picking off the seemingly endless supply of enemy troops with his Walther. Constance was on one knee firing her own pistol but she would find it hard to hit a barn door. Slowly they found the returning fire to become less frequent and they had fewer targets to choose between. The inevitable was finally happening and the remaining German soldiers downed their arms and surrendered.

"Where were you going?" Pierre translated his English comrade's words. After finding that the surviving Nazis were merely privates with no intelligence of any value and no information on the trains orders or the reason for the cattle carts, or if they did they hid it well. So they had to interrogate the collaborating train driver and his assistant, surely they would know the locomotives destination and purpose. After a few threats of torture they were only too happy to oblige, but they were unable to give any new information. They claimed that they were to be given instructions by a Gestapo officer before leaving.

"Gestapo? Was he on the station?" screamed James, Pierre was translating the best he could.

"*Oui, oui*, the station," the driver replied nervously. James strode back to the top of the ridge and looked over the sea of dead Nazis, it was an image of a bloodthirsty massacre but they could spend weeks searching for the Gestapo officer and still not find the man. James observed the battlefield. The fight had not been won without the loss of resistance troops. Many of the Maquis fighters were now cradling the heads or crying over their fallen friends and family members, father, sons, mothers, daughters, husbands and wives, none had been spared by the Nazi war machine, but justice prevailed. The only piece of useful information the driver and his young assistant divulged was that they were going to pick up some Free French prisoners of war, this was of great interest to them. It was also disconcerting news, the only reason to move prisoners of war would be to make room for more captured soldiers and possibly sending these existing ones to death camps as traitors. They could not even be sure that these Free French soldiers were being held in France, these tracks could lead to Poland or even to the heart of Nazi-occupied Europe, the capital city of Germany, Berlin.

Before leaving, the two resistance armies met up, executed the remaining Nazis to keep up morale and set explosives on the enemy searchlight as well as the train tracks to blow them both. Further along the tracks mines were laid beneath the girders so that when a train travelled over them the mines would detonate, blowing both the tracks and the train together, permanently demobilising them so they could not be used, at this time or for a considerable amount of time afterwards. Before setting the explosives to the searchlight, James pulled the body of the young soldier from the top, only to realise that the light was on during the execution and the intense heat of the lamp had burnt the soldier's body and singed the boys' skin, it was now covered in disgusting blisters. James could not help but vomit the contents of his stomach.

The decreased resistance fighters bodies would be taken to be buried by friends and loved ones.

It was late evening by the time they had reached their Paris resistance base, many of the men and women fell asleep once the adrenaline that was running through their veins had waned and the fatigue that followed hit them like a sledgehammer. James and Pierre were unable to drift off to sleep, the news of the Free French prisoners of war warranted more attention and the sight of the burnt-up soldier prayed on James' mind, he could not help seeing the young man's deformed corpse every time he shut his eyes. So for much of the night, they poured over countless maps of France.

"Where could they be keeping them?" Pierre shouted in a rage, slamming down his fist on the wooden table that they had planned the previous attack on.

"It could be anywhere," commented James, rubbing his eyes which were growing heavy, he was exhausted from the constant deliberation. "We don't even know that they are in the same country, they could be in Italy or even Yugoslavia for all we know."

"He is correct," said Édouard, appearing from behind a curtain, he had one arm in a sling. "We need more information, we must find out more," he insisted.

"*Oui*," agreed Pierre in thought.

"I agree, we do not have enough to go on," agreed James, he looked at his comrade Pierre who was lost in his own thoughts.

"I have got a contract," the French commander finally spoke. "He is a barman at the SS officers-only bar at the top of the Eiffel tower, we cannot contact him at his home as all the staff are watched. We will have to meet him at the bar, he may have heard something," Pierre spoke slowly as he expressed his thoughts.

"Are you mad?" retorted Édouard. "Only the SS are allowed, you go up there then you will be shot!"

"Not if we were in disguise," interrupted James. "It is worth taking the risk; as you said, we have to try." Édouard just shook his head in disbelief.

"We must sleep on it, *mon amie*," suggested the large man. James could not agree more, he could feel his bed calling him. The three men took their leave.

James walked into an annexe of the underground headquarters and found Constance writing in her journal by candlelight, she placed down her book and rose to great her English friend.

"Are you hurt?" she asked, checking James' sleeve which had a distinct tear right up to his shoulder.

"Blast it," the Englishman said angrily. "I must have snagged it on that bloody shed!" He removed his dark coat; the tear was unrepairable.

"Wait here," the French maiden demanded and elegantly walked to a coat stand laden with lot of various coats. She removed one and handed it to James, it was a black leather coat, it could be called a biker jacket but was still casual enough not to be noticed. There were some slight markings where sewn on emblems had once been. James would not have been surprised in the slightest if he learnt that this once belonged to a Nazi biker messenger. The Englishman slipped on the coat, it felt strange, totally unlike this previous jacket, but it was a perfect fit. "It makes you look handsome England," she giggled in her schoolgirl way.

They sat together on the settee, she laid her head on his lap as sleep took them both.

Chapter 19

"Are you sure they are going to fall for this?" James asked, he had real concerns for this plan, it was riskier than anything they had done in the past. Pierre just smiled broadly and nodded, it was a bold plan.

"Yes, we will use this." The Frenchman produced a partially torn poster. "Your wanted poster." It was the first time James had seen this flyer, it was very bland with a silhouette of a man in a flat cap, it could be any man you pass in the street, and some bold French writing. Seeing his man trying to decipher the writing, Pierre translated it for him. "It says: 'We are searching for an Englishman who is working for a group of terrorists and is believed to have been involved with many acts of terrorism against the Third Reich. We offer a reward for this man, dead or alive.'" James recognised the last bit: '750,000 $\mathcal{RM}$'.

"This could be any Tom, Dick or Harry." James laughed; being called a terrorist did not bother him, he was used to being called that by the invaders and if he incited terror in them then all the better. "It could be anyone!"

"And that is why it will work," agreed the French leader. The duo had been discussing the plan for the best part of the morning, it was an ambitious plan and involved the stealthy assassination of two SS officers, not to mention their driver.

Later that same day the two men were seated side by side having their hair cut and being cleanly shaven with straight razors. A female comrade named Francine dealt with Pierre, whilst Constance had insisted on shaving James. Without his ponytail, Pierre looked quite different, as did James being cleanly shaven. The two females found the transformation amusing but it was a necessity if they were to pull off this daring plan.

Before leaving the headquarters, Édouard took James to one side and gave him a black leather, businessman style suitcase and told him to put it in the toilets of the Eiffel tower with the express instruction not to tell Pierre. This order made James feel uncomfortable but he promised to his friend that he would not say a word.

By late morning the two men were on their way to a local French cinema named *La Cinémathéque Française*. They were being led by Yosef and were followed at a distance by another car of five resistance members. It was a small family owned cinema but one of the few which remained open for business. As the occupation of Paris had continued, western made movies had become illegal and only German movies, full of Nazi propaganda, with glamorous blond women and true Arian men, portrayed as the heroes, were permitted. As many smaller cinemas refused to accept such programs they were promptly closed down along with the many Jewish family-owned establishments. Even though this was only a small cinema, the SS had requested the managers' office for their own use. The resistance had been informed that the German officers had spent many late nights, drinking wine and eating a large consumption of French cheese.

James and Pierre casually strode into the cinemas reception area, attempting to remain casual, James dug his hands into the pockets of his leather jacket, and seeing, standing as bold a brass, two black-clad SS officers, displaying their iron crosses and red swastika armbands, he slipped his fingers through the holes of his knuckle duster. Seeing James tensing slightly, Pierre whispered, "Be calm, my friend, do nothing until we are in the office." James just nodded, keeping his eyes on the two strongly built Reich officers. He turned to say something to his friend but his gaze was not reciprocated, so he thought better of it.

Pierre was looking dead ahead and led the way towards the enemy officers, James followed him a single step behind, looking around him at the Victorian architecture, trying his best to act casual. He watched as Pierre got out the wanted flyer and spoke to the two men in French. The soldiers deliberated for a brief moment before leading the two men through a side door into a small room. There was a round table in the centre of the room, on it sat a decanter of red wine, two used crystal wine glasses, a beautifully decorated terracotta beer stein with a metal lid and a rectangular cheese board with just a few crumbs of cheese remaining. As one of the officers questioned Pierre about his claim of knowing where this British agent resided, their greed was evident, James gripped his brass knuckles ever tighter. Then without any warning, Pierre lunged at one of the German soldiers and the pair rolled around on the floor wrestling for control. At the same time James revealed his brass armed fist and smacked the second German across the jaw, cutting open the flesh on his cheek, he then delivered the second blow to the man's nose, breaking it, the man grabbed his nose with a cry as it gushed with blood, James then delivered another punch to the man's gut, dropping him to his knees, with that James thrust his knee into the man's face, pushing the man's broken nose up into the crippled man's brain, killing him instantly. James then turned his attention to the two brawling men rolling on the floor. He removed his silenced pistol and aimed it at the head of the Nazi officer who was now astride Pierre with his hands at the resistance leaders throat.

"No! No blood!" cried Pierre, seeing his friend's actions, he was right, they could not risk damaging the uniforms. James did not have time to think, he jumped on the officer who tumbled off Pierre and was caught in an arm lock that James had initiated, the German officer tried to struggle as James ever tightened the lock around the man's throat. After a minute in that position, the soldier went limp in James lock and only then The Frenchman nodded to James.

"Thank you, my friend," he panted, pulling himself to his feet with a helping hand from James. They began stripping off their clothes and wrapped them into a bundle in their jackets, they replaced them with the highly offensive uniforms of the Nazi SS officers. They had hardly redressed when there was a tapping at the single window which led to the secluded alleyway, two slow knocks and three rapid knocks in quick succession. James had now associated this knock with safety. He strode over to the window and drew open the curtain to reveal three men waiting for them outside. James lifted the window open, checked the alleyway which revealed a black Kaiser convertible staff car, unlike the one they had used at the book barbecue at the *Arc de Triomphe*, this one would have been altered to be bulletproof. On the muddy ground lay a naked man with a short pyramidal moustache and a deep gruesome gash on his throat, this would have been the driver of the officer's staff car. Two of the men removed a drainage grate and continued to drop the dead drivers' corpse into the sewage drains below, it was not uncommon to find corpses in the sewers, many would be Jews that had been ruthlessly murdered at the ghetto. James passed the men the bundles of clothes which they loaded into the boot of the newly acquired vehicle. Yosef, who was now wearing the deceased chauffeurs uniform, was sat in the driver's seat. They then passed through the heavy corpses of the murdered officers, the three resistance members then repeated the procedure of lowering them down into the sewer, reuniting them with their driver, the rats and toxins would destroy any distinguishing features and no one would expect to see some Nazi officers in the sewers. Before James closed the window and drew shut the curtains, the two men continued dressing into the satanic uniforms.

"Looking sharp," jested James, looking at his comrade dressed in the black officer's uniform. When Pierre turned to check himself out in the full length, oval mirror, James grabbed Édouards package making sure he did not misplace or leave it behind. He didn't know what his friend had given him but he was sure the Germans would not like it and any soldier would have to have nerves of steel to ask to search an officer of the Schutzstaffel. The two men did a final straightening of their disguises which were completed with the black, peaked officers hats on their heads, which displayed the skull and crossbones emblem of the '*Toten Kopf*' and exited the office, ignoring the French civilians who looked towards them in disgust, not knowing their true identity. The two men stepped out onto the Parisian streets where Yosef had already parked up the armoured staff car and was stood holding open the back-passenger door, saluting his comrades, with a raised arm, they could never be too sure who was watching and it may seem suspicious to any witness if a driver did not stand on ceremony by saluting his superiors. Once they had both taken their seats in the back of the car, Yosef closed the door and entered the driver's seat.

"Relax, my friend," said Pierre calmly. "Just act as if this is normal, talk, return salutes and enjoy the luxury of this automobile," he said, resting his arm on the car door and holding up a hand in a salute as a passing soldier gave the ancient Roman fascist salute adopted by the Third Reich. James had to admit that his comrade had totally adopted his role. As they travelled down the streets, James began to relax. The Nazi officers truly travelled in comfort, they could not even feel the cobbled streets as they drove along. It did not take them too long to arrive at the iconic Eiffel Tower with the giant, white letter 'V' fitted on the outside. The 'V' for victory was used widely by the resistance and allied forces, so much that the Germans also adopted it for their own purposes.

Yosef stopped the car outside the guarded entrance of the French landmark, where the common Nazi banners surrounded it, jumped out and opened the passengers' door for the 'officers' to disembark. "I will talk to you in German so they will not dare to interrupt us," whispered Pierre, as the two of them straightened their jackets. "Just pretend you understand what I am saying." With that they approached the entrance with James speaking in German, as far as James could make out, he was telling him something about a girl from the regular use of the word fräulein. Pierre had been totally correct, apart from a couple of salutes the two men were given a wide birth. A pair of green-uniformed guards stumped out their cigarettes and stood to attention as they marched past and entered the elevator and the lift ascended.

Chapter 20

"*Dritte Etage?*" asked the young Nazi lift operator.

"*Ja,*" replied Pierre and the lift jolted to life, taking them up three floors. Pierre continued the German conversation to James ignoring the young soldier.

"*Die treppe führte dich zur Offiziers stange,*" the operator said as the elevator doors slid open revealing the metallic third level, Pierre just gave the young man a nod in response, as they left the lift James could hear music and what sounded like a party above him. There was a single soldier patrolling the perimeter of the level who did his best not to notice the two men. Pierre led James towards an unmanned set of stairs which spiralled upwards.

"What did he say?" asked James in a hoarse whisper, they had got this far without any trouble and the last thing they needed was to be discovered now, a normal soldier in the Nazi army would be shot for coming up here without permission, James did not even want to think what would happen to them if they were caught.

"He said, the officers' bar is up the stairs," replied Pierre, stopping at the bottom of the staircase and looked up above him. "Do not worry, my friend, if they had suspected anything we would have not got this far, everything is going as we had planned." This did not inspire much confidence, all their plans seem to work fine at first and then someone would throw a spanner in the works and one day they would not be lucky enough to escape with their lives.

They slowly began walking up the dense metallic spiral staircase and stopped again once they stepped onto the maroon red, plush carpets of the officers club, neither man had been too sure what to expect but this was beyond anything they could have imagined. The wooden bar at one end was decorated with four swastikas carved into the wood with the design of the iron cross in the centre, a Nazi flag hung on the wall behind the bar, in front were four occupied leather stools, the backs were stylised with the leather-covered Armenian runic SS symbol. The entire floor was swarming with Schutzstaffel officers in either dark green or grey combat uniforms or black or grey dress uniforms, each with a red Nazi armband, some wore their peaked caps while others, lucky enough to get one of the few tables, lay their hats upon them as if they were on display. Nearly every man had an overly made up women in a colourful dress, most wearing a long pearl necklace or feather boa, on their arm. Most of these women would be prostitutes, paid an excessive amount to entertain the troops on the bill of the Third Reich. Through a pair of open French windows that lead to the observation deck, overlooking the Nazi-occupied capital city of France. As much as James' mind was screaming at him to get the hell out of there, they could not turn back

124

now, it was too late, they were deep in the lion's den. Behind the bar were two young men in their mid-twenties, they were struggling to keep up with the constant stream of orders placed by Nazi officers. Both young men had long bright blonde hair, they wore black shirts and Hitler youth armbands, which unlike the regular armband was light brown with three black and white lines running through the centre and a black swastika. James, following Pierre, walked up to the bar, Pierre locked eyes with one of the young men. Another Nazi officer, an SS *Sruemscharführer* (SS-Assault platoon leader) barged past James trying to get to a table which had just become vacant but James did not give in, his insignia showed that this man was a lower rank than James was pretending to be, he was an SS lieutenant general so James had to act his rank. The young officer turned to look at the man who was staring daggers at him. The man stood quickly to attention, clicked his boots' heels together and gave the undercover SOE a Nazi salute. "*Es tut uns leid, Herr Generalleutnant.*" James scanned the young apologetic officer, the undercover SOE kept quiet, calm and signalled to the young man's undone collar, which he hastily fastened it. James gave a nod and raised his hand as a salute before turning his attention back to Pierre.

"Well done, my friend. Give me one of your gold coins," Pierre whispered, James had anticipated this and had pocketed three of his coins before leaving the headquarters. He dug one from his trouser pocket and covertly passed it to his French comrade. Pierre signalled to one of the young men to meet them at the far end of the bar and the three men casually moved out of the way of the abundance of Nazi troops trying to order their chosen beverage. James watched as the two men spoke in French and Pierre slid the gold coin across the bar, the young man put his hand over it and took a look around to make sure they were not being watched, he flipped his hand half up to inspect the item then grabbed it up and slipped it into his own pocket before continuing his conversation quietly with Pierre. James patted his comrade on the shoulder and whispered

"I need to go to the toilet and then I will meet you on the balcony." Pierre nodded once without turning and replied in French, forgetting James' limited ability of the language, but James got the idea.

"*C'est par là,*" said the Frenchman pointing down a small corridor, directing him to the officers conveniences. James followed his friends directions and made his way into the bathroom. The room was nearly as lavish as the bar with a navy-blue carpet and a Nazi swastika on every fifth primarily white tiled walls, which were so clean they shined. He was welcomed by an overweight man sitting by a table of various French *eau de toilette*. James acted his part and gave the man a quiet nod, he walked directly into the first cubical, which to his surprise was a proper box and chain toilet, it was as clean as the walls. This style of toilet was not usually used in public conveniences as most were just holes in the ground and what was more, these toilets were also equipped with real toilet paper when the majority of the French population were making use of torn newspaper, this was one of the perks of being an officer of the occupying forces. James nearly wished he had needed to go to the toilet. He locked the door behind him, sat on the rim of and opened the flap of his case, he took out Édouards package and unwrapped the content. When he saw what he had been given he could not help but give a small chuckle under his breath, this was Édouard all over. He had given James a roll of eight sticks of dynamite, with a timer fuse. This had enough power to destroy the entire level, not to mention causing a rude interruption to anyone trying to relieve themselves. James set the timer for fifteen minutes, hoping this was enough time, and stuck the explosives under the circular toilet bowl, it would not be noticed unless some Nazi wanted to inspect the plumbing.

He calmly flushed the toilet and walked from the cubical, washed his hand, was handed a soft towel to dry his hand by the plump man and dropped a couple of Reichsmark coins into the toilet attendants silver coloured ashtray, the large man beamed a smile and said, "*Danke*." He was blatantly overjoyed by this officers generosity, not a trait many SS officers were known for. James just returned the smile and gave the man a friendly pat on the back, this man's day was about to get a lot worse.

The Englishman strolled back down the narrow corridor, Pierre noticed his friends return but James ignored his friend who was still talking to the young man in hushed French. He went straight out of the French windows onto the metallic balcony that encircled the bar area. The cool breeze awakened James, he pulled down his officers' hat, securing it in place, the walkway was deserted, why go outside and look at the view when you can stay warm inside and see the view through the giant windows? James slowly walked to the front of the balcony and the view took his breath away, he could see the whole of Paris from up here. As he scanned the great city, he could see the building that hid the Paris resistance headquarters, the red-light district, to his left he could see the *Arc de Triomphe* and could even make out in the distance the vine fields where the communist resistance was based. From this scene, he could see the reason why this city was worth fighting for.

"Quite a view, is it not, my friend?" said Pierre, appearing out of nowhere, as he often did, next to James. He leaned against the barrier, James dropped the case beside him and the duo looked out to the city of light together.

"It is beautiful," agreed James.

"And you, my friend, will help liberate our great city and then help restore it back to its former glory." James looked at his friend; he seemed unusually proud of himself.

"I take it you got the information we wanted," James asked eagerly, turning his attention back to the unique scenery.

"Indeed, I have foun—" Pierre was interrupted by a strong German accent.

"Do not be moving!" The duo looked at each other through the corner of their eyes and turned to see an overweight SS officer in a bulging black dress uniform showing that he had grown since the uniform had been issued to him. He was pointing a Luger pistol at them, but keeping it low, by his side so that anyone looking through the giant windows would just see three comrades talking, the gun being totally obscured by the man's heavy tuned body. "You are English?" *If I had a penny for every time a German asked me that, I would be a millionaire,* thought James, but knew better than to argue with this Nazi officer; their cover had been blown.

"And you are German?"

"Of course!" The man looked at the two men before him, totally unamused, but he had a glint of excitement in his eyes. "You are the Englishman we have been looking for?"

"Maybe, you know the picture is not very clear," provoked James.

"Why do you fight with these terrorists?" He gave Pierre a deathly stare. "This is not even your country."

"You know, you are totally right! This is not my country," James said as if he had just come to terms with the fact, "but if I can help free these good people from that Charlie Chaplin look-alike maniac in Berlin you call the führer, then I will be willing to fight and, if need be, die beside them to help them achieve that!" The officer looked deeply offended by James' reference to his leader.

"You now come with me to Berlin!" the German said, having got fed up with the pleasantries. "I will allow our glorious führer decide your fate." The man was blatantly proud of himself or maybe it was the thought of the bounty and a probable promotion waiting for him.

"Not bloody likely!" spat James, keeping up evil stares with the officer in front of him as he unbuttoned the strap which held his own luger in the holster which had previously been the property of the officer whose uniform he now wore. Noticing what James was intending to do, Pierre put his hand on James' arm, stopping him from drawing the pistol, a single shot would bring down every intoxicated officer in the bar down on them like a ton of bricks.

"Non! No, my friend," he whispered. "Live today, fight tomorrow!" the Frenchman urged.

"I would listen to your friend." The Jerrie soldier smirked. "You will come nicely now, I do not want to be sharing the reward and if I give you to our marvellous leader alone, I will get another medal." James looked at the man's breast which was already decorated with countless medals. "You be coming now!" prompted the officer, James looked a Pierre for permission to end this hindrance, Pierre reading James' mind gave a small shake of his head. "Both be coming now!" ordered the officer. But James was not going to move fast under the order of any Jackbooted invader. The two resistance fighters took a single step forward when there was an overpowering explosion. It blew out all of the windows of the bar, making the metal walkway shake perilously and the metallic structure creak. The officer had dropped to the floor at the sound of the eruption. James and Pierre reacted instantly, jumping through the window frames and followed a frantic stream of soldiers rushing for the exit at speed. The bar once packed with playful oppressors of freedom was now in disarray. There was glass all over, not only from the windows but from the smashed drinking glasses that had been dropped in shock, tables and chairs had been knocked over and hats had been abandoned in the rush of the evacuation. There were a few bodies of Nazi officers either knocked out or dead, some with cut up faces from the exploding windows, in the frenzy, it was hard to tell if they were still living. Very soon James and Pierre had mixed in with the other soldiers getting the elevator to the ground floor. Having heard the deafening explosion, Yosef was already waiting, holding open the passenger door, impression was even more important now than it had been because eyes would be searching for the perpetrators, so the slightest thing out of place would be noticed. James and Pierre jumped in as other officers boarded their own vehicles and Yosef sped off with the line of Nazi vehicles, none of them wanting to be at the aftermath to be interrogated by the unmerciful Gestapo, who would undoubtedly take charge of the investigation, even an officer's rank would not spare them the torture chambers that the Nazi secret police were so famous for.

Yosef kept up the pace as military police raced past them in the opposite direction for five blocks. Once the other cars had turned off and disappeared he finally slowed and stopped the car in a tight alleyway. James and Pierre had to clamber through the window to disembark as it was too tight to open a door, they opened the trunk and began to hastily change back into their original everyday clothes. Once they had changed, out of the shadows, three men made their presence known. An unshaven man who stank of diesel fuel, old chewing tobacco and body odour, wearing the stereotypical French clothing of a stripped back and white shirt and a black beret, approached James.

"Pierre?" he asked gruffly. James corrected him by moving aside and presenting his friend. "*Je m'appelle Vincent,*" said the man. James was quite happy with himself, he understood this, the man was introducing himself as Vincent. But James' pride was short-lived; as Vincent began speaking at a fast pace, he was saying something that lost James totally.

"*Merci* Vincent," said Pierre, then turned to James to give an explanation. "They will take care of the car, that is what they do."

"Take care of the car? What do you mean?" James asked, a bit confused.

"They take apart the car that people want to disappear and then put together new cars with the parts for resistances or anyone who need a vehicle cheaply," explained Pierre, chucking the Nazi uniforms in the trunk and slamming it shut. "They will also destroy the clothes, after they have removed the medals to melt for scrap." James was amazed by the simplicity, he could no help to think the communist resistance could use a similar system, it would be more productive than blowing up every vehicle they wanted gone. It seemed that the war had produced more jobs, even if they were illegal. "I believe that the explosion was the thing that Édouard had given you?" James looked a Pierre, surprised; he had explicitly been told that Pierre must not know about it.

"I don't know what you mean," the Englishman lied.

"Come, my friend." Pierre gave a wide smile. "I would not be a good leader if I did not know everything that was going on," he said with a laugh as the trio left the alleyway and began to make their way back to base. The streets seemed glum and gloomy, it was as if he had been viewing a different city from his elevated position earlier.

Once they had finally got back to headquarters and sat around in an annexe joined by the two lieutenants André and Bastien, Constance, Édouard and the young Spaniard, Manuel, who had begged to be more involved with resistance operations. Since coming to Paris Manuel had been part of the youth resistance writing pro-resistance, anti-Nazi slogans on walls and tearing down Nazi propaganda posters. When he learnt that the Paris resistance was forming he did all he was able to join the ranks. But since being in the resistance he had mostly been putting up propaganda posters and not been involved in any real action, apart from being the banner bearer at the daring attack on the train station. He wanted more responsibility so Pierre allowed him to sit in at the meetings with the explanation that everyone has to start somewhere. For James' benefit, the leader spoke in English, with the occasional French translation to aid their colleagues.

"The Free French soldiers are being held in the town centre of Troyes, there is a forest neighbouring the town," he said, interpreting what he had been told by the French barman. "It will be too far to travel there and back in one day and we must survey the area first. There is a gypsie refugee camp hidden in the forest, I have had some dealing with them before. They have been hiding there for a while and may be able to give us some information and a place to stay."

"How many of those fascist sons of bitches are we going to be facing this time?" asked James.

"We will not know until we get there, will we Englishman!" replied Bastien in a gruff throaty voice, he had never warmed to James and never hid the fact. James shook his head in disbelieve, removed a cigarette and lit it.

"So, just so I understand your plan, we are going somewhere else, going to sleep in the woods and then go up against an unknown number of enemies, to free some Free French soldiers from prison. Is that right?" James asked, not too chuffed about the prospect of not knowing how many Nazi soldiers they could be facing, again. Pierre nodded his agreement.

"I know it is not a lot of information, my friend, but we have to do this, we have to rescue those brave soldiers of *De Gaulle*."

"And they will join our ranks," added Édouard, "and build up our forces." James smiled at his friend's confidence and fast recovery as the large man was no longer wearing his sling.

"Well, if we are going to do this then we have to act quick." James took another drag on his cigarette before continuing. "They were planning to move those POWs yesterday so it won't be long until they attempt to move them again," he insisted.

"So when do you think we should do this?" asked Constance.

"We should leave tonight," Pierre answered for his friend.

"I agree," confirmed James, André grunted his approval as the others present agreed with their two comrades.

The remainder of the day a group was arranged for the plan and the designated troops spent the day cleaning their guns and lubricating all the pieces so that they worked smoothly. The six members who had attended the meeting had all volunteered to go, so they were going to go with the eleven other resistance members, making a group of only eighteen strong, this was not a huge force to take on an unknown amount of enemy troops but Pierre said he wanted to attack this mission with stealth and secrecy, not that it had worked well in the past. A large number of people moving would only cause suspicion and leave the Paris resistance zone deserted and unprotected. The Paris resistance now controlled around forty per cent of the city and had small squads of resistance members who were continually making small level attacks on Nazi targets, patrols and the occasional officer assassination, not including the lone attacks and this could not diminish or the enemy troops would become suspicious that there was a larger plan in motion.

Chapter 21

The troops left the underground headquarters in what used to be a bread delivery van, it had a faded picture of bread loaves and rolls on the side with '*Pains de Dieu*' in elaborate writing, which roughly translated as 'Loaves of God'. James and Constance sat beside Pierre who had taken on the role of the driver. The journey was uneventful and they kept, as much as possible, to the quiet back roads, through small country hamlets, passing the sea of green fields and pastures, it was a different atmosphere to the hustle and bustle of the big city, it was quiet and peaceful. The patrols were few and far between, they were near unnoticeable. James was very relaxed, even so far as to say too relaxed, he had one arm over Constance's shoulder and the other hanging out of the open cab window holding a cigarette, you could almost forget that there was a war on, they passed over a small bridge where children were jumping off into the creek below, they watched cautiously as the van passed by but soon continued their youthful games after receiving a reassuring smile from James and a playful honk on the vehicle's horn from Pierre.

"It is almost as if there is no war," said James envious of the children's ignorance.

"To these country folks the war is something which only happens in the city," replied Constance calmly. "The Jerries never come this far out, they have no business out here so unlike the city there is no constant reminder."

"When we get closer to Troyes you will begin to see more Germans, my friend," added Pierre, not wanting his English comrade to get a false sense of security.

Pierre was not wrong, as they got to the outskirts of the town, there was an immense amount of Nazi soldiers and as they travelled further into the town the number of troops also grew, outnumbering the locals twenty to one, not that many locals dared to leave the sanctuary of their own homes, not even in Paris were the odds this bad and they only had eighteen men under their charge, you did not need a qualification in maths to know that the numbers were not on their side. They were driving towards the centre of town when Pierre made a sharp turn to the left and before they knew it they were driving along a muddy, hole-riddled dirt road.

"Hold on!" cried Pierre and before James could speak the Frenchman had turned off the dirt track and they were now driving cross country. The uneven ground threw the van up, jolting the passengers violently in their seats, the old van had no real suspension so the ride was not comfortable. Pierre was seeming to enjoy himself as he narrowly missed trees and hidden pits. James hastily wound up his window as the branches from trees and bushes were getting dangerously close to taking out his eyes and tearing his arm to shreds. When the van finally stopped, James was relieved, the hostile movement of the van had seriously hurt his back, if it had gone on much longer he was sure his spine would have collapsed. Even with his back in agony, when he saw where he was, he sat up straight and looked around in amazement, they had entered a clearing in the centre of the forest, which was still covered by a canopy of trees. The trees that had at one time been growing here had been felled and made into bunkers, which had been dug into the ground and covered with branches as camouflage, James could count five of these makeshift disguised log bunkers. Hidden among the tree line, surrounding the camp, on three sides, were elaborately painted red, yellow, green or blue wooden, horse-drawn caravans decorated with painted flowers and bells. The resistance fighters remained in the vehicle, as rough shabby, unshaven, dirty looking men with tanned skin and women wearing decorative head scarfs, with large hooped earrings, who looked just as shabby and unshaven as the men, all brandishing rifles, encircled the van, stopping it from advancing or reversing.

"They are bloody gypsies!" exclaimed James, he had found it hard to believe Pierre when the French leader had first mentioned it, he had always hoped, subconsciously that it was a joke.

"Ssh!" Pierre said angrily. "They understand English. We must show them politeness and manners. They are easily offended and will not have any conscience to stop them from shooting us and leave our bodies in the forest for the wolves." James removed his arm from Constance's shoulder and began to withdraw his pistol. "Non, my friend, they will see that as a challenge; remain calm."

"Calm? Great!" replied James sarcastically, forcing a smile at a grim looking woman with a sour face looking through his passenger window, misting it up with every breath, but he got no reaction. A man stepped forward from the ever-growing armed crowd. He was a tall pencil thin man wearing a brown suede flat cap, a matching jacket and green trousers, that James recognised as previously belonging to an enemy soldier, he also noticed the man had an unsettling lazy eye that seemed to linger on him. He carried an Enfield rifle slung over his left shoulder, a Luger in his right hand and had an unlit hand-rolled cigarette hanging from the corner of his mouth. As he approached the drivers' side window, his grim face cracked into a crooked smirk. Pierre steadily rolled down his dirt covered window.

"Anton, please ask your grandmother if we could have her blessing to stay among your fine people and if we may share your food and fire together," Pierre asked respectfully.

"*Pourquoi parlez-vous Anglais?*" the man questioned. Pierre gave a sharp nod in James' direction.

"You are English?" the man, Anton, asked, looking at James.

"Yes, that is correct," said James, hoping to sound polite but it came out more pompous and he instantly regretted opening his mouth when a simple no would have sufficed, but the gypsy did not seem to notice. "Is that a problem?"

"Non, *Pas problém*. What do you do here Pierre?" Anton asked, turning his attention back to their leader, it was obvious that they were talking in English for James' benefit.

"I have come with a team to free the Free French soldiers from the German jail, I am told they are being held in the town centre."

"How many men do you have?"

"Eighteen." The Gypsy laughed at this.

"Come, we will speak with Grandmother," said Anton. "She is weak and cannot leave her caravan."

"Stay here, I will be back," insisted Pierre, getting out of the van and slamming the door shut, they watched as he followed the male gypsy to a yellow caravan. James looked around, not one of the assailants had moved a muscle, they looked like statues. The Englishman couldn't deny that being threatened by this number of weapons, by a malicious looking gypsy hoard, made him awfully nervous and on edge.

"Grandmother?" James finally asked, turning to Constance, trying to act calmly and ignore the countless eyes and guns trained on them.

"Anton's grandmother is the head of this clan. Nothing will happen without her say so, she will choose if we stay or go," she said. The French maiden was seeming a lot more relaxed than he was or she was at least hiding her fear well. "We just have to hope Pierre makes a good impression, one wrong word could ruin everything." This did not inspire James with confidence. They then sat together in silence waiting for Pierre's return.

Half an hour passed with no news, James was feeling less and less comfortable, the assailants surrounding the van had hardly moved, their stamina was impressive.

"What the hell is taking so long?" James asked, getting ever more nervous as every second passed, patience was not his strong point.

"They have to share a tea together and then she will ask God and wait for a reply," Constance explained, not moving her eyes from the caravan as if she could see through the wooden panels into it. "Some say she is a witch, they say she is one hundred and two years old."

"Bloody hell. Okay I get it, she is ancient, but does it really have to take this long?"

"It is a test and to seem impatient would be seen as a rudeness and then they will not help us!" Even though it was clear she was getting annoyed with his constant complaining he could not believe she was being so calm about the whole situation. James got out a cigarette, offered one to Constance who declined, he lit it and wound down his window so not to fill the cab with smoke and was greeted by the face of the sour-faced women who had been observing him intently for the last half an hour without a single glance away. James quite calmly opened the end of his packet of cigarettes and offered one to the women, without tearing her eyes from James' face, the lady took out two cigarettes, she put one in her mouth and tucked the second one behind her ear under her headscarf. James wanted to take back one of the cigarettes, but the words of Pierre rang in his head and he did not fancy the idea of being eaten by wild wolves, so instead, he lit the lady's cigarette, who puffed on it as if her life depended on it. James gave a second attempt of a pleasant smile but the grim face still remained. It was only now, that he had wound down the window, that he noticed the whole area was eerily quiet, there was not a sound, no bird song, no rustling of leaves, no dogs barking, no children laughing or crying, even the open campfire did not make a sound, it was as if the whole forest was holding its breath with hesitation, the only way James was sure he hadn't gone deaf was from the gypsy women dragging loudly on her cigarette. This made him all the more wary of his surroundings. Finally, Constance gave him a sharp nudge in the ribs with her elbow and nodded towards the caravan where Anton and Pierre had finally emerged. Anton said something loudly in French to the crowd that James did not understand, but was relieved as their aggressors lowered their weapons and began applauding and cheering. James turned to the sour-faced women who was now grinning broadly, showing nine rotten teeth. Pierre approached the truck.

"They have allowed us to stay for as long as we need," he proudly announced.

"Thank God, about bloody time, old chap," blurted James uncontrollably. "My arse was falling asleep," he joked and opened the passenger side door. The gypsy woman patted him on the back, before she wobbled, as that is the best way to describe how she walked, back into the forest camp. James walked around the back of the truck and opened the back door, only to be accosted by the nervous passengers, once recognising James they lowered their weapons and began disembarking, each one looking around, taking their first sight on the gypsy woodland home, where they would be spending an unknown amount of time.

Each resistance member was welcomed like an old friend, even though the only ones known to them was Pierre and his younger sister. The hospitality could not be faulted, they were invited to join their hosts around a large fire pit, a flagon of home-made alcoholic spirit, burning the throat of even the most experienced drinker, was passed around, it was a vile concoction, unlike anything James had ever tried and killed off your taste buds. They were each given a bowl of wild rabbit stew and a chunk of home-made flame-baked bread. They claimed that they were mostly self-sufficient, they kept chickens to lay eggs and anything else the forest could provide for them, but they never denied stealing some essentials from local farmhouses, claiming that the local population were all Nazi collaborators. When they were alone, Pierre later explained that it was a common misconception because of the abundance of Nazis and denied the gypsies claim. According to Pierre, "the residents of the town are good true French people, just trying to live their lives as best as they could under the difficult circumstances."

They had passed around multiple flagons of the eighty per cent strong concoction refusing to reveal the recipe, just saying that it was an ancient gypsy mixture handed down by word of mouth from father to son and mother to daughter, never to be altered. James had considered that these people may have heard of him and the price on his head so might try and make him pass out so they could hand him over to the Nazis and collect the five-thousand-Reichsmarks bounty, but Pierre trusted these people, even though it had been proven that he was too trusting of people James had to trust in his French counterparts' decision or his paranoia would drive him insane.

By the end of the night it was clearly proven that no matter how used to this vile alcoholic beverage you were, in the end, you would succumb to its strength and if not instantly pass out, then loudly sing English or American songs or stumble around like a blind man until you fell over, urinated in your trousers where you lay and fell asleep under the influence. James, like many of the other resistance members and gypsies, had fallen asleep in an alcohol-infused slumber where he sat around the fire pit.

The crowd began to rouse late the next morning, it was well past eleven when James rose and like a great many of the others, was suffering from the previous nights' merriments. His hangover was colossal, James could not remember the last time he had a hangover, at least not as devastating as this one. The gypsies were prepared for this eventuality and had put together another concoction, given to them by their 'Grandmother', it was an ancient remedy that looked like the contents of the waste disposal pipe that James had wade through when escaping the Nazis and tasted like tar, it set off an explosion inside their bodies, but after half an hour they were happily back to their original selves.

Pierre pulled James aside once the medication had taken effect, away from any over inquisitive ears, to discuss the plans of today's operation. "You and I must go and observe the area where they are holding our brave soldiers of *De Gaulle*," whispered Pierre, his throat was hoarse and raw as a punishment for the night before.

"Can't these guys give you any information?" queried James.

"Non, my friend. They don't leave here unless they have to and then it is only to the outskirts. We must do this ourselves," Pierre insisted. James got the impression that his comrade did not entirely trust the words of his friends, after all, they were gypsies and not the most trustworthy or honourable of people.

The two men slipped away from the camp, only informing Édouard to take charge and Constance, so she would not become worried about where her brother and close friend had gone. Pierre seemed to know these woods like the back of his hand and they were soon walking down the streets of Troyes. As the two friends walked casually down the desolate streets they noted the many different divisions by the insignia they each wore and determined that this town was housing at least six different military companies. The duo stopped a street newspaper vendor and Pierre purchased a newspaper to appear inconspicuous, after all, this was only a reconnaissance mission.

The centre of town was an intimidating spectacle. The centre of the square was surrounded by sandbags and vicious metallic anti-tank blockades. In the centre of this 'restricted zone' was a wooden shed-like building, this would be the guard room and at the far end were two heavy duty cages which each housed twenty worn, beaten, weary, Free French Forces soldiers. Behind the sandbags were a number of German guards and overlooking the entire area were four tall guard towers which even now, in the midday light, scanned the zone with their bright lamps. James timed the scans on his watch. A two-minute scan every ten minutes, at night he assumed it would be the same and this would be their window of opportunity. James and Pierre continued casually over to a wooden bench which overlooked the prison post and as James got out another cigarette and lit it, Pierre pretended to read his newspaper, occasionally turning the page, but always surveying their objective, stealthily making mental notes.

"What do you suppose they are keeping down there?" asked James, motioning to a small road just down from where they were sitting, which had a portable concrete block to stop anyone gaining entry.

"Vehicles." Pierre sounded confident. "With the number of troops and lack of vehicles, have you not noticed, my friend? There are Nazi troops all over but no cars, lorries or even tanks, so I would assume they would keep them in the same place where they could access instantly if they needed to." This sounded a reasonable assumption. James turned back to their objective.

"It will not be easy," murmured James to his comrade.

"Non," agreed Pierre, "but it is not impossible, my friend. You see how the guards move?" James watched the two patrolling Nazi soldiers who walked parallel to each other with their backs to the cages, passing on the near side of the shed, obscuring the cast iron cells from view. They would then share a few words or a cigarette and pass a lighter between them before returning along the same path. "They lose sight of the cells for around five minutes," explained Pierre. "Three minutes when they are walking away and another two when they are this side of the building."

"Five minutes does not give us much time to pick the lock and get them out," noted James. Pierre's eyes were now fixed on a young soldier who had just exited the wooden guard post and was striking a match to light a hand-rolled cigarette. Without taking his gaze from the young soldier, the French resistance leader said in a trance-like tone,

"We could always use a key."

"Of course, why don't we just go over there and say, 'Excuse me, but would you mind giving us the spare key to your cells?'" James said sarcastically, he received an unimpressed look from his French associate.

"*Oui*, exactly, just wait here, my friend." The Frenchman rose. "Give me a gold coin," he said. These were disappearing fast; between paying his tab with Édouard and the constant bribes, James was beginning to regret telling this Frenchman about them. Pierre took a deep breath and walked calmly over to the heavily guarded area. *What the hell was he doing?* thought the Englishman in a sudden panic, he had only been kidding! Had this Frenchman finally lost his mind? He watched, holding his breath as Pierre caught the attention of the refreshed young soldier and motioned to him, the teenage boy took a quick glance around and approached Pierre. James watched with bated breath as the two men talked as if they were old friends, he saw Pierre open his hand and the young Nazis soldiers' eyes widened as he saw the gold coin, but the Frenchman did not hand it over, instead he replaced it into his own pocket before turning and walking quite coolly back to where James was sat. The Englishman looked up to each guard tower, the guards seemed less than interested in what was happening below them and had probably not even noticed the two resistance fighters 'scoping out' the restricted POW post which James was sure they would soon regret. "Come, my friend," said Pierre, James slowly rose and walked with his friend back the way they had come. James kept looking towards his comrade for an explanation yet Pierre did not say a single word and ignored James' glances until they were once again walking through the heavily wooded area. "The fate have smiled upon us, I helped his father escape the Nazi death camps." James looked at his comrade confused. "The young soldier, I helped his father escape," he confirmed, but James was puzzled. "He would never tell his superiors but his father is a Jew. The lad's name is Achim, he heard how I had assisted with the escape of *General de Gaulle* and that I was running the escape routes into Spain so he asked for my help."

"Blimey! They would crucify him if they ever found out!" exclaimed James, this was a wake-up call. "So you blackmailed him! What is he going to do?"

"You will see tomorrow," laughed Pierre, the Frenchman liked his surprises. "But do not tell the others, we must keep this between the two of us for now." Pierre had totally changed his face from the chuckling Frenchman to a serious leader of the French underground.

The pair wondered back into the camp as if they had just been for a relaxing stroll. They had only been gone for a couple of hours and people went missing for a lot longer just when going to the bathroom and losing their way, to the untrained eye the woods all looked the same. So nothing was amiss when people noticed the two men returning to the camp from the deep dark forest.

That afternoon was the same as the previous night, with everyone sat around the fire-pit, drinking the strong home-made beverage. Later Anton got out a gramophone with a large horn speaker and put on some American music, James and Pierre would not have felt comfortable with the loud sound, but they had drunk too much to care by this stage. Édouard and James even got up and began dancing with some of the younger gypsy maidens. Édouard was dancing with two teenage gypsy girls who were sandwiching the giant man between them whilst James danced with a girl in her mid-twenties. Constance watched jealously until she got up and cut into the dance with James, by this time the majority of the gypsies, as well as all the resistance members, were up on their feet, going along with the musical tones. Everyone eventually passed out of exhaustion and intoxication.

James awoke the following morning in much the same place and condition as the day before, his head was banging and muffled as it was full of cotton wool. A gypsy male was already handing out the vile potion and the resistance members would pull grim faces as they took the medication, with a few even running into the woods to vomit the contents of their stomachs but the gypsies did not seem to mind the taste with some even licking their lips after taking a dose. After James had taken his course of treatment he rushed over to a steaming pot of coffee on an open grill, poured himself a cup and downed the hot liquid with the hope that it would dull the taste of the tar-like medicine. James wondered around aimlessly for a couple of minutes, waiting for the concoction to take effect, trying to regain momentum in his legs and recall what had happened the night before.

"We must leave in an hour, my friend," a voice said behind him, James spun round to see Pierre standing behind him looking surprisingly refreshed, but there was also a sense that he couldn't handle many more nights like the one they just had and James couldn't agree more.

"What? Why? Where are we going?" James groaned, the ancient gypsy medicine had not yet taken effect.

"To see our young friend Achim," explained Pierre. "I believe he may have a small gift for us."

"I say, I do not believe you can count on this kraut!" blurted James, recovering like a thunder storm clearing the air.

"Well, he has a lot to gain and lose," Pierre continued and then saw James' questioning look. "I offered him your gold coin, soldiers do not get paid enough and if that didn't tempt him enough to help us then his superiors may get an anonymous letter, revealing the secret of his Jewish heritage." Pierre had a sly smile on his face.

"Blimey, would you actually do that?"

"Non, but he does not know that." Pierre laughed, patting James on his arm. The Englishman had to admit his friend was devious.

"You will need a different coat," said Anton, stepping out from behind a tree. Pierre looked cross when he learnt of the eavesdropper. "Not many people wear this kind of coat out here, it is a city coat. They will recognise you. Come, come." James was confused.

"Will they not just recognise me by my face?" he asked; the gypsy laughed.

"No, to them you are just another Frenchman." Anton led the two men towards a green painted, wooden caravan where a bearded man was sitting on the steps leading to the entrance, he was smoking a beautifully carved meerschaum pipe of a pair of prancing ponies, which complemented the gypsy way of life, but this man could never afford a smoking piece like this, which told James the man had most likely requisitioned it from some rich French household, but the Englishman preferred to think that it had previously belonged to some wealthy Jerrie officer. The head gypsy whispered a few words to his friend who just nodded slowly and Anton led his two counterparts inside. The inside had a strong smell of burning sandalwood incense, which covered the ceiling in a cloud of smoke. Along one side of the caravan stood a clothes rack which went from one end to the other, it contained a large assortment of dresses, suits and coats including military and Nazi attire. "Try this one on," Anton said, chucking James a tanned suede coat which fitted him perfectly.

Once again leaving Édouard in charge, the duo left for the town square. Pierre, who was also wearing a different coat, stopped at the end of the street where they could both see the restricted zone.

"Wait here, my friend," suggested Pierre. "We do not want to scare him." This was a plausible explanation so James casually leant against a small tree, lit a cigarette and watched his associate carefully. Pierre walked calmly to the bench where they had sat the day before, he placed the newspaper he had purchased the day before beside him, placed the coin inside it and folded it in half. They then had to wait, the longer they waited the more anxious James became, he would have felt more at ease if they had more members for back up, or even if he had made sure his silenced pistol, which was still in the back of his trousers, had a full magazine. Just in case the young soldier had been caught and cracked under interrogation or decided to tell an officer about Pierre's offer of the gold coin and the request for the cage's keys, this could all be a setup, the young man could not be trusted, after all, he was a Nazi.

James breathed a little lighter when he saw the young soldier walk from the German compound and sit beside Pierre, they did not say a word or even nod to each other. James watched intently and noted the discreet switch, unless you were watching for it you would not have noted anything suspicious. Pierre abruptly rose and strode straight past James who followed two paces behind him. They walked at speed until they got to the outskirts of the forest and the French resistance leader revealed what had been given to him, it was a small gunmetal box.

"It does not look like much of a key," said James dully.

"It is not." Pierre smiled, opening the box to reveal clay inside with a couple of imprints; they were blatantly the two ends of a key head, showing the thickness and shape of the key. "It is the imprint of the key, so we can make our own."

"Really? How?"

"Our gypsy friends can help with that." Pierre smiled, closing the box and replacing it in his pocket.

An hour later the resistance members were leaning against one of the caravans watching as two of the gypsies were furiously filing away at a couple of pieces of metal that were fitted in a couple of clamps. They watched with bewilderment as the keys took shape.

"Are you sure these will work?" James whispered to Pierre.

"These people are the best key makers in the country," he replied proudly.

"Of course they are," said Édouard, standing on the other side of James, puffing on his wooden pipe. "They are all thieves so if they couldn't, they would not make a living." James couldn't help but crack a smile at his friends comment, a month ago this giant man lost himself at the bottom of a bottle but he had now returned to normality.

"Édouard show some respect!" Pierre butted in angrily. Édouard just gave a grunt.

"I was just saying I admire their skill," he murmured and then continued smoking his pipe in silence.

"We will leave this evening at sunset," Pierre said sternly. "Two of the gypsies have volunteered to cause a distraction by blowing up some of the vehicles and firing machine guns to give the impression of a fight, this should distract the guards." The two gypsies finished the keys and passed them to Pierre who compared them to the imprint the young German soldier had given him, they were impressively accurate.

"How the hell will they get to the vehicles without being seen? The only entrance to them is through the town centre and that's swarming with those jackbooted bastards!" James noted.

"They will enter over the rooftops," replied Pierre. "They are the best climbers you could find in France." Édouard grunted.

"Of course, they are, they are all thieves." He received a glare of daggers from Pierre.

Chapter 22

In the front cab, Pierre and James were accompanied by the two gypsy associates who were bunched up between the two men. The bakers van steadily rounded a corner and smoothly continued down the street that Pierre and James had walked down the previous day. It was eerily quiet, no locals, no soldiers and not even the newspaper vendor was open. The sun was setting in the west, illuminating the sky in fluorescent orange and pink, it was a sunset assembled from dreams. James looked over to his comrades, Pierre was his normal relaxed self-focusing on the road. Anton was gently humming a tune to himself, James did not recognise it and assumed it was some gypsy tune handed down through the generations, besides Anton sat a fourteen-year-old gypsy named, Viktor, who Anton had introduced as his cousin, which was no real surprise as many of the travellers were related by blood in some way or another. This young boy was looking more and more hesitant as he fondled a set of ivory prayer beads that he wore as a necklace. James was somewhat relieved that he was not the only one who was nervous about the extraordinary lack of military presence. Could they be falling into some Nazi trap? Had Pierre's young German friend babbled? Had one of the gypsies betrayed them?

Halfway down the street Anton whispered something to Pierre who nodded obediently and following his orders, pulled the large vehicle up against the pavement and cut off the engine. James looked at the head of the French underworld for instructions.

"This is where our friends get out," explained Pierre, then turning to the two brave gypsy volunteers, he shook their hands with a '*Bon Chance*', James opened his side door and jumped out of the cab to allow their comrades to disembark.

"Good luck," he said, shaking their hands. James then pulled out his German MG 42 machine gun and watched the street behind them in case any soldier or patrol should come round the corner and spot the suspicious actions of the gypsies who with great ease clambered up a tree on the pavement and then jumped up onto a red tiled roof, making nearly zero sound, they then clambered across it on all fours like a pair of cats until they reached the top and disappeared over the other side, this only took them a matter of seconds and James could not help but chuckle to himself, they made it look so easy. The second the two gypsies had vanished from view, he jumped back into the front of the truck and Pierre swung the vehicle around, he turned left down a side road and left again, they did not want the Nazi forces to notice the van crammed with heavily armed resistance members. If everything went to plan the enemy soldiers will not notice the van at all, though this would be unlikely. Pierre swung the van right and then left again, stopping the van just at the opening of the heavily guarded town square of Troyes. James once again jumped out and opened the back doors allowing his comrades out to the sweet air. Pierre handed one of the two replicated keys to Édouard and a clump of dynamite sticks with a timer fuse to James. The small resistance army crept in complete silence, being mindful to keep close to the buildings, to the end of the street, where around the corner stood the fortified restricted area. James went into his trouser pocket and using the last few rays of the sun, flashed a hand held mirror twice towards the roof of the building opposite, signalling to Anton and his young cousin that they were in position. Moments later he saw a couple of small flashes in return.

"They are ready," he whispered to Pierre behind him.

"Tell them to proceed," came the reply, after the French leader had a brief check that everyone was ready to act. James gave a single nod, confirming that he had understood the order and gave three short flashes of his mirror, he got two in response, confirming that they too understood the command. James then replaced the mirror in his pocket. All they had to do now was wait and put their faith in their gypsy counterparts, which was not the most comfortable position to be in.

Once the distraction had been successfully performed, the resistances quest would be in three stages; the first objective was given to the young keen Manuel who once the guards' attention was distracted by the bogus attack would climb up the nearest guard tower, the only people who may notice what was happening were the prisoners in the cages beneath them. He would take out the guard, strip him down and put on the deceased guards uniform to disguise himself, he would then keep his attention on the other end of the complex, the Nazi troops below and in the other guard towers. James had given the young Spaniard his McLaglen Peskett close combat weapon to assist him, it had served James well in the past and was a quiet weapon, it was ideal for his mission. The second would be to unlock the cells and release the French Prisoner and get them into the back of the truck that Constance would be driving and finally blowing up the centre command shed and causing enough distraction for everyone to escape.

There was an ear-shattering, cataclysmic explosion followed by rapid machine gunfire and then another explosion. The operation was underway and the distraction had the desired effect, the spotlights from the four guard towers flooded the street entrance with light, down on to the vehicles, multiple sentries abandoned their posts and ran to assist their comrades who were guarding the Nazis means of transportation. James was surprised with the ease that the soldiers rejected their posts, this may be easier than he had hoped. The Paris Maquis urged Manuel forward and after a reassuring pat on his back from James, the young Spaniard ran like a leaf caught in a breeze, ducking from cover to cover and as quiet as the wind, the teen raced to the guard tower. He climbed the metal ladder, carrying the SOEs close combat weapon between his teeth, taking each step carefully, one at a time, assuring that he would not be detected by any of the few soldiers that remained on guard in the restricted zone or the guard above him, this was not a big risk as everyone's attention was drawn to the opposite end of the street. James had to admit that this youth had true grit. James recalled how it was the first time he had come face to face with a real fascist Nazi, he had nearly wet himself.

It was a week into his tour behind enemy lines when he and a fellow special operations executive agent named John Treen were tasked with destroying a German communications post in the Austrian Alps and assassinating the commands operator inside to stop an alarm being triggered. The trek through the knee-high snow had been simple enough, evading a couple of enemy, skiing patrols. James stood guard as John entered with a knife to cut the throat of the unfortunate communications expert and plant the explosives. James had just started to relax when he heard the sound of crunching snow to the right of him, he swung round to come eye to eye with the aforementioned communication operator who was returning from making a call of nature, he was hunkered over breathing into his hands in an attempt to warm them. Seeing James, he stopped as if he had turned into a sculpture. Both James and the Nazi stood stock still, neither willing to risk causing their opponent to become hostile, the two men just stayed frozen in their place, sizing each other up, not daring to move. This was the very first Jerry James had had contact with. Only a couple of minutes had passed when John exited the wooden hut.

"It is bloody deserted!" John chuckled; his laugh was cut short once he observed what is partner was staring at. Unlike James, John did not hesitate and drew his Colt 45 revolver, at the same time the operator pulled out his own Luger revolver and the sound of the two pistol shots rang out across the mountains as both men fired simultaneously. John had been hit in the leg and fell to the floor with his hand clasped around the wound as blood seeped through his fingers. The German had been hit in the abdomen and was clasping it with one hand, still holding his revolver in the other. James could not hesitate another moment, he drew his own pistol and fired two more shots into the man's chest, this caused the man to collapse back. James tended to his comrades wound. He removed John's hand and blood sprayed over James' face like water from a squirt gun, the bullet had severed his carotid artery and unless it was clamped and fixed within the next five minutes he would die of blood loss. James had only had very basic medical training from his time at a chemist. He looked down at his friend who just looked back with understanding in his eyes, they knew that there was no hope. "Morphine," croaked John, James got out a syringe and injected it into his fellow SOEs leg. James got out a second and administered it and a third. His friend John Treen died crying for his mother on the snow-covered Austrian Alps. James dragged his comrades' corpse to a thicket of trees and buried him under a mixture of piled dirt and snow. He watched as the communications shed burst into a cloud of splinters, all that remained was the smouldering foundations. If there was one thing that John had been good at it was demolition.

Manuel stabbed the Nazi guard through the back of his neck, cutting the man's spinal cord and killing him instantly. The young Spanish resistance member placed the Nazi coal scuttle on his head and put on the dead man's top, he then took control of the searchlight, pointing it in the same direction as the others so as not to arouse suspicion. James rechecked the town square. The raucous of the gypsies simulation of a gun battle was still going on and as it continued the sentries became all the less concerned with their duties and were more concerned with what was happening on the other side of the buildings. The Free French prisoners of war, as if they could smell an escape attempt, were up on their feet, except for a few badly wounded men. They were scanning the area for any sign of their rescuers. James watched as more soldiers dispersed down the alleyway in pursuit of the aggressors.

"Constance, you take the van in, the rest of you follow it into the centre and take cover, do not shoot until necessary! Then you can follow us out," commanded James, Pierre translated for the resistance soldiers that did not understand the English language. Constance jumped up into the cab, James along with Pierre and Édouard, climbed into the back, keeping the doors ajar. The engine gave a dull low hum, unnoticeable over the gunfire. Constance drove at a steady pace into the town square and did a sharp U-turn behind the tower so that the van was facing back the way they had just come from and was ready for a quick getaway. The three comrades jumped from the back of the bakers' van and slid between the barriers into the restricted zone. If they were caught then they would be shot on the spot and their only reinforcements were the fifteen resistance fighters, covering them from behind benches, concrete flower beds, trees and even lamp posts. The Free French prisoners were totally aware of what was happening and kept their voices low and quiet, not allowing the exciting prospects of escape to overwhelm them, to a volume that would not compromise the operation to the Nazi forces, chosen to guard them. Pierre and Édouard unlocked one cage each and cringed as the hinges on the cast iron grate doors screeched loudly. James was setting the timers on the dynamite and placing it on the back wall of the wooden command shed.

James withdrew his silenced pistol and with his back against the wall of the shed watched in case any of the enemy soldiers decided to glance behind them and sounded the alarm. Édouard and Pierre helped a barefooted Free French officer, whose feet were so swollen he seemed unable to walk out of the cages and into the back of the van with his other compatriots. He was the last of the escapees to get out.

Édouard and Pierre had joined Constance in the cab, James was about to jump up to sit with them when he froze, his face turned marble white and his blood ran cold as he looked at his comrades. The resistance members were all looking at each other in worry. The shooting from the gypsies distraction had ceased, it had been replaced with an eerie ear-splitting silence. This could only mean one of three things. The two men were either lying dead on the ground riddled with Nazi bullets, they had been caught and arrested, or the number of troops had become overwhelming and they had no choice but to retreat. James could only hope it was the latter, the former was unimaginable. The silence was broken by the sound of a whistle being blown frantically. They had been discovered! James sprung into the cab of the van and before he could even close the door, Constance slammed her foot down onto the accelerator and sped into the side street as a battle ensued behind them.

"Stop!" ordered James. "Stop the van!" Constance braked hard, throwing the passengers forward and back. James grabbed his Sten gun from the footwell and jumped from the cab. "Get these guys back to the camp. I will help our men and we will meet you back at the gypsy campsite."

"I will come with you, *mon amie*," Édouard said pulling out his own monstrous MG 42 machine gun; James gave an appreciative nod.

"I come too," said Pierre, making a move to join his two comrades on the street.

"No, Pierre," James stopped him. "You have to protect Constance and the soldiers and get them back to safety." He looked at his friends, the underground resistance leader was evidently disappointed not to join the fray.

"You are right, of course, my friend," Pierre said dully, slamming shut the door and the two comrades watched as the van sped around the bend and out of view.

The two men glanced at each other before running to re-join their Paris resistance fighters who were frantically fighting against an overwhelming barrage of Nazi troops. There was a continuous stream of soldiers filtering from the small blocked off street where they had gone to fight the non-existent army, the young Manuel had remained in the watchtower and had already shot out two of the spotlights that had been turned towards the attackers and shot the guards who had manned them. One of the corpses was hidden from view while the second guard was hanging dead by his belt that had been caught on the metallic structure. The wooden military building in the centre of the restricted area exploded, blowing debris up into the air with a dark cloud of smoke rose from the remains. James saw at least eight enemy soldiers had been felled by the blast, it was initially meant to be a signal to their gypsy resistance friends that they had completed their mission and for them to make their escape. James and Édouard opened fire from the corner of the building, towards the flow of soldiers returning to the town centre from the narrow alleyway, killing many before they even had to take cover from return fire. James' Sten gun had a terrifying effect, embedding its rounds into the walls and shattering the concrete blocks. Manuel was firing at the third occupied sentry tower but it stood just out of range, at the opposite end of the square. James saw the lieutenant, André, fall with a gunshot to his left upper arm.

"Édouard, cover me!" James shouted the order to his friend who began firing wildly into the town square as the Englishman, leaving his weapon, ran as fast as his legs would carry him, weaving to avoid the onslaught of enemy gunfire getting a lock on him, over to his fallen comrade. He grabbed the man by his collar and dragged him to cover behind a concrete flower planter. "Are you alright?" James asked, checking the man's wound, André just gave his normal grunted reply. It was a clean wound. James aggressively tore at the man's sleeve, which came away after three ruthless. The Englishman cut the sleeve down the centre and made it into a makeshift sling which he fitted around the man's neck and without considering the wounded man's pain, slipped his left arm through the loop. He passed the wounded man his Walther PPK revolver, André would not be able to fire a rifle while his arm was in a sling. There was a colossal ear-splitting explosion as the guard tower Manuel had been manning turned into a blazing inferno. James looked up from his secluded spot, what on God's earth had the Jerries brought to the table that had caused such a devastating effect, resulting in the young Spaniard of the French resistance to lose his life at the tender age of seventeen. An armoured Nazi Sturmwagen had turned up and was nestled by the very same tree that James had leaned against earlier that day. These menacing armoured vehicles were not armed and were only troop transports, nothing more. As James observed the enemy forces before him he searched for the weapon that had just obliterated the aforementioned watchtower, he watched three dark green motorbikes race into the square and the riders jump off and scramble for cover before the bikes had even come to a standstill. That is when the Englishman saw it, hiding behind the armoured enemy vehicle was a soldier armed with a Panzerschreck anti-tank weapon, this was a giant rocket launcher used primarily to take out opposition tanks and with great success, many allied attacks had been nearly foiled, thanks to the use of these terrifying weapons of war. James grabbed André's Karabiner 98K, it was a single shot weapon which meant that James could get a steady shot without too much recoil. He took aim and fired towards the concealed soldier, each shot missed the target and caused a spark as the bullets were deflected by the armoured vehicle.

André groaned. "We must go!" He suddenly spotted what the English resistance fighter was firing at. "Now!" he blurted. It was against James' instincts to give in but they were outmatched, not only by the number of troops but also by the variety of arsenal, any further confrontation would not only be futile but could cost more lives of resistance members to no avail.

Before too long the remaining resistance members were running at a steady unwavering pace along the streets towards the forest. Behind them, the battle against the now non-existent resistance army was still raging on.

Chapter 23

It was well after dark, by the time James and the remaining resistance fighters had returned to the gypsy camp yet it was a hive of activity, lanterns and torches were lit around the camp. The many gypsy healers were crowding around the Free French soldiers, that had previously been rescued from incarceration by the Nazis. They applied herbal creams and ointments to the bruises, cuts and other various injuries the French escapees had received. Édouard accompanied James to give their report to their captain, Pierre, who was standing over the Free French officer that he and Édouard had helped into the van previously. James now realised why the man had not been able to walk, the man's feet were swollen, twice their normal size, they were red, blistered and a bleeding red and black mess with most of the man's toenails missing. A gypsy woman was dabbing the feet with cold water to clean them and a second helper added an ointment to them and bandaged them up, making the man wince with every touch. "Those scum tortured him. They burnt his feet with a blow torch to get information," Pierre explained, James was utterly stunned, he knew that the Germans could be sadistic but he had never expected them to be evil to this extent.

"Jesus Christ!"

"But he did not give in, he did not tell them anything." James had to admit that he was impressed. The Englishman would have done all in his power to resist during interrogation but if he had been submitted to unimaginable torture such as this he was not sure how long he would have been able to hold out for. Pierre continued, "That is the power of our resolve, my friend." James led Pierre to one side.

"Manuel is dead," this time it was Pierre's turn to be in shock.

"Manuel?" he asked, finding it hard to resister, James nodded.

"And we have five wounded," this was a glum report and not one that James had enjoyed giving. "How are Anton and Viktor?"

"No news of them yet," replied Pierre, still trying to come to terms with their loss, it had been his decision to allow Manuel to get involved.

"No news? Nothing?" questioned James, surprised. "They should have been back hours ago!"

"*Oui*, I know. We have sent one of the gypsy children to see if they can find out what had happened," Pierre replied in a frustrated tone. James decided that it was best he left Pierre to his grief, the death of a comrade was never easy to bear but to lose one at such a young age was an utter tragedy. James saw Constance sitting out of the way on a tree stump, alone, cutting and eating an apple with a small pocket pruning knife. James went and sat beside her, without a word she cut another slice and offered it to her English friend who accepted the sweet, crisp fruit slice, before slicing herself another piece.

"So many men hurt," she said solemnly. "Is it true that Manuel is dead?"

"I am afraid so," replied James sadly, looking at the men, lying all over, being cared over by medics.

"We will not be able to get them all back to Paris, there are too many." She was clearly distressed by the situation and not handling the pressure well. He put his arm around her shoulder to comfort her, she snuggled into his embrace and buried her head into his shoulder.

"We will find a way, we always do," James said in a soft comforting tone, but he could not deny that he had noticed the same problem.

"*Ils ont été Pris*," came a hysterical yell as a young black-haired boy ran from the woods and continued yelling, "*Anton et Viktor ont été capturés.*"

"What is he yelling about?" asked James, not happy about the interruption, he was rather enjoying his consolidation. Constance wearily raised her head from where she had nestled her it on James' shoulder, her eyes were red from crying, she had quite obviously been more upset than James had first realised.

"He said that Viktor and Anton have been caught." James rose to his feet; how much more of this could they take? The situations were getting worse by the second, after all, they had hardly just escaped with their lives. James strode over to where Pierre was being briefed by the young lad. Édouard, being the unsentimental style of man, fired question after question at the boy. Only after an intense few minutes of interrogation did they let the child depart.

"Well?" James pushed the resistance captain, Pierre, for further information.

"The boy said that Anton and Viktor will be hung in the morning by the Nazis, by the town well, as a warning to all the people of Troyes."

"Well, why can't we rescue them tonight, under the cover of darkness?" James asked. "They wouldn't expect an attack so soon after the last."

"Non, *mon amie*," Édouard replied abruptly, "they are in the Gestapo headquarters; it would be suicide!"

"Gestapo? Shit!" James exclaimed. "Well, we have to do something! You saw what those sadistic sons of bitches did to that poor bastard!" James said angrily, pointing out the Free French officer, he was enraged. "How long do you think it will take them to crack and give up this location?" There was no reaction. "We at least owe it to them to try!" James urged. Pierre replied, he had already decided and was adamant.

"We cannot, my friend. As Édouard has said, they are being held in the Gestapo headquarters, it would be like a fortress, it—"

"It would be easier to walk into Hitler's Eagles Nest," interrupted Édouard, getting an evil stare from Pierre. Édouard was referring to a hilltop retreat made for Adolf Hitler, near Berchtesgaden in the Bavarian Alps on the Austrian border which was only accessible by a gold-plated elevator.

"Yes, well," Pierre continued, ignoring his comrades' interruption, "the ruthless Gestapo will be on guard." This comment would make the bravest of men quiver but James could not believe his ears, he had never heard Pierre being so negative. The Englishman was not going to accept this, these gypsies had volunteered to help them and it would have made the situation much harder, with a larger loss of life if it had not been for their effective distraction. The ex-SOE did not want to defy his friend and leader, but neither was it in his British nature to stand down.

James voiced his concerns to Édouard, in private later, in the wood just out of the camp, he did not want to be seen by Pierre as he tried to convince his friend to disobey their captains' orders and act. Édouard was beginning to understand and sympathise with his foreign comrade and evidently was not entirely comfortable with the situation either.

"We cannot just let these guys be executed and then go on and act as if nothing has happened!" James ranted, lighting a cigarette. Édouard took a couple of deep drags on his wooden pipe in thought before saying,

"These are not normal police, *mon amie*, not even normal Nazis, they are the Gestapo. The Nazi secret police."

"I know who they bloody are!" spat James, a bit more hostile than he had anticipated but he was getting truly fed up with his comrades' defeatist attitude. "Where is the Gestapo headquarters?"

"On the other side of town," came a voice from behind him, James spun around, instinctively reaching around his back for his pistol, but dropped his hand as he saw three of the male gypsies approaching them.

"How far is it from the town well?" queried James.

"Nearly five kilometres," replied the man, James did a quick calculation, it was about three miles.

"So I take it they would have to transport Anton and Viktor to the execution by a lorry?" Édouard gently nodded; in his head, he was following James' train of thought.

"Yes, of course," the gypsy replied. James turned to his black-market friend.

"We need a truck to transport the *De Gaulle* soldiers back to Paris." Édouard just nodded in response, an unusual smirk growing across his face, anticipating James next comment. "We will hi-jack the lorry."

"We are going with you," the gypsy said in English, after sharing the plan with his two associates who did not speak English, he spoke in a hoarse whisper and they gave their agreement.

"You are more than welcome," smiled James. You could never fault the heart of a volunteer.

Fifteen minutes later, one by one the five men slipped away from the camp and by the torchlight met by a small cluster of trees where the gypsies explained the plans for the routes and the best places to ambush the transport lorry. They spoke in French, leaving Édouard to translate for James. Every member of the congregation submitted ideas but every plan of rescuing the two men from the gallows, from attacking the truck the second it left the Nazi secret polices compound to raiding the Gestapo jailhouse, were overly risky for James to feel comfortable with. "How many guards will they have with them?" he asked eventually, the gypsies looked to Édouard for a translation and then replied in French,

"They say two guards for each prisoner, a driver and sometimes there is another man seated beside him, but not always."

"So five or six?"

"Yes," replied the English-speaking gypsy. James' mind was racing.

"Will the Gestapo know the soldiers?"

"No, they do not want to be associated with normal soldiers."

"What are you thinking *mon amie*?" Édouard inquired, puzzled by this new line of enquiry.

"What if they hand the guys straight over to us?" James cracked a smile, impressed with himself; it would be a bold risky ploy. "We take out the krauts who are meant to escort them, dress in their Nazi gear and let the Gestapo hand them straight over to us and no one will have a clue what has happened until it is too late. Dangerous but simple."

"No German uniform will fit me," Édouard replied gloomily, "the trousers are always too short and tight."

"Just put on the hat and shirt, then stay in the driver's seat," shrugged James as if it was the least of their worries. The three gypsies deliberated James' plan in French for a few minutes before the English-speaking one asked, "And we drive them here?"

"Exactly," James spouted cheerily. "We drive back here before the Jerrie know what has happened and be home in time for breakfast." The group chuckled at James' wording but agreed with the plan. "Now this will have to be a stealth attack." This seemed to be the story of James' career in the French resistance. "So we cannot use un-silenced guns." The two non-English speaking travellers looked at their foreign associate quietly. James removed his pistol and unscrewed the suppressor showing the silenced gun to the two men, he shook his head and then replacing the silencer with a nod. He then got out his knuckle duster from his pocket and chucked it into the lap of one of the men who slipped it over his fingers and admired it, still not totally understanding until the giant black-marketeer explained, the men nodded in understanding. The man went to hand the brass knuckles back to James but he motioned for the man to keep it, so that he could use it during the future operation.

"What time will the transport truck be at the Gestapo headquarters?"

"Well the hanging is at six o'clock," mentioned Édouard, squinting, trying to read his friends' mind.

"They will be there at about four hundred hours," the gypsy said.

"Four o'clock?" The gypsy nodded his confirmation. James checked his watch; it was twenty past twelve. "Okay, we will take it there, it is the last thing they will expect. We will meet back here at three o'clock and be ready to go." Édouard translated and once they had all agreed the five men individually blended back into the camp.

The five men reconvened at the secluded spot. The gypsies had collected together an assortment of hand to hand and close combat weapons which consisted of multiple hunting knives, a wooden clot, a hatchet axe and a twelve-inch heavy metal mace. The troop shared out the weapons and set off in silence through the woods, no one had anything to say, they were about to walk into one of the most feared areas in the region, not even the Nazis dared enter unless they were ordered to. They skirted around the outside streets of the town, ducking behind hedges or melting into the shadows as troops passed. They may not be in the city of Paris or even close to the centre of the town, but there was still a curfew in effect, now even more strict, after the rescue of the Free French troops, the opposing army had become ultra-vigilant. As they approached a grey brick building, James was handed a dear-horn handled knife with a beautiful engraving of a hunting scene on the blade, by Danior, the eldest of the three gypsies. The building was connected to a knee-high matching brick wall that encased the Gestapo owned courtyard. James cautiously glanced around the corner of the building which all five of men now had their backs flat against. Directly by them on the other side of the wall were a pair of smoking Nazi soldiers talking in hushed voices, parked behind a sleek black Mercedes Benz Gestapo staff car sat the dark grey Nazi lorry for the transportation of the condemned prisoners. James swapped places with the man beside him, Danior, so the man could observe the situation before the two men began their covert assault. The Frenchman gave James a nod and then counted down from five on his skinny, dirt covered fingers. Once the final finger dropped the two men vaulted over the stone wall directly on top of the two German soldiers. James spent no time stabbing the blade between the victims' jaw, killing the man instantly but not daring to remove the blade so to avoid the blood being soaked into the collar of the uniform, he would be wearing this uniform and it wouldn't do for some eagle-eyed Gestapo officers to notice a blood-stained uniform. Beside him, Danior had assassinated the other soldier, at the same time disfiguring the poor middle-aged soldiers' face by ploughing the heavy mace into his skull. James turned to scan the courtyard and just twenty feet away from them, standing stock still, stood another Nazi soldier, he looked at them with pure horror at the assault that he had just witnessed. The young soldier, who must have been in his late teens, nervously moved his hand round to a small whistle which hung on a silver coloured chain around his neck, he was about to sound the alarm and alert the whole base to their presence, they could not allow this. James hastily reached around his back and drew his silenced pistol, he took his aim as the young lad put the whistle to his lips but before James could squeeze the trigger the lone man collapsed to his knees with an eight-inch hunting blade embedded in his skull straight between his eyes. James turned in surprise to see one of the other gypsies with his hand still in the 'follow through' position after throwing the blade accurately, James would have applauded the man but as they were all aware that there were at least two more Nazi soldiers in the vicinity. Danior and James began to strip off the clothes from the deceased men and dressed into the dark green uniforms with the chamber pot style helmets to complete their disguise. In the meantime their three comrades had also jumped over the wall and as one of the other gypsies was changing into the other Nazi uniform, the final pair of men dragged the dead, stripped corpses, to a dark corner of the courtyard where the bodies would not be found until it was light and by that time it would be far too late. The five men remained crouched by the wall, they knew there were more men here but no idea where. That was until they saw a light in the cab of the truck, someone was lighting a cigarette, Édouard acted, he casually walked up to the cab, opened the door and grabbing the man by the back of the head he smacked it savagely against the dashboard several times, knocking the man unconscious before dragging the body over to his comrades and began disrobing him, once the body had been undressed, James slit the man's throat without hesitation, allowing the blood to seep into the man's white vest. Before James could drag the corpse to join its deceased comrades, the fifth and final soldier walked out from behind a tree, doing up his trouser flies and oblivious of the five intruders, he walked calmly over to the lorry to investigate why the door, which Édouard had left open, was ajar. James was getting weary of this and fired a suppressed shot into the back of the man's head, the man collapsed into the cab of the truck, the final gypsy repeated the process of dressing in the soldier's uniform.

"Any of you speak German?" James asked Danior, the Englishman could have kicked himself for not thinking about it until now.

"Yes, Alphonse can." James breathed a sigh of relief.

"Okay Édouard, get in the driver's seat. The rest of us will wait for them at the bottom of the stairs. When they hand Anton and Viktor over, Alphonse will do the talking. Everyone understand?" He was worried he may have given this order too fast for his comrades, as his mind was racing, but never the less he received a nod from Édouard and Danior nodded before translating the orders in a whisper to his French-speaking comrades, who in turn nodded enthusiastically and with that everyone took up their positions.

James lit a cigarette and stealthily checked the time on his watch using the flame of his lighter to illuminate it, the time was five twenty-eight, the execution was scheduled for six o'clock and if nothing else the Jerrie forces were always prompt, so it would not be much longer until the handover. As if confirming James' thoughts, the thick brown wooden entrance at the top of the concrete steps opened, spilling light out into the mundane courtyard. A square-shouldered stocky man wearing a brown leather coat, his greasy black hair in a side parting and a grim look on his face exited the property followed by a much skinnier man wearing a black suit with a matching fedora, a pair of thin wire round spectacles and carrying a black file case. They looked down at the waiting men, who all stood to attention, they had to make this charade look good. Alphonse ascended up the steps and gave the men the fascist salute, the two men returned it by raising their right hand. James could hear the Gestapo agents asking the undercover Frenchman questions in German, he assumed they were making sure he understood their orders, the skinnier of the two men opened his file case and handed a piece of paper to Alphonse who saluted with a Heil Hitler, folded the piece of paper in two and placed it in his shirt pocket. James dared not look in their direction as he remembered that he was a wanted man and even though the posters were overly vague it was possible the Thirds Reich secret police may have more details about him. The stockier man then shouted something into the building and a blindfolded Anton was roughly pushed through the open doorway.

"*Du und du legst ihn in den Lastwagen!*" commanded Alphonse pointing to James and Rener, the third gypsy, gesturing to the back of the lorry. They could simply decipher that he was ordering them to put Anton into the back of the lorry so the two men ran up the steps and so as not to cause suspicion, roughly dragged their comrade down the steps and into the back of the lorry, followed by Danior and Alphonse with the struggling, blindfolded, young Viktor.

The group stayed in complete silence as the four men jumped into the back of the large truck and it rumbled to life. The lorry slowly left the complex, nobody dared say a thing, until they were a safe distance away from the Gestapo headquarters, they had got away so far but they dared not make a stupid mistake which could get them caught now.

After a couple of minutes travel, when they were sure to be out of view of the intimidating Gestapo command post, James gave a faint sigh. He had had the terrible premonition that the bodies of the executed Nazi sentries had been discovered and the German secret police would have pursued them and easily caught them in their souped-up armed Gestapo cruiser, but there were no cars following them, the roads were bare. Even though they were not out of harm's way just yet, the Englishman lowered the open flap to the lorry and the disguised men turned on their torches, using their hunting knives they severed the men's bonds, which were so tight they were cutting into the two gypsies wrists, before they removed their filthy blindfolds. The duo looked around the lorry but stayed silent, it was clear that they were unaware of the four men's identities. James removed his helmet, followed by the three other men. Viktor's face changed to a picture of shock and Anton's to a laugh as he identified his saviours and then turned into a roar of laughter when he realised what had just happened. James and his comrades laughed along with the man. James, unstable on his feet with the rocking of the truck, stumbled to the front of the cargo bay, to a small grill which connected to the lorries cab.

"Take us home Ed," he called through the grill.

"*Ja wohl, herr unterfeldwebel!*" replied Édouard getting a bit carried away, jokingly calling his British comrade a staff sergeant. James smirked at his friends' witticism. The Englishman steadied himself by holding a rope suspended on the ceiling and offered his fellow counterparts a cigarette, Anton, Alphonse and even the fourteen-year-old Viktor all accepted one thankfully. After lighting his own cigarette he passed around his silver lighter, keeping a close eye on it. They were his comrades and he had just helped them escape, but he had to remember that they were gypsies and were well known for the theft of items of value. James was relieved when Viktor, who was the last to light his cigarette, returned the lighter to him. The Englishman fell from his feet onto one of the wooden benches when Édouard made a sharp turn to the right onto a hole-riddled mud road, heading towards the wooden forest base camp. They had travelled cross country through the evergreen, fir tree forest for another twelve minutes when Édouard braked so hard it jolted the passengers violently.

153

"Bloody hell Ed!" James said loudly through the grill. Without turning and in a tone that made James think that he was trying to speak without moving his lips Édouard said,

"I think we may have a small problem." James could make out Édouard raising his hands on the other side of the mesh grating.

"Have we arrived at the gypsy camp?"

"Yes... but I think, they think we are Nazis." James had not thought about arriving into a resistance-controlled base in an enemy vehicle, dressed as Nazis, or how it may cause some problems. Maybe they should have told someone. It was a stupid mistake. He carefully walked to the back of the truck and peered through the flap, first to the right and then the left. Approaching the lorry was a huge abundance of armed vicious gypsies, Paris resistance and rescued Free French soldiers, all with their weapons aimed at the dark grey Mercedes military lorry and their fingers poised on the triggers. "Anton!" whispered James. "Go talk to these buggers, tell them that we are not bloody krauts!" The gypsy commander hesitated and looked at each of his rescuers before piping up,

"I do not think they will believe us, after all, we were arrested by the Gestapo." James could not believe what he was hearing.

"So let's just stay in here and be shot full of holes then!" James said angrily, full of sarcasm. Anton did not argue, he flung open the rear flap and jumped out, followed by Viktor. He heard the gypsy commander talking to his comrades. Meanwhile the four disguised men were brutally dragged from the lorry and forced to their knees. James rose his head to see Édouard at the front of the truck, also on his knees, he rolled his eye and James gave a mild smirk. He could not believe it, this was the third time he had found himself on his knees about to be shot by supposed allies since the day Pierre had joined him at the bar and offered him the opportunity to join the Paris resistance. The three disguised gypsies were pleading with their friends, tearing off their Nazi clothing, whilst Anton tried to explain to his overzealous friends, who were eager to assassinate these apparent German soldiers, that they had been rescued. The growing angry crowd came to an abrupt stop when a loud order was made in French.

"Silence!" The five would be victims looked up at the sound of the voice and saw Pierre, with his younger sister hanging on his arm, approach from out of the woods.

"Pierre! Thank God!" James cried. "Can you tell these sons of bitches who we actually are?" James requested with relief. Pierre barked at the gypsies, resistance members and Free French troops, who lowered their weapons and helped the men back to their feet. Pierre walked up to James and embraced him, which made the Englishman feel very uncomfortable.

"I am glad you are safe, my friend, we became worried when we could not find you," he said, releasing his English comrade.

"Sorry we did not tell you, old chap," James replied, confused by Pierre's coolness. The resistance commander did not reply but approached Édouard and gave the giant man the same welcome. Constance flung her arms around James and to his total surprise gave him a passionate kiss on the lips. As her soft lips connected with his, his head became fuzzy with desire and for that brief moment, there was nothing, no war, no occupation, no resistance and everything around them disappeared. There was just James and Constance. As Constance broke off the passionate connection, he looked over to Pierre who was looking at the couple with a stern, inquisitive look, whilst Édouard beside him looked at the two with a broad smile, in a way which said 'it is about time'. James was mildly embarrassed by the crowd who was watching them but he had very much preferred receiving this welcome to the one he had received from her brother.

Anton, Viktor and the five comrades were ushered around the campfire where they were passed a flagon of the strong, home-brewed, alcoholic beverage and the French speakers began telling the tale of how they had rescued two men from the custody of the Gestapo, without firing a single shot.

Chapter 24

Pierre, along with Anton, had left the group who had congregated around the campfire, early on and had retracted to one side, out of the way. They were talking in hushed tones, with constant glances towards their friend James who kept his eyes on the two Frenchmen, he was sure they were discussing another way for him to put his neck on his line for their beloved France. He was only picking up a few of the words of the excitable gypsies as they repeated the story of their daring rescue; even though James was finding it difficult because the gypsies had a strong accent and had already had plenty of the strong beverage, the insulting charades of the Nazi troops and Gestapo officers helped. Constance sat on the floor resting her head on James' lap as he sat on a log, laughing along with the woodland travellers. As it was getting dark and their hosts started lighting lanterns to illuminating the camp, James was summoned by the two commanders, he slowly rose and joined the two men.

"James, my friend." Pierre was hesitant, which James assumed was confirmation of his suspicion, he was not likely to like what was coming. "Anton wishes to grant you with a rare privilege for saving him and his nephew, even against my instructions." James dropped his head as if in shame, but this was not what James had been suspecting.

"Well, you know, I was only doing what I thought was the right thing," explained James.

"*Oui,* quite. Anton wishes to honour you with a gypsy wedding, it is a unique opportunity, never offered to people outside the gypsy community." Anton smiled as Pierre explained.

"Wow! Hold on a second, old boy!" said James, shocked by this sudden turn of events. "Who am I meant to be marrying?" He could hardly believe that these two men were trying to marry him off.

"*Constance, bien sûr,*" said Anton without a second's pause. James looked a Pierre who confirmed with a gentle nod of his head.

"She has made her feelings clear," Pierre added; it seemed as if he had come to terms with marrying off his younger sister to this English fighter. "She has already accepted it, my friend, it is now up to you, do you feel the same as her?" This was beginning to embarrass James; of course, he had strong feelings for her, but marriage? It had not even crossed his mind, not since his English fiancée had died in the blitz.

"Of course, I have strong amorous feeling towards her b—"

"*Bon*! It is decided," interrupted Pierre. "Because you marry my sister, you will become my brother." Anton shook James' hand vigorously in congratulations, then Pierre took hold of James by his shoulders and gave him a peck on each cheek before waving over his sister who had been watching them intently ever since James had joined them. Pierre had a few words with her in French, her eyes lit up with the news and without any indication she pressed her soft rose lips against James' in their first kiss as an official couple. It was once again surreal; James was useless to resist so all he could do was reciprocate the clear sign of affection.

The following day the preparation for the duo's betrothal was in full swing. The framed lanterns were covered in coloured films whilst Chinese style paper lanterns were being set out outlining the forest camp, a small band were preparing their rustic instruments and tables with various types of seating such as wooden chairs, tree logs, hay bales and piles of pillows, were all being set up either side of the tables for the celebrating guests that would be joining them. They had opened eight more fire pits which at his time had various pots bubbling over them as well as a couple of overly sized cast iron pans as they would fry a mixture infused with homegrown garlic bulbs. In the larger of the pits, they were preparing a spit to cook the main meal of the celebration, a large male boar that a troop of gypsy hunters had caught in the early hours of that morning. There was a large number of children coming and going with sacks of vegetables which had been relieved from some local farmhouse and were emptied into the boiling pots. Everyone seemed in high spirits. Some of the excited female gypsy women had ushered Constance away a few moments after she had risen, to prepare her for the forthcoming nuptials. James felt like a spare wheel, wondering about the camp aimlessly. Every time he tried to aid or assist anyone he would be intercepted; it was not the custom for the groom to be involved with the preparations for his own wedding festivity, even if it was helping to move an overly heavy table.

"I have a wedding gift for you," said a nervous French voice just as James had given up all hope of any conversation. He spun around to see the young Viktor holding out a rectangular wooden box. James smiled at his boy's consideration.

"That is very kind of you, lad," said James accepting it gratefully, he opened the box and his jaw dropped open. It was a case of Montecristo cigars, the nicest cigars in existence, not to mention a case of these were more than a standard two months wage back home in England.

"I say! Where on earth did you get these?"

"The Americans," stuttered Viktor.

"The air drops." Anton laughed, appearing behind his young cousin. "One of these cigars would make any Nazi bring you Hitler's moustache, but, they are a wedding gift, so you must enjoy them," he advised the Englishman, looking at them jealously.

"No problem there, I certainly will, thank you lad." James smiled, admiring them before snapping shut the lid so Anton didn't get any ideas on how he could relive the Englishman of his newly acquired tobacco. The rest of the day James was getting small gifts in dribs and drabs. Édouard had presented him with two bottles of Johnnie Walker whiskey, from the gypsies he had received a matching pair of silver goblets, a wine decanter and other silver or crystal, stolen dining ware and five German Luger pistols, which James truly appreciated. Lugers were greatly desired by the allied forces and you could normally name your price but James had decided to hang on to a couple of them, they were dangerous but beautiful weapons and nearly never jammed.

The big occasion quickly came around. Constance wore a ravishing cream dress made from the silk of a parachute which had been cut to show off her immaculate curves and a floral crown on her brown hair, which they had curled. James, on the other hand, had been given a black pinstriped suit, a black Fedora and black loafers with white spats, he felt like a spiv as he stood at the front of the gypsies, Free French and Paris resistance members.

The music played and James turned to see Pierre leading a snow-white pony, carrying the stunning bride who sat side saddle, down through the crowds, James was in awe, Constance was a radiant beauty. Pierre helped her from the steed and handed her hand to James, giving him a quick 'I am trusting you' stare as a young gypsy removed the pony. As James had insisted on giving his sister away, Édouard played the important part of the best man and had produced a pair of yellow gold wedding bands for the newlyweds.

The feast was a banquet of medieval times. It began with a rustic vegetable soup, followed by what James had been told was garlic fried snails, they tasted better than James had expected and he had to admit that he had rather enjoyed them. There was an excessive amount of wine and champagne flowing and as the starters were served both Pierre and Anton gave speeches in French, which Constance had to translate for James as both men were beginning to slur their words, both of them had had their fill of alcohol. Then the main course of the roast boar which had been slowly cooked on the turning spit all afternoon was served with roast potatoes which had been cooked in the embers of the fire pits. The meal ended with a collection of cheese and French port. They all ate their fill, so much so that James was hardly able to perform the first dance with his new bride, but before long the party looked like a carnival. James and Constance soon retired to a gypsy caravan that had been donated to them for the night, to share a marital bed and a night of ecstasy.

It was late by the time James awoke and it took him a good couple of minutes to recall where he was. He turned to see his new bride lying beside him, she looked angelic in a dreamless sleep. Making sure not to stir her he carefully rose from the bed and was about to redress himself in his civilian clothing when he saw his Nazi uniform hanging from a coat hanger and the plans for today poured back to him. They were to travel back to Paris, disguised as Nazi soldiers, escorting the freed Free French prisoners of war, so in case of an inspection of the lorry, there would be no suspicion. It was a daring rouse and one that would need every ounce of courage they could muster. James slipped into the dark green, much hated and in some cases feared military uniform, taking care not to wake his French bride and stepped out into the open air. The cool breeze was bracing but he welcomed it, he had only just noted how stuffy the caravan had been. Many of the merrymakers of the night before had not yet woken from their alcohol-fuelled sleep and were strewn around the camp where they had passed out. James took a couple of deep breaths of the sweet country air, lit a cigarette and weaved through the anaesthetised bodies into the dense forest. He needed some alone time to gather his thoughts, the events of the previous day had all happened so quickly that he had not had time to register it all. He was now a married man and his brother-in-law was the head of the Paris resistance. Being in the resistance was no longer a matter of respect but a family commitment. Walking through the dense forest was peaceful, there was not a sound except for the creaking of the trees straining against the gentle breeze, one could get lost here and not be found for days. He had wandered about for a good couple of hours when he was brought back to reality by a sound, there was a low drone of planes above in the sky, James looked up.

"Your boys coming back from Germany, my friend," said Pierre appearing from behind a tree.

"They're leaving a bit late," smiled James.

"So how are we this fine morning?"

"I am good, thank you, old boy," replied James. "When are we setting off to the base?"

"In half an hour, my friend."

"I best go awake sleeping beauty." James chuckled, thinking of his spouse still in the caravan in her restful slumber.

There was a sudden rustle behind them and James swung round aiming his pistol in the direction of the sound, Pierre acted swiftly, lowering James gun as one of the gypsy children ran from the brush yelling loudly.

"*Allemands! Avions Allemands,*" he ran straight past the two men as if they were not even there.

"What the hell was that all about?" James asked.

"He said… they were German planes. But they are coming from the East," said Pierre confused.

"We should get back to the camp!" James said with some urgency, there was something clearly wrong here.

"I agree, my friend!" said Pierre and the two men strode hastily back to the deep forest camp.

By the time they had arrived back to the woodland realm many had awoken, the Free French troops had assembled in their uniforms around the newly requisitioned Nazi Mercedes Bauer lorry, Édouard was seen wearing his German military shirt and three of the eighteen strong resistance army were wearing the other Nazi uniforms, these would be the men accompanying James in the back of the motorised wagon whilst the others would be hidden in the back of the bakers van that they had arrived in. All of the people in the camp had their eyes to the sky, having heard the droning of the aircraft above. Before anyone knew what was happening James heard the high-pitched whistling sound, it was unmistakable, it was the sound that had given him nightmares for months after it had killed his previous love, it was the sound of bombs.

The woods around them began erupting, trees were obliterated in explosions as the bombs fell to the camp. A lot of the residents jumped into the underground, wood reinforced bunkers as others jumped into the two trucks. Before he could even think, James ran to the caravan that he had occupied the night before, Constance had just stepped out into the open, he grabbed her arm and dragged her roughly over to the Bauer, chucking her in the cab, he was being a bit harsher than he had meant but utter panic had hit him. James then jumped into the driver's seat and Pierre jumped in the other side, beside his younger sister.

"*Va Vite!*" shouted Pierre, as a bomb hit the caravan that Pierre had entered when they had first arrived, leaving nothing but a crater. James did not need any encouragement as the two vehicles sped deeper into the forest. James was in a blind panic, he had not even realised that the cataclysmic onslaught behind them had ceased and he only calmed when Constance put a tender hand on his leg and said tenderly,

"It is okay *mon amour*, you can stop." James braked and stopped the large lorry. Pierre and James jumped from the truck to where Anton was waiting, he had sped the baker's van from the area.

"They must have seen the lights from your wedding," he said disappointedly.

"I am sorry," said James, feeling responsible.

"It is not your fault, Grandmother has died, these are my people now," he said.

"Do you want to come back to Paris?" Pierre asked. "We could use your help."

"Non, thank you. We are travellers, so we will move," laughed Anton dryly. They watched as he and the other gypsies that had been saved began walking back to the demolished camp. Meanwhile, James and the other members disguised as Nazis jumped into the back of the Bauer with the Free French soldiers, with Édouard as the driver, whilst the others hid in the back of the bakers' van.

Chapter 25

The unusual two-vehicle convoy stopped at one of the common military checkpoints on their way back into the grand city, they had left the quiet streets behind them and could hear the common rumble of some decrepit workhorse truck following them, blowing out plumes of oily black smoke from its exhaust engine and raining down a trail of rust from the undercarriage as it travelled on its way. James listened carefully as the bread van was waved through with absolutely no trouble, the military lorry jolted forward and came again to a halt, he could hear Édouard speak to the Nazi guards in his limited German, only saying a few words so not to give himself away. The back flap was thrown open by the sentries and the Free French 'prisoners' were counted to confirm Édouards story of transporting Free French prisoners of war. James sat back in relief once the flap was thrown shut and the lorry was allowed to continue its journey. After leaving the city centre entry control point, the resistance members undid the shackles of their French counterparts who were wearing them on their wrists and ankles to complete the deception that they were being transported to a new prisoner of war camp.

The lorry came to another stop and James looked through the side of the flap and then swung it open to see that they were parked in the metallic complex that housed the Paris resistance beneath. He never thought he would feel so happy to see this old building again. Staying at the gypsy camp was nice enough but did not feel quite right. As soon as he had jumped from the back of the lorry he dropped the back tailgate down to allow their comrades to unmount the personnel carrier. He could see by the faces of his comrades that he was not the only one to be happy and somewhat relieved to be back. Many of his comrades walked from the large building full of glee into the warm sun. James felt a sudden emotion run over him and fill him up like a cup being filled to the brim. He walked at a fast but still trying to act casual pace to the opposite end of the building and ducked behind a pile old empty packing crates which had been left from when the building had been a factory or warehouse of some sort. James could do nothing but break down into tears, in the last couple of days he had lost count of how many times he had almost lost his life and it had just all rushed back to him like a thunderbolt. He could not let anyone see him, the emotion was demoralising and that is the last thing they needed. He could not believe it, his adrenaline had waned and he had transformed into a shivering wreck. He had to snap himself out of it, he could never defeat the enemy if this was to be the result. James dried off his eyes and rose to his feet, he wiped a hand over his face and strode back to join his comrades. As he stood looking out of the large metallic property his beloved turned up by his side and clung to his arm, clasping his hand as they walked into the underground command post. Seeing the couple enter, the occupants of the headquarters rose to their feet and gave thunderous applause to the newly betrothed couple, congratulating them and giving them both pats on the back or a kiss on the cheek and their good wishes.

They were stopped in their tracks by Yosef. "My congratulations," he said and presented the couple with a silver Jewish Hanukkah candelabra. "A gift on your wedding, we rescued it from the ghetto before the scavengers got it," he confessed. It was not unusual for scavengers to dig through the rubble at the burnt-out ghetto for any valuables, some of the scavengers were even said to have paid off the French police to turn a blind eye, because, under the German Nazi regime any property on these sites belonged to the Third Reich and the Fuhrer. The couple accepted the Jews gift with thanks before disappearing into an annexe and sinking into the settee, they were both relieved to be back. Pierre and Édouard went into another annexe and spoke quietly to the captains that they had left in charge during their escapades in Troyes. The adrenaline that had been pumping through everyone veins had dissipated and was replaced with fatigue or delayed shock, so as some raced for a bucket, the majority fell asleep, as the newlyweds did in each other's arms.

They could have only been asleep for a mere matter of hours when, as usual, Pierre interrupted their much-deserved slumber.

"James, Constance, there is no time for rest I am afraid," he said, pulling aside the tattered sheet which was acting as a curtain to separate the annexe from the rest of the room. Rousing the comatose couple he looked at them for a moment, James thought that he must be finding it hard to accept the new relationship that his younger sister was now in. "I have received a message from one of our print houses, they need us to collect the new flyers. I ordered them before your wedding, after your gallant rescue of our gypsy friends. They have been printing non-stop since."

"Blimey. Won't the police get suspicious from all the racket the printing press makes?"

"Non, They play music on a gramophone to mask the noise, my friend." James just rolled his eyes, it was so simple. "I need the two of you to drop them into the *Saxe-Breteuil* market from *le Balcon*… the balcony. They will also give you sticky labels for you to put around our fair city."

"You have a true skill, old boy," said James, finally rising from his seat. "You can make any task so simple and luxurious." The three friends laughed together in unison.

"There is not much risk, my friend. You just must avoid any Nazis. I have a man who will play 'The Pathetique' on his box, I believe the term is organ grinder, when the coast is clear and if the Germans turn up you will just act like a couple who have been caught up in the romance of Paris."

"You have thought of everything!" James had to admit this sounded simple enough and much less risky than the past missions he had been assigned to, but then again Pierre's plans always seemed simple and most of the times proved

162

anything but… Pierre's demeanour suddenly changed into a much sterner, harsher version of the man he knew.

"Édouard and I must go to *La Belle de Nuit*." James looked at the man, there was something about the way his brother-in-law had said it that sounded venomous.

"Why? What is going on?"

"I will tell you soon, but not now!" Pierre nearly spat the words, this was a totally new unseen side to Pierre that the Englishman had never suspected. With that, the French underground leader walked from the underground headquarters followed by the giant Édouard who tiredly trudged behind, blatantly James and Constance were not the only ones exhausted by the previous few days adventurous shenanigans.

The newlyweds changed back into their everyday Parisian clothing to disguise their identities and left for the secret resistance printing press.

The printing press was in a small apartment, there was creased up paper with black ink smudges all over the family home, a gramophone playing Beethoven but James had never been a real admirer of the classics. Constance spoke to a middle-aged woman wearing a pair of ink-stained dungarees, she had an equally ink smudged face, she pulled up a large travel case and opened it, showing that it was packed to the brim with A4 promotional flyers.

"They are written in both French and English so any English or American airmen who are stranded in France can read it, if they are like you and do not speak French," Constance explained. James picked up one of the flyers and began reading the typed English text.

'We can no longer wait for or rely on the Allied army if we are to liberate our beloved France, we must hinder and hurt the invading forces at any chance.' It was short and to the point, which was essential, anyone caught reading these could be arrested and interrogated by the Gestapo. At the bottom of the flyer was a small black and white cartoon, even though James could not read or understand the subtext which accompanied it, he could understand the story by the pictures alone; it was the daring rescues of Anton and Viktor from the Nazi secret police, it had been a bold stroke against the Nazi regime and a great victory for the French resistance. Along with the liberation of the Free French soldiers it would be a demoralising defeat to the invading German army. The printing girl passed James another sheet of paper with multiple circles, which contained a large letter 'V' in the centre and words in red encircling it: '*Prenez les armes pour la liberté de la France*'.

"It says to take up your weapons to fight for Frances' freedom," whispered Constance looking over her husband's shoulder. "They are labels, they can stick, we will put them around town," she explained. This made sense. The duo folded the sheets of stickers and put them in their coat pockets for stealthy use, closed the case of flyers and took their leave. James was carrying the weighty suitcase in one hand and holding his lovers hand in the other. They walked together in total silence. Constance took the lead, she guided the way to the market, it was not unusual to see couples moving belongings. So the couple did not arouse too much attention from the eagle-eyed sentries who watched everyone with suspicion. The markets were not only a place the public could pick up their everyday items but was also a place for a lot of black-market, under-the-counter trading, where a secret word, phrase or gesture would alert the market trader that the customer was after more than just half a pound of onions, everyone had connections and were involved in the back-alley transactions, even if they were law abiding citizens.

James and Constance weaved through the market traders wooden, wheeled wagons and ascended a large granite stairway to a concrete balcony that overlooked the marketplace. They opened the tanned suitcase at the back of the balcony and as James kept watch, Constance removed two piles of the incriminating flyers. She then put the half-full case upright against the wall and passed over one of the bundles to James, they then walked to the opposite end of the balcony, James could see the organ grinder. A man in his mid to late sixties with a long tangle grey beard, wearing a straw weaved hat and a black waistcoat adorned with pins, over a white shirt with his sleeves rolled up, he would give them the signal as to when they were least likely to attract the enemy soldiers' attention. The married resistance fighters watched the world go by below them, people bartering with the market traders and examining the legal wares for sale. James' ears perked up, between the noise of the crowds, the organ grinder had started playing 'The Pathetique', this was the signal. The duo lifted their bundles onto the concrete balustrade and with a decisive shove, pushed them over the edge, littering the street below. As expected this act of defiance enraged the Nazi troops who went berserk and ran at speed up the stairs to find these 'terrorists' who were spreading these messages against the 'great regime' and 'glorious Fuhrer'. But all they found was a loved-up couple, embraced in each other's arms, enthralled in a passionate kiss, James could see one soldier, through the corner of his eye, hesitate, possibly considering to ask this couple if they had seen anything but decided against it and continued his search. After a few minutes in their intimate embrace, the two split to see the soldiers, unsuccessful in their search, either returned to their guard duty or picking up as many of the illegal flyers as possible, before they could be picked up by the public. James quite calmly picked up the suitcase and followed Constance down the stairs, not without sticking a resistance sticker onto one of the white painted pillars first.

The two undercover resistance members continued travelling down the streets, slipping flyers through letterboxes and sticking labels in public places around the town, so they would be seen by the maximum amount of people. It was a scary proposition with Nazi troops roaming the streets.

By late evening they had distributed all the leaflets around the city of light and were on their way back to the resistance headquarters when a maroon red Gütmann car drove towards them at full speed and handbraked to a stop before them. The couple hesitated briefly, what on earth was going on, the sun was setting and there was an ominous feel in the air. The lovers chose to continue on their way and walk past the car, they could not arouse suspicion. The drivers' side door opened and Pierre stepped out.

"James get in! Constance get back to the headquarter!" he ordered in a strong, harsh tone, James had never seen Pierre like this.

"What is wrong?" Constance asked, her voice sounded feeble as if she was pleading with him. "What is going on?" James knew that she was speaking in English for him. Pierre looked at them with a stern face then said to his younger sister, in a near shout:

"Constance, *rentre à la maison!*" His tone was nearly one of hostility. James turned to Constance and took her by the shoulder. She had tears in her eyes; seeing her brother like this obviously scared her.

"Go, I'll be back," he said solemnly, "don't worry." And with that, he got into the passenger's side of the car. He could not deny that the way Pierre was acting scared him; had he been told that James had done something? Had he done something to upset his brother-in-law?

Chapter 26

The two men drove along in complete silence, the stretching shadows had disappeared into the darkness when James could no longer hold the suspense.

"What the hell is going on? You have been a different person since we got back from the gypsy camp! Is it just my marriage to your sister? Or is it just something else? Because I must say, I am not too keen on the new you!" James ranted, faster than he had first anticipated but it was clear by Pierre's shocked glances at James' outburst that the Frenchman had understood his English friends' remarks clearly. It still took the Englishman's brother-in-law a couple of minutes before replying, after a few deep breaths he said,

"I am sorry, my friend," his voice had reverted back to his normal gentler tone. "Whilst we were in Troyes, we got a message from your army that the British, American and Canadian forces will be invading the Normandy beaches on 6 June."

"Well that is good news, surely?" replied James, a bit unsure why this would be an explanation for Pierre's sudden change in attitude. James' mind was racing. "Normandy?" This explained a lot, this is the reason he nearly died for the British Military Intelligence, he could hardly believe it. But he had to put this thought out of his mind.

"But, that is only in two days' time, they want our help to delay the German reinforcements. There is much to do but no time to do it." This explained it, the pressure of assisting with a massive assault that could bring the end to the war was strong enough to crack anyone. "Édouard has taken some men to cut down trees and sever telegraph wires on the outskirts of Paris. André is in the city and has got men digging up the streets to delay the Nazi troops and the rest is up to us."

"Us? It sounds to me that you have everything covered."

"Non, we must go to the *Gare de Paris* and disable the trains," said Pierre.

"The trains? How on earth are we going…" James stopped, in the back-seat of the car was a bulge hidden under a dark grey wool cover. He pulled it to one side to reveal half a dozen explosive devices with five sticks on each bundle with a timer attached to each. There was also a Viper SMG, a silenced sniper rifle, it was a beautiful but deadly weapon and as silent as a wisp of wind. It was the kind of weapon that James liked to call a 'one shot, one kill weapon'. "I say!" were the only two words he could summon. Just then Pierre swerved the car into a dark lay by, the two men disembarked. The cool summer air woke James, he looked up to see the waxing moon shining brightly in the sky, he would not be working under the full cover of darkness then.

"You put the explosives on the trains and I will cover you with the *Fusil de sniper*," said Pierre in a whisper, grabbing the Viper rifle. James looked around, on one side was a six-foot high wooden wall with a small brick shack-like house and on the opposite side of the road was farmland as far as the eye could see, but with the truth being told, in this dim light, he could not see too far at all.

"So, where is this train station of yours?" James asked his brother-in-law. The Frenchman cracked a smile and opened the trunk of the car chucking James a tanned satchel.

"Fill it with explosives, my friend." So James did as he was bid, he then looked towards his counterpart who had also removed a sixteen-inch crowbar from the boot of the car and was now slinging the silenced sniper rifle over his shoulder, James was deeply puzzled. Without a word the head of the Paris resistance went over to the tall wooden fence and using the crowbar, pried open one of the wooden planks.

"*Gare de Paris*," he whispered, James went beside his friend and peered through the gap and behind a barbed wire fence he saw the dimly lit train station with three matt black trains parked out on the tracks. "Come, my friend," Pierre urged, squeezing through the gap and dropping to his stomach, James had learnt better than to question his brother-in-law, once Pierre had an idea in his head nothing could change his mind, so the Englishman followed suit. The ground was harder than he had expected and his body made a thump as he hit the ground. The two men leopard crawled forward. The four-foot high barbed wire fence was made up of three wires fitted through supportive rods, with rustic Bavarian mountain cattle bells fitted every eight meters, the theory being that if an intruder was trying to enter the restricted area it would set off each bell, alerting the German troops of their presence. Beneath the lowest wire, two feet off the ground was a coiled barbed wire and this would be James' entry. Pierre withdrew a pair of wire cutters from his rear back pocket and began snipping at the wires with occasional French obscenity as he snagged himself on the sharp spikes, eventually, he cut through and the two men rolled the unalarmed wire aside, making sure not to touch the wire above.

"Go, my friend, *Allez!*" urged Pierre in a low harsh whisper, James had to take in a deep breath of the night air to calm his nerves before advancing at a crawl on his stomach until he was well past the fence. He turned to see his French comrade nimbly clambering up to the roof of the small building. This was not his concern, he had his job to do, he had to fix the explosives to the train engines without being caught, he could not help thinking how much easier it would be if he was wearing a Jerrie uniform, it would not be the first time. The Englishman crawled up to a large red fuel tanker and only then did he carefully rise to his feet. He peered around, the guarding of the Paris train station was very lax, the guards on the platforms seemed more interested in talking than guarding their posts, they clearly had not heard about the impending invasion which would have put them on high alert.

Sprinting in a crouch and cringing as the gravel crunched under the feet, he moved from his hidden position to the next behind a metallic pillar and then to the dark trains. James covered the ground in good time and wasted no time fitting two rolls of dynamite and setting timers to the first engine and then carefully set the second roll of explosives to the second engine, he had just set the timer in the engines cab when he heard a young male voice behind him and the metallic clicking of a rifle cocking.

"*Nicht bewegen! Hände Hoch!*" James slowly raised his hands.

"You don't want to be doing that lad," he advised, his voice still low. There was a quiet whirling of wind and a thump as a bullet from Pierre's rifle hit the young soldier in the back of the skull, James turned just in time to catch the fallen Nazi to avoid the sound of him clattering to the ground. The Englishman was shocked to see the boy was no older than fourteen years of age, he must have been a member of the '*Junge Wehrmacht*', the 'Young Army', this was Hitler's final desperate last line of defence, to enlist all the young members in the Hitler Youth. The ex-SOE rolled the child soldier under the train and gave a salute of thanks in the direction of Pierre, James could not see his brother-in-law but he was sure Pierre could see him through his telescopic sight and once again making sure the coast was clear he continued planting of his explosives.

Fifteen minutes later the two friends stood, side by side along the fence as the clocks hit zero and the German transport erupted into an apocalyptic fireball, erupting the fuel tankers. The heat singed their unshaven chins and the fumes of burning fuel filled their nostrils, but even so, the atmosphere was one of success.

Chapter 27

On Tuesday, 6 July 1944, as promised, the British, American and Canadian forces stormed the beaches of Normandy and despite the tremendous loss of life and thanks to the French resistance delaying Nazi reinforcements, the Allies were victorious and pushed on into France. Over the next fortnight the underground Paris freedom fighters listened on the wireless radio endlessly for the updates on the allied forces insurgence, they heard how the invaders took more and more land as they liberated town after town and came ever closer to the city of light.

On the night of the nineteenth, the battle for Paris began. A barrage of gunfire and explosions could be heard on the suburbs of the great city, the night sky was lit up as an endless barrage of tremendous force was exchanged back and forth between the two armies. Even though it was clear that their eternal struggle against the Nazi oppressors was close to an end they could not sit back and relax, if anything their real fight had only just begun. Every night, under the cover of darkness, they would leave the safety of the French undergrounds, clandestine, lower-level, basement, armed with axes, pickaxes, shovels and sledgehammers. They would then split into various groups to continue digging up the cobbled roads or dismantle railway tracks with the sole aim of disrupting the German troops hastened advance to the front lines. They continued this process tirelessly every night until 25 June when the Nazi army machine surrendered the city of Paris to the United States Army.

Epilogue

25 *August 1944*

As the German army marched from the French capital in defeat, they were spat on and jeered at by the people the Nazis had held under their jackboots for the past five years. The Americans were cheered into the city as conquering heroes, receiving kisses from the enthusiastic French females and pats on the back or embraces from the male residents. The blue, white and red tricolour flag and American stars and stripes were being waived by the unwavering throng of Parisian residence who had gathered onto the streets to welcome their liberators.

Watching the procession from a flat rooftop sat four figures. The previous head of the French underground, Pierre, his sister Constance, his brother-in-law James and good friend Édouard.

"The war is over for us," said James as he watched a couple of Sherman tanks laden with young French maidens roll into the city. "So what are you going to do Ed? You won't be able to sell your wares anymore." The giant man looked down at the armies below as he took a couple of deep drags on his pipe before responding.

"You see the Americans as freeing us from the Nazis," he replied boldly. "I see a lot of new customers." The group laughed as they could almost see 'dollar signs' appear in the large man's single good eye.

"What about you, Pierre? What are you going to do now there is no need for the resistance any longer?" continued James.

"Non, there is no need for the Maquis any more but a new group has been formed, the real '*Forces Françaises de l'Itérieur*', to look for hidden Nazi officers, collaborators and Nazi sympathisers. I was proud to have led the Paris Maquis and will continue to serve my country and bring our great city back to its former glory," said Pierre, reverted back to his old self and as determined as ever. "What about you, my friend? Will you be taking my sister back to your home in England?" James looked first at his bride and then out to the skyline of the city of Paris. Then, to everyone's surprise, in perfectly fluent French, James said:

"*Je suis à la maison* (I am home)."

The Facts

While most of the characters in this book are fictional, there are some who were real, but their demeanour or demise may have been altered for the book. So here are the facts:

Winston Churchill:

Sir Winston Leonard Spencer-Churchill was a British politician, army officer, and writer, who was Prime Minister of the United Kingdom from 1940 to 1945.

Adolf Hitler:

Adolf Hitler was a German politician, demagogue, and Pan-German revolutionary. He was leader of the Nazi Party, and rose to power in Germany as Chancellor in 1933 and Führer in 1934.

Oswald Mosley:

Sir Oswald Ernald Mosley, 6th Baronet of Ancoats was a British politician who rose to fame in the 1920s as a Member of Parliament and later in the 1930s became leader of the British Union of Fascists.

Dietrich Hugo Hermann Von Choltitz:

He is chiefly remembered for his role as the last commander of Nazi-occupied Paris in 1944, when he disobeyed Hitler's orders to level the city, but instead surrendered it to Free French forces. He has been known as the 'Saviour of Paris' for preventing its destruction.

Marie-Madeleine Fourcade:

Marie-Madeleine Fourcade was the leader of the French Resistance network 'Alliance', under the code name 'Hérisson' after the arrest of its former leader, Georges Loustaunau-Lacau, during the occupation of France in the second world war.

Otto Abetz:

Heinrich Otto Abetz was the German ambassador to Vichy France during the Nazi era and a convicted war criminal. He died on 5 May 1958, in an auto accident.

Charles de Gaulle:

Charles André Joseph Marie de Gaulle was a French army officer and statesman who led the French Resistance against Nazi Germany in World War II.

Heinrich Himmler:

Heinrich Luitpold Himmler was Reichsführer of the Schutzstaffel, and a leading member of the Nazi Party of Germany. Himmler was one of the most powerful men in Nazi Germany and one of the people most directly responsible for the Holocaust.

Joseph Goebbels:

Paul Joseph Goebbels was a German Nazi politician and Reich Minister of Propaganda of Nazi Germany from 1933 to 1945.

Hermann Göring:

Hermann Wilhelm Göring was a German political and military leader as well as one of the most powerful figures in the Nazi Party that ruled Germany from 1933 to 1945.

William Joyce (aka Lord Haw Haw):

William Brooke Joyce, nicknamed Lord Haw-Haw, was an American-born, Anglo-Irish Fascist politician and Nazi propaganda broadcaster to the United Kingdom during World War II. He took German citizenship in 1940. He was convicted of one count of high treason in 1945 and sentenced to death.

Rose Antonia Maria Valland:

Rose Antonia Maria Valland was a French art historian, member of the French Resistance, captain in the French military, and one of the most decorated women in French history.

Pablo Picasso:

When the second world war came to France, Pablo chose to remain in Paris, unlike many other artists who fled from the German occupation. On one occasion, while the Nazis searched his apartment, a Gestapo officer saw a photograph of one of Picasso's most famous works, Guernica. The painting depicts the bombing of Guernica, a city in Spain attacked by the German and Italian fascists at the direction of Francisco Franco and the Spanish nationalists. When the Gestapo officer spotted the photograph, he asked Picasso, "Did you do that?" Only to receive the artist's answer: "No, you did." His friends within the French Resistance supplied him with smuggled bronze. Picasso returned the favours of the French Resistance by providing shelter to anyone who was sent by them.

Ernst Hermann Himmler:

Ernst Hermann Himmler was a German Nazi functionary, engineer and younger brother of Reichsführer-SS Heinrich Himmler.

All other characters in this book are totally fictitious and any similarity in appearance or demeanour to anyone, dead or alive, is totally coincidental.